PRAISE FOR THE
CHRISTOPHER WORTHY/
FATHER FORTIS MYSTERIES

LET TH E DEAD BURY THE DEAD

"A readable and engaging novel. Carlson's characters are real and relatable. The quality of a mystery series lies not in how well-crafted the first book is but in how well-written the second is. In this case, the second installment matches the first in quality."

—Rich Gotshall for the *Daily Journal*

ENTER BY THE NARROW GATE

"Carlson takes great care with his depiction of the state's history and culture even as he fictionalizes and conflates small details for dramatic effect. Every character receives this respectful treatment as well [....] The novel, while grounded firmly in theological and spiritual themes, is not a Bible-based mystery but an exploration of humanity [....] Lest anyone perceive *Gate* as a quiet book focused solely on the contemplative and monastic, rest assured that the mystery takes a spectacular twist. Lives are endangered, and the threat of the apocalypse hovers over a few of the characters, putting others high in the mountains at risk."

—Jennifer Levin for *Pasatiempo, the New Mexican's Weekly Magazine of Arts, Entertainment, and Culture*

"The novel's prose is rich with religious references and imagery, which add to the unique depth of the novel....The rapport between Worthy and Fortis is easy and enjoyable, and the double case ensures that *Enter by the Narrow Gate* never slows in action."

—*Foreword Reviews*

"The real joy in reading this mystery lies in Carlson's exploration of how faith shapes reasoning and actions, rather than simply the action itself. Thus Father Fortis can proudly take his place in a list of religious detectives that includes Father Brown, Brother Cadfael and Rabbi David Small."

—Rich Gotshall for the *Daily Journal*

"The cultures of New Mexico and its Native American population are explored in depth, offering many insights into the region and its inhabitants while providing a background for this intriguing mystery.... Enter by the Narrow Gate is the first novel in the Christopher Worthy-Father Fortis mystery series, and it gets these two characters off to a chilling but entertaining start."

—Toni V. Sweeney for the *New York Journal of Books*

"I didn't want to let go of Christopher and Father Fortis.... We need sleuths like this. They're intelligent and not afraid to share that intellectualism with each other. How refreshing!"

—Christine DeSmet, award-winning writer and author of the Fudge Shop Mysteries

"A consistently compelling and entertaining read from first page to last.... highly recommended."

—Mason's Bookshelf, The *Midwest Book Review*

"Father Nicholas Fortis and Lieutenant Christopher Worthy are both out of their element the instant the two friends get to Santa Fe from the Midwest, and that ratchets up the suspense in this excellent mystery.... Author David Carlson has created a great team in Fortis and Worthy. The priest's kind, open manner and knowledge of scripture and theology complement Worthy's hard-nosed pursuit of killers."

—Rich Zahradnik, author of the Coleridge Taylor Mysteries

Let the Dead Bury the Dead

Let the Dead Bury the Dead

A Christopher Worthy/Father Fortis Mystery

———◆———

DAVID CARLSON

cp

coffeetownpress

Seattle, WA

coffeetownpress

Coffeetown Press
PO Box 70515
Seattle, WA 98127

For more information go to: www.CoffeetownPress.com
www.DavidCCarlson.org

This is a work of fiction. Names, characters, places, brands, media, and incidents are either the product of the author's imagination or are used fictitiously.

Cover watercolor by Kathy Carlson
Cover design by Sabrina Sun

Let the Dead Bury the Dead

ISBN: 978-1-60381-395-2 (Trade Paper)
ISBN: 978-1-60381-396-9 (eBook)

Library of Congress Control Number: 2016962688

Printed in the United States of America

To two communities that anchor my life:

First, Holy Trinity Greek Orthodox Church, Carmel, Indiana, a loving and accepting community where people's lives—including mine—have been transformed.

Second, Franklin College, which over the past thirty-nine years has taught me that being a professor is about student learning, not about me.

ACKNOWLEDGMENTS

To Kathy, my friend, wife, and first editor, I owe the most. She has spent nearly as much time with Christopher Worthy and Father Fortis as I have, and she shares my love for these characters. I also wish to thank Sara Camilli, my agent, for her constant belief in this series. Thanks also to Catherine Treadgold, Jennifer McCord, and Becca Eskildsen of Coffeetown Press for their patience and excellent advice.

To Leif, Marten, Mandy, and now Felix, please know how much joy you bring to my life.

I am grateful to Franklin College, a gem of a liberal arts college that has been my home for nearly forty years. Through various grants, Franklin College generously funded travel that was essential to creating this series.

Finally, I wish to thank all the English and writing teachers who encouraged me to read, read, read, and who responded with kindness to my early attempts to fill the blank page.

"Jesus said to him, 'Let the dead bury their own dead, but you go and proclaim the Kingdom of God.' "

—Luke 9:60 (NIV)

Also by the author from Coffeetown Press

Enter by the Narrow Gate

Coming Soon

Let These Bones Live Again

CHAPTER ONE

———◆———

A HUSH FELL OVER THE SANCTUARY OF St. Cosmas Greek Orthodox Church as Father Fortis bent down next to the flowers on the carpet.

The parish council president, Mr. Margolis, sighed heavily, and in a trembling voice said, "Yes, Father Spiro was killed right here, in front of the very altar he served for thirty years.

"Right below the icon of the Virgin Mary," Mrs. Filis added, her false teeth clacking.

The piece of new carpet wasn't large, little more than the size of a plate, but Father Fortis imagined that death by strangulation wouldn't have left much blood. A shiver passed through him as he remembered what Mr. Margolis had said over the phone. In the middle of their conversation about his duties as St. Cosmas' interim priest, the old man had suddenly blurted out, "We can only imagine how angry the killer must have been. You see, blood flowed from poor Father Spiro's eyes and nose."

Father Fortis struggled to his feet, aware of the eyes of the other parish council members on him. He looked toward the altar. Even when a priest died under normal circumstances, a parish was swamped with pain, sorrow, and regrets. And this priest's death had been anything but normal.

"Let us offer a prayer for the repose of the soul of Father Spiro," he said as he bowed his head. "In the name of the Father, Son, and Holy Spirit," he began and then paused for a moment of silence. As he offered the prayer for the recently departed, he recalled his abbot's caution. "Please remember that you are to be pastoral, Father Nicholas. I trust your background with murders won't get in the way of this sacred charge."

Then he should have sent someone else, he thought to himself. Such as

Father Basil, a fellow monk-priest with a dry cough. Basil would have been the murdered priest's contemporary, a fact that might have been of some comfort to this community. Or the abbot could have sent Father Gregory, a young and eager priest who'd just completed his degree in philanthropy. He might have helped St. Cosmas turn their sorrow in a more generous direction. He finished the prayer and heard Mrs. Filis sniffling. One of the men coughed too loudly. No, for some reason the abbot had sent him. Even in his role as interim parish priest at St. Cosmas, he would quickly learn from parishioners what the victim, Father Spiro George, had been like. Could he be faulted if part of his brain listened for clues about who would have wanted him dead?

"Shall we return to our meeting?" he said, looking around the circle.

The group stayed where they were, still looking at the flowers.

"Poor, poor Spiro. Such a lovely man," a woman in her forties with thick glasses commented.

"Yes, he was a giant, really," Jimmy Angelo, another older member of the council, added. His eyes blinked rapidly as he looked around the circle for support. "We won't see his like again. Part of a dying breed. Oh, please forgive that."

"We know what you mean, Jimmie," a fourth voice added. "But if Father Spiro could speak, he'd probably ask us why we're not listening to Father Fortis and facing the decisions in front of us."

Father Fortis glanced up toward the voice of reason. It was Dr. Pappas, the cardiologist who had been the first to introduce himself when Father Fortis had entered the library a half hour before. Father Fortis wondered if the man had been the dead priest's physician.

Knowing that he'd have plenty of time to return to the scene of the murder later, Father Fortis stepped around the flowers and moved toward the side door. "Back to the library, then."

In the hallway, Mrs. Filis called from behind him. "Did you ever meet our Father Spiro?"

"I regret not," he replied. If the council was any indication, it wasn't going to be easy for the parish to focus on anything but their loss.

As if to prove his point, the younger woman on the council chimed in, "But I thought he brought a group to St. Simeon's, your monastery, a couple of years ago."

"That's very possible," Father Fortis said. "You see, we receive many guests in the course of a year."

Once back in the library, the group took their places around the large table. Fourteen in all, Father Fortis counted. Two women and twelve men, with an even mix of retirees and younger professionals. Fourteen seemed to him a large number for a parish council, something that could indicate a thriving parish … or a distrustful one.

From the center of the table, Dr. Pappas cleared his throat. "Metropolitan Iakovos called yesterday and said something quite astute, surprising as that may seem." A few chuckled nervously around the table. "He said that when a beloved priest dies, some parishioners step back precisely when they're most needed to step forward. We can't afford that here, and that's why we're so happy that you're with us, Father Fortis."

"Of course, His Eminence is right," Father Fortis replied, looking from the doctor to the others around the table. "But I would add that in extraordinarily tragic circumstances such as these, the parish is looking to you, their parish council, for leadership. They don't know me, but they do know and trust you." Even as he said it, Father Fortis wondered if that was true. Greek Orthodox churches were not immune to infighting, and sometimes the fighting was most intense within a church's council. He would certainly find out soon enough.

"The last thing Father Spiro would want is for his death to result in the death of this parish," Dr. Pappas added.

The younger woman with the thick glasses squinted. "Of course that's right, but—"

"And this council will do its part, I assure you, Father," Jimmie Angelo interrupted, pounding his fist on the table. "Please, Father Fortis, let us know how we can help you, you know … find time to help the police."

Father Fortis looked down at his hands. So, news of his rather odd past had leaked out.

"Let's remember that the police haven't asked for any help," Dr. Pappas said by way of clarification. "In fact, from the way the police have acted so far, I'm sure they wouldn't welcome it at all."

"Ooh, that horribly rude Lieutenant Sherrod," Mrs. Filis said, her teeth clamping down on the name.

"In that regard, some of us would like to ask a hypothetical question, Father," the younger woman said.

"Remind me of your name again," Father Fortis interrupted.

The woman smiled nervously. "I'm Dr. Lydia Boras."

"Ah, another doctor. A Greek mother's dream come true."

The woman raised her hand as those around the table laughed. "Not a real doctor, at least according to my mother. Classics professor at Allgemein College."

"Ah, yes. I've heard of the school," Father Fortis said. "Please pose your hypothetical question. Maybe I'll have a hypothetical answer."

"Ah, nicely put, Father. Our question is this. If the police were to ask for your assistance, what would you say?"

"That's easy. I will offer whatever service I can, but we all know that my greatest challenge will be as your priest. Not an easy task for an out-of-practice monk."

Dr. Pappas leaned forward on the table, and Father Fortis noticed how all eyes turned toward him. "But we were told that you've assisted the police before. In fact, we heard you've worked with some of our own police force in the past. We naturally assumed—"

"It's true that I know one detective from Detroit. In fact, I count Lieutenant Worthy as one of my closest friends. But I don't know the officer you named a moment ago, so it seems a moot point," Father Fortis added hurriedly. The last thing he needed was for everyone at St. Cosmas to expect him to be doing exactly what he intended to do—poke around and discover what he could about the grisly murder.

"Ah, yes, we're back to Lieutenant Sherrod," another man offered. "Sorry, I'm Dr. Stanos, and I'm just a professor too. What I think the parish council might be overlooking is that while Lieutenant Sherrod is a bit brusque, he seems quite competent."

"I'm sure you're right, Dr. Stanos, and that's my view as well," Father Fortis said, emphasizing the point with a gentle tap on the table. "I promise to stay out of the way of the police, even as I'd expect them to stay out of my way as your priest."

He reached to touch his pectoral cross and give those sitting at the table as pious a look as he could muster. If his half-truth was taken as gospel throughout the parish, all the better for him.

THE BOXES LINING THE WALL OF Captain Lorraine Betts' office suggested someone near retirement, someone recently fired, or someone recently promoted. It was, in fact, the last, and this was Lieutenant Christopher Worthy's first meeting with his new boss.

Worthy had spent his entire fourteen-year career under the worrying gaze of Captain Joseph Spicer. Captain Spicer was a detective's best friend and key supporter when he handed out a case, but as soon as pressure came down from above, the captain's infamous memos would begin. From demanding daily progress reports to questioning mileage reports, Spicer had done his best to make his staff feel the pain of his own ulcer attacks.

Spicer had objected particularly to what had become one of Worthy's key rules of detection—that progress on a case happened when witnesses weren't rushed, but rather given time to pass through their shock to recall the important clues. And important clues for Worthy were precisely those that didn't at first seem to fit. It had been Spicer's barb that he'd named two of his ulcers after Worthy.

So he wouldn't miss Spicer, though he knew there was no guarantee that Lorraine Betts, his new captain, would be any better. She'd been recruited out of Indianapolis, and the scuttlebutt was that she'd made the short list because of Detroit's gender imbalance on the force. Having seen her the day before from across the room, Worthy wondered if that could be true. Something about the look in the eye and the set of the mouth of the middle-aged, substantial woman suggested that she'd deserved every promotion.

When Captain Betts entered her new office, Worthy rose respectfully from the chair to his full height of six feet two inches. It was a chair he'd occupied many times before—when he'd been dressed down and when he'd received commendations. The drab office even held an echo of his being threatened with dismissal, and that echo wasn't all that long ago.

It was in this same chair, eighteen months before, that Spicer had reassigned him to Siberia—Siberia being the academy, for a second teaching stint. Spicer had spoken of Worthy's natural talent for teaching, his proven ability to influence new recruits for the better, but Worthy had taken the assignment for what it was—a punishment for not returning from New Mexico on his last case with the missing college girl. That he'd found a serial killer out in New Mexico hadn't counted for much. He had failed—as far as everyone in Detroit knew—to complete his assignment. Now he wondered if it was too much to hope that this meeting was more than a social call.

Captain Betts tapped on an open folder with a pencil. "I've been reading your personnel file, Lieutenant. Of course, I'd heard of you before I got here." She looked up at him over half-frame reading glasses. "But from first impressions, I'll say this. You're not exactly what I expected."

Worthy made it a point not to move in his chair. "Oh?"

"Relax. I'm confessing my problem, not yours. I'm one of those who superimposes the known onto the unknown. In your case, I assumed you'd be like my top detectives in Indianapolis."

"I'm sorry if I don't quite live up to that."

She seemed to be studying his face. "Let me put it another way. You don't match what I'm used to in terms of my best cops. The ones I know tend to be nasty. I mean, nasty on the first meeting and nasty from that point on. But then," she added with a smile, "maybe you're just good at hiding that. Yes, hiding. Maybe that's what your file adds up to."

Worthy shrugged. "You're better than me, then. I've never been able to figure out what my file adds up to."

"No? How about this? You're a bit of a magician, and you have a pattern of working best when working alone."

Worthy could have objected to the last remark. In his opinion, his best work had been his work with Sera Lacey in New Mexico a year and a half before. But he had to admit that his career in Detroit had been a different matter. "I'm sure my file also describes the way I've fallen flat on my face," he said.

Captain Betts studied him again. "Yes, that's here too. Gutsy of you to begin with your weak points. But the magician part gets the press clippings, don't you agree?"

Having no possible response to that, he didn't bother to offer one.

Captain Betts took off her glasses and let them dangle from a beaded cord. "The two of us would have met eventually, maybe on a visit to the academy. But I've asked you to come in for a particular reason." She waited, as if expecting him to respond. "Aren't you at all curious what that might be?"

Worthy shifted in the seat. "Only if it gets me out of the academy. I need a case, Captain."

Betts smiled slightly and sat forward. "I may have that, Lieutenant, if you can finesse matters a bit."

Captain Betts passed a case sheet across the desk.

Worthy studied the top of the form, noting the incident's date, January fourth. "This murder is two weeks old," he said, scanning the sheet. "It's the strangulation of the priest. That's Sherrod's case." He moved forward to pass the paper back.

She raised her hand to stop him. "It *was* Lieutenant Sherrod's case, and it still would be if he had his way." She gazed toward the room's one grimy window and exhaled slowly. "That's where the finesse part comes in. You see, I've been told—no, I've been warned—about you and Sherrod. The petty jealousies, I mean."

"Not on my part," Worthy interrupted. "In my world, Sherrod doesn't count."

"That's not a response that shows much finesse or respect, Lieutenant. You can't see how your record would rankle someone like Phil?"

Phil, is it? Worthy thought. Would he become Chris to whomever she talked with next?

"Why would anyone, even Sherrod, be jealous of my being exiled at the academy?" he asked.

"I've had only one meeting with your colleague, and I wouldn't say it went all that well. But I can see his point. You see, Sherrod isn't the only one tired of seeing your picture in the paper. You may not have found that missing girl in New Mexico, but you did catch a serial killer."

Worthy studied his hands. He didn't need a reminder of how isolated he'd become at the precinct over the past five years. "How does any of that relate to the murder of the priest? Did Phil blow the case already?"

"Lieutenant Sherrod was doing just fine," she answered evenly. "He was working it with Sergeant Henderson, who apparently is known as 'Hoops' around here. Know him?"

Worthy thought he did. A guy ten years younger than him, an ex-jock who looked like he still worked out. An African-American, at least six feet, five inches. Very quiet. He recalled something going around the precinct about Henderson, but he'd never heard the details.

Captain Betts sat back in her chair. "Henderson remains on the case, but Sherrod has been requisitioned to assist on a federal case. The body found in the iron ore boat last summer."

Worthy shook his head. "Nope, don't recall that. That must have been when I was overwhelmed with challenges at the academy."

Betts seemed unfazed by his crack. "The feds think that body is part of something bigger, a racketeering scandal. So they want Phil back as the local guy. Probably just for a few weeks."

Worthy groaned. "I don't know how it works in Indianapolis, Captain, but around here, a takeover case is a no-win. If I solve it, it looks like I stole Sherrod's glory. If I fail, I'll be blamed for screwing things up."

"Remember finesse? I want you to solve it and do so in a way that brings credit to the entire department. Be a team player. Unless, of course, you'd prefer to stay at the academy."

Worthy leaned forward. "Here's a better idea. Give me a fresh case, one with an intact site and helpful witnesses, one with nobody's nose out of joint."

"That's not what I'm offering, Lieutenant."

Worthy rubbed his forehead. "You and I both know the priest case should logically be given to the second in charge. Henderson, isn't it?"

"I can't do that, and I think you know why."

Worthy tried to read his new captain's face. "Well, I don't."

"You really are out of the loop, aren't you? The day after I moved into this office, Henderson decked Pescatelli in the locker room. Broke his jaw in two places. That was my welcome to Detroit."

Worthy shook his head. "Anything else you can say to make me want to take this case? Look, you said it already, I work best alone. My luck with partners has never been so great, even the non-violent type."

"I come with a different viewpoint, Lieutenant. You're a senior investigator, a highly decorated one. In addition, you've trained recruits at the academy. Henderson needs some—what's the word—mentoring? From where I'm sitting, you're the perfect lead on this case."

Worthy heard the plea for cooperation but didn't fall for it. "With all due respect, ma'am—I mean, Captain—it sounds like this Henderson needs a departmental leave."

He saw the color rise in his new superior's cheeks.

"I think you should work with him a bit before you tell me what he needs." The two sat in awkward silence before she added, "I look at this as a chance for you as much as for Henderson."

"For me? Chance for what?"

"Lieutenant Worthy, let me tell you the first thing that I noticed in your file. It was your ten requests to get out of the academy. I saw those the day before the priest was found strangled. And I thought about them when two reporters called and asked if I was going to assign you. Secondly, in Indy, we call that 'name recognition.' But my superiors figured the case would be straightforward, and we agreed that there was no sense adding to the resentment around here. So I gave it to Sherrod."

"I don't see how that answers my question. How is this my chance?"

She shook her head slowly, as if Worthy were being deliberately dense. "You have a chance to help a fellow officer save his career. You can see that, can't you?"

Worthy sat quietly. Now it was a charity case?

"And you, Lieutenant Worthy, should see that saving someone's career could be especially appropriate for you. You've known success, but you've also known struggle. The way I see it, both of you could learn something. Who knows, it may even change your Lone Ranger image around the department."

Worthy leaned back in his chair, trying to read between the lines. If Sherrod had been close to solving the case, he'd still be on it. That meant the case wasn't as straightforward as everyone first expected. And what did he have to teach Henderson except maybe new ways to hate his job? Worthy's last two partners in Detroit had complained loudly that he didn't confide in them, didn't include them in what the department called "direction-setting."

What I didn't do was buy their drinks, Worthy thought. He had about as much chance of mentoring Henderson as he did of reconciling with his ex-wife, Susan. But what was the alternative—the academy?

"What do you say, Lieutenant?" Betts asked.

"I think this is a total disaster waiting to happen."

Captain Betts opened a folder on her desk and turned over a few sheets of paper. "I was led to believe you'd like the other person involved in this case."

Worthy couldn't believe what he was hearing. *Another person?* He pictured the red-headed Cunningham, top recruit at the academy, dogging his heels.

"No, no, Captain. Maybe that's how things work in Indianapolis, but—"

"A third? Give me a little credit, Lieutenant. I'm talking about this note I received yesterday, about the priest they've brought to fill in at the Greek church."

The tightness in Worthy's chest eased. Was what he was thinking possible?

The paper-shuffling stopped as Betts drew out a sheet. "Ah, here it is," she said, stabbing the name at the top with the bow of her glasses. "One thing you'll learn about me, Lieutenant, is that I never forget a name. So, when I saw that Father Nicholas Fortis, a monk from Ohio, was assigned to St. Cosmas, I went back into your file. Isn't that the priest who worked with you in New Mexico?"

Chapter Two

———— ◆ ————

WORTHY SAT AT HIS DESK AND reread the note. Yes, it was true. Father Nicholas Fortis—Nick, to him—had been assigned to St. Cosmas Greek Orthodox Church. That fact alone didn't cancel out the crap he was sure to get from Sherrod, if not from this Henderson, but it certainly trumped it.

He had worked with Father Fortis for the first time four years before, when a novice monk originally from Detroit and in his second year at Father Fortis' monastery, St. Simeon's, was found with his throat cut in an Ohio farmer's field. Father Fortis had been the monastery's novice master at the time. To the surprise of both Father Fortis and Worthy, they had worked together as well as Worthy had worked poorly with his colleagues in the precinct.

The two men could hardly seem more different. Worthy didn't see himself as shy, although everyone around Father Fortis would seem so by comparison. Father Fortis was an overly talkative, sumo wrestler of a man with a trailing ponytail. Because of his habit of breathing heavily through his mouth, Father Fortis advertised his preference for spearmint candies, the smell of which wafted from his heavy black beard.

On the other hand, Worthy was lanky, fair-haired, slightly slouched, and just beginning to gray. The stories in the papers over the past five years—at least the flattering ones—tended to refer to him as quietly ambitious, and he really couldn't argue with that assessment. Worthy's assigned partners in Detroit could vouch for his ambition but had tired of his lack of communication as well as his stunning successes. What surprised Worthy was that, in their work together, Father Fortis had reacted so differently to his taciturn nature. It wasn't that Father Fortis—or Nick, as he preferred Worthy to call him—

understood Worthy's intuitions any more readily than others, or that Nick was any less critical. No, the difference was that, for some reason, the very silences that irritated his usual partners did not bother Father Fortis. Father Nick had an uncanny ability to be talking and at the same time listening deeply. Worthy knew that his own silences were not spent listening to others as much as pondering the clues of a case. He had come to understand that Father Nick somehow understood that his silences tended to precede intuitive leaps.

Of course, Nick would have expressed his attitude in another way. He would have said that his trust in those difficult and ambiguous moments wasn't so much trust in Worthy's methods as in God's truth winning out. Faith was something Worthy had repeatedly told Nick he no longer had, but even that chasm between them had only brought a knowing laugh from the priest.

And now Nick was serving at St. Cosmas, the site of a grisly murder that still rocked Detroit. Father Spiro George, a priest old enough to retire, had been brutally strangled at nine in the morning and in broad daylight. The method used by the killer had apparently been to grab the vestment piece that hung around the priest's neck and tighten it until the old man's heart stopped for lack of oxygen. Not a pretty way to go and not a pretty way to kill—face to face until the last second.

Worthy would like nothing better than to drive out to the church and hear Nick's initial theories—of course, he would have several, and all of them would be interesting—but department protocol prevented him from going anywhere until the case was formally turned over by the last team. And that was set to happen in fifteen minutes, back in Captain Betts' office.

He looked out his office window at the cars whizzing by on I-94. His entire fourteen years on the force had been spent in this very office, but he'd noticed as little about the cars and trucks that flowed by as the colleagues who'd come and gone from the precinct.

Self-absorbed? That's what his ex-wife, Susan, would say, and in his low moments he tended to agree. After all, there had to be something terribly his fault to cause his marriage to end. Now, nearly five years later, he still wasn't precisely sure what that was.

At other moments, he felt her criticism to be far from fair. He thought of himself less than anyone else, if that were possible. If fault lay anywhere, it had to be in the way he approached his work. From his first months in homicide, he'd spent his waking moments trying to understand the mentality of those he was looking for. Over the years, he'd entered deeper and deeper into their darkness. He imagined them dreaming their deeds, planning the way they'd kill their victims, and finally gathering the courage to carry out their plans. That had been the extramarital affair that had ended his marriage.

So, what kind of person would strangle a priest with his own vestment? And did the odd weapon point to a crime of passion or an accident gone awry? The time of day and the sheer violence of the method suggested a lack of planning, a spontaneous eruption. But the newspaper story reported that not a single fingerprint, other than the victim's, had been found on the vestment. That meant gloves, and gloves suggested a level of premeditation.

He glanced at his watch. Still five minutes before he met Henderson and had to face Sherrod again. He reached into his desk drawer for a legal pad, wanting to jot down his initial questions before Sherrod detailed his own theories.

He began with "Murder site: sanctuary" as one heading and wrote below: "How did killer go unnoticed? Any significance to where body found? Why kill this way?"

Under a second heading, "Relationship," Worthy wrote two questions for later consideration: "Did killer know victim?" and "What was on the victim's appointment schedule for that Tuesday morning?"

Worthy suspected that Sherrod had barely considered such questions, if he'd thought of them at all. Lieutenant Philip Sherrod took the standard approach. A murder happens. The goal is to solve it as quickly as possible.

And how is a murder solved quickly? The approach followed by Sherrod and others was to chase after all known leads before they got cold. Worthy called it the "Hurry and Look Busy" approach. Sometimes it worked. The killer was sometimes caught hours after the crime, the evidence still in his possession. But even when that approach failed, as Worthy suspected it must have done on this case, it was sure to safeguard the department from criticism by the mayor and the media.

Worthy knew the method because that had been his own for his first years as a detective. But then something odd had dawned on him, changing his outlook completely. Kneeling over the bludgeoned body of a city councilman in a sleazy flophouse, it came to him that murder had a lot in common with falling in love. The face of the victim, frozen in death, often held the same look of surprise as on the face of someone experiencing that first kiss.

What Worthy had come to believe over the following years was that, in death as in love, the intersection of the two lives in question was rarely haphazard. Something in the past—some prior hope or decision, something perhaps quite small and made in secret—had made that kiss, or that knife in the heart, inevitable.

The trick was to uncover those past decisions, and that took time. Worthy painstakingly, and often maddeningly for his partner and for Captain Spicer, retraced the decisions made by the victim over the final days, weeks, and sometimes months. He collected long lists of names of those the victim had met, had wanted to meet, or was afraid to meet. But he also unearthed the odd hopes and frustrations of the victim, those tiny clues initially dismissed by witnesses as unimportant.

His approach almost invariably led to early criticism. He was dawdling, giving the killer time to leave town, or ignoring the "hot" clues. But Worthy had learned to stick with the material he was gathering, convinced that within the victim's hopes and frustrations, the killer would be found. The three commendations on Worthy's wall proved that his approach often worked. Other parts of his file attested to the fact that his approach was hardly foolproof.

Worthy closed his notes and exhaled deeply. Two approaches, each at odds with the other. He stood and straightened his tie, realizing as he left his office that he'd just described the real cause of the tension between Sherrod and him. It wasn't simply that Worthy was a college grad and Sherrod had worked his way up from the neighborhood beat. Nor was it that Worthy frequently had his picture in the paper, though that didn't help. The bottom line was that Sherrod was the poster child for the hurry-up approach. When he solved a case, he bragged as much about how quickly he'd made the bust as about the arrest itself. For Sherrod, police work was a race. The first to cross the line should win. *And that is why he hates me,* Worthy thought, as he headed down the hallway. *And that's why this won't be a fun meeting.*

Sherrod was already waiting in Captain Betts' office, as was an African-American who was staring out the window. *This must be Henderson,* Worthy thought. The room was quiet when Worthy entered, but Sherrod looked up from cleaning his nails as if he'd already given Henderson an earful.

"Well, look who's back?" Sherrod said. "I thought you'd died or at least been transferred."

Worthy made no move to shake hands. Sherrod was one of those guys who, while not fat, had a fat man's face. Round, with a comb-over and a wispy mustache to complete the look. Pushing forty, Sherrod was a year ahead of Worthy on the force and a detective's generation ahead of Henderson.

"No," Worthy replied, choosing a chair closer to Henderson's side of the room. "They have me out at the academy."

"Oh, right. Teaching them how you fucked up that missing person's case in New Mexico." Sherrod shot a glance at Henderson. "Hear about that, Hoops? Worthy caught a killer out there. Didn't find the missing girl, but hey, what the hell."

"Morning, gentlemen," Captain Betts said, coming through the door. Sherrod stopped the chatter as their new captain took her seat behind the desk and adjusted her half glasses.

Looking up, she said, "Everyone know each other here?"

Worthy stood and took a step toward Henderson. "I'm Chris Worthy."

Henderson barely glanced his way as he shook his hand. "Uh-huh."

Captain Betts cleared her throat. "For the record, Lieutenant Sherrod has quite emphatically expressed his wish that he have two more weeks on this case."

"Maybe only one," Sherrod interjected. "Hell, Captain, give me the three days left in this week, and it could be wrapped up." He raised a hand, thumb and finger forming a closing vise. "We're that close."

Captain Betts leaned back and gazed at Sherrod for a moment. "Given all the work you've put into the case, your desire is natural. But as I made clear this morning, this meeting is for you to turn the case over to Lieutenant Worthy. Apprise him of the most significant developments and demonstrate the collegiality I know you're capable of by giving good counsel. As everyone in this department will find out, collegiality is key for me."

"All I'm saying is that I'm this close." Sherrod's thumb and finger remained aloft.

"I'm sure you meant to say that Sergeant Henderson and you are that close."

Sherrod looked puzzled. "Isn't that what I said?"

Worthy noticed Henderson's attention remained on the view outside. Was he even listening?

"Proceed with your summary, Lieutenant," Captain Betts suggested.

"No problem." Sherrod moved to the edge of his chair. "What we have here is a robbery gone sour. The file describes the article stolen as an altar thingamajig, a piece of silver of some considerable value, but what's the market around here for something like that? Anyways, I figure—we figure—the perp or perps came over from the projects, from Suffolk. There've been three break-ins in the neighborhood over the past ten months, and after a little pushing on some contacts I have over in Suffolk, three names keep popping up. We were in the process of bringing them in for questioning when the feds requested my assistance. One of them, a guy named Bales, is a real nutcase. Picked up twice on battery, once on assault. So, Hoops, start with him and lean hard." Sherrod looked in Henderson's direction. Getting no response, he turned back to Captain Betts. "Like I said, if you could give me a few more days …."

Captain Betts jotted down a note. "So you're going on the assumption that the priest interrupted a burglary."

"Assumption? No, it's a fact, ma'am," Sherrod replied, looking pleased with himself.

"Why would anyone break in at nine on a Tuesday morning?" Worthy asked. "Why not the night before when the place is empty?"

"Because they're stupid fucks," Sherrod said, glaring at him.

"But smart enough to leave no signs of forced entry. Not even a fingerprint."

Sherrod's eyes narrowed. "Ever heard of gloves and dumb luck? Look, we did our homework, smart guy. It was friggin' cold that morning—nine miserable degrees. So they wore gloves. And we figure the priest turned off the security, so they just followed him in."

Worthy could feel Captain Betts' eyes on him and remembered her appeal for finesse. *Welcome to the real world, Captain*, he thought. "If I have this right," he said slowly, "you're saying this robber or robbers knew the old man was around because they followed him in. But then this same priest surprised them a few minutes later in the sanctuary, so they killed him."

Sherrod shook his head, pointing the nail file at Worthy. "Look, they did fucking surprise him. The priest must have come in and gone down to his office. Maybe then he hears something in the sanctuary. Like maybe they dropped the piece, okay? So he comes in, and they realize he could ID them. Work for you, Einstein, or you gotta better theory?"

Worthy looked down at the questions on his sheet. "I don't know. I wouldn't say there's a lot here from the interviews at the church."

Sherrod stood up and glared down on Worthy. "Look, I'm telling you, those church folks are only going to get things balled up. Hell, half of them don't even speak English. Hoops will tell you that none of them know nothing. And please, for Christ's sake, have the basic courtesy to read the report. That will tell you that the priest was there alone that morning."

Worthy nodded. "Of course, of course. Well, I don't see why Sergeant Henderson shouldn't carry on with your three suspects from Suffolk. I don't think the interviews will take more than a few days."

Sherrod stood, red-faced, as he ran a hand through thin strands of hair. "Look, Worthy, it won't be interviewing, but re-interviewing. I give you a case practically done, but you can't just tie the bow and be done with it, can you? No, you have to over-complicate things."

Captain Betts cleared her throat.

"No, let me finish, Captain," Sherrod said, hands planted on his hips, his right hand gripping his holster. "Look, Worthy, almost everyone we arrest in this city is, at bottom, a simple fuck. There are no great ideas floating around in their heads. No masterminds out there; that's what I'm trying to say. That morning, this guy or guys figures the easiest way is to follow the old priest in once he gets there. That way, no alarms go off. You see, it's simple."

Worthy kept his eyes on his notes.

"Okay, fine," Sherrod said. "Screw things up, if that's what you need to do. But I'm out of here."

Worthy sat silently as Sherrod left the room, slamming the door.

Nicely done, Worthy thought. Now everybody in the precinct knows exactly where things stand.

Captain Betts took her glasses off and looked over to the window. "Sergeant Henderson, we haven't heard anything from you."

Henderson didn't respond.

"Did you hear me, Sergeant?"

"Yes, ma'am," he said. "I don't see nothing wrong with the two of us going our separate ways. I'll take Bales and his buddies from Suffolk. The lieutenant can take the church."

Betts raised her eyebrows and turned her attention to Worthy. "Lieutenant, because I'm sure Sherrod will make his displeasure known to my superiors, maybe you'd be so good as to tell me what you hope to gain from interviewing the same people at the church over again."

Worthy sat forward in his chair. "I just want to make sure we don't have this whole thing backwards."

Henderson turned toward him.

"Go on," Captain Betts said.

"What if somebody made it look like a robbery? I mean, what if the priest was having problems, maybe even some at the church. That's all I want to find out."

"Okay," she said, unconvinced, "but churches usually give their ministers or priests ulcers. They don't generally kill them, Lieutenant. Any other thoughts, Sergeant?" she asked.

"Like I said, I'm fine with it."

"Fine, fine, fine," Captain Betts snapped back. "Tell me why you're fine when somebody suggests a completely contradictory theory to what you've been pursuing for two weeks."

For the first time, Henderson met his new superior's gaze. "All right, here's what I think. But remember, you asked me. I think Worthy's angle is full of day-old shit, but yes, I'm fine with that. Because at the end of the day, it's going to make me look all the better."

FATHER FORTIS HIT THE PRINT COMMAND on the church office computer so hard that the keyboard jumped, but for the third time nothing happened. He felt like the new schoolboy, having to ask the church secretary, Mrs. Hazelton, how to do something. The monastery in Ohio had only four computers, and Brother Basil guarded them jealously.

The buzzer beeped on his desk. "Yes, Mrs. Hazelton?"

"Father, there's a policeman here to see you."

Father Fortis took a deep breath. So it was time to meet the infamous

Lieutenant Sherrod, the detective who'd managed to alienate nearly everyone at St. Cosmas. He stood, straightened his robe, and managed a serious scowl. *Let's see how he does with me,* he thought.

The door opened, and Christopher Worthy walked in. Father Fortis let out a yell and scampered around the desk to lift his friend off the ground.

"Easy on the ribs, Nick," Worthy said, laughing.

Father Fortis set him down and laughed in return. "Did you like that look on my face when you came in?"

"It looked like you had gas."

"It was supposed to intimidate you. I thought you were someone named Sherrod."

"Intimidation, huh? You couldn't scare anyone if you tried."

"Sit down, my friend, and bring me up to date. How are things with you? More importantly, how are things with Allyson? The last time we talked, you were hoping to make some headway."

Worthy shook his head, not knowing what to say about where things stood with his older daughter. After the case in New Mexico, he had indeed returned to Detroit more committed than ever to connecting with his troubled daughter. Two and a half years before, Allyson had run away, and for five months Susan and he had no idea whether she was dead or alive. Then one day, she walked back into the house as if she'd just come home from school. She'd told no one—not her mother, her father, her younger sister, or her counselor—where she'd been in those months or how she'd survived.

Despite Allyson's stonewalling, Worthy had come back from New Mexico with a pledge to give their relationship another try before Allyson went away to college. But his renewed attempts over the last eighteen months to talk with Allyson had made no headway. Until four days ago, that is.

"All I can say, Nick, is that I've tried a new tack. I had to do something. The counselor kept saying the same thing to me, through Susan. 'Don't upset your daughter. Don't put her in a corner.' It was like the safest thing I could do was never talk to her again."

"So what did you do?"

Worthy sat down in the chair. "Maybe something really stupid. I just don't know. Anyway, it must have been last Monday when I stopped at the house after work. Allyson was alone in the kitchen. To use her words, Amy had conned Susan into buying her more clothes for school. So I took a deep breath and asked if she'd go up some weekend to the cabin. Just the two of us."

"And she said yes?"

"Not exactly, but at least I didn't get the standard 'you have to be kidding' response. She wanted to know when, exactly. So I said the weekend after next, and then I stupidly added we could leave on Friday night if she wanted. As soon as I said it, I realized how that sounded, like I was saying she didn't have anything better to do than spend the whole weekend with her dad."

"So she said no?"

"Well, she ignored me for a few minutes. I'm used to that. She finally told me that Amy would make better company. She said the cabin is boring."

Father Fortis sat down next to Worthy. "I'm so sorry, Christopher."

Worthy shrugged. "It may not be over yet, Nick. I told her that Amy and I can go another time. The way I figure it, Amy is only twelve and hasn't yet decided that I'm the cause of all her problems. So I told Allyson that I know the cabin can be boring, but with it being mid-January, we could go skiing or ice fishing. I tried to crack a joke, saying we could be bored together for a while, just like the old days. She rolled her eyes at that and told me to skip the 'good-old-days stuff.' "

"You never fail to make me glad I'm celibate, my friend," Father Fortis said. "Teenagers' brains are much too quick these days."

"No argument there, Nick. That's when she really opened up on me. She said she had a theory as to why I was asking her to go. In talking with Rachel, her counselor, she'd worked out that my time out in New Mexico had changed me. How I'd been sent out to find a missing girl, and how I'd failed. So I'd come back worried that she'd run away again. I don't know if that's her thought or the counselor's, but I can't say she's completely wrong."

"You haven't told her what actually happened in New Mexico?"

"Not in so many words. The fewer people know what really happened out there, the safer things are. Anyway, just when I thought she was leading up to a big 'no' on the cabin plan, she said she'd think about it. With my luck, she'll say yes just about the time my new case ties me down here." Worthy shook her head. " 'Just like the old days,' she'll say."

Father Fortis sighed. "This is Allyson's last year of high school, right?"

"Yes, and after that, who knows?"

"Blessings on you, my friend. I truly mean that. And congratulations on getting a case, although I suppose that means someone's been murdered."

"Any case is better than being at the academy, Nick. And I think this one could be a challenge. It's complicated, though not everyone agrees with me on that. But speaking of complicated, I understand you've got your own problem here."

"Indeed we do. That's why I thought you were this Lieutenant Sherrod. Do you know him, by the way?"

"Oh, yes. Sherrod and I go back a good ten years. Unfortunately, we've never actually been friends."

"Well, he hasn't made a very good impression around here."

"He never does. Sorry you have to deal with that." A smile played across Worthy's face.

"You find something funny?" Father Fortis asked.

"I'm just jacking you around. What if I told you Lieutenant Sherrod isn't your problem any longer?"

Father Fortis studied his friend's face. "He's been reprimanded?"

"Better. He's been promoted to a federal case."

Father Fortis' heart leapt for joy. "Thank you, St. Nicholas or St. Cosmas, or St. Whoever! I don't suppose you know who's taking his place?"

Worthy's smile widened.

"Christopher, don't tease me."

"Think we can work together again, Nick?"

Father Fortis jumped up and planted a big kiss on the crown of Worthy's head. "Watson reporting for duty, Holmes."

"Better, I'll be that Flambeau guy and you be Father Brown," Worthy countered.

"Well, now I know you're teasing me. No, it's going to be hard enough trying to be a good parish priest. That's a bit of a stretch for this monk, let me tell you. Nothing to keep me awake at night like remembering that I've been given the care of over three hundred grieving families. So, I'll settle for a very weak impersonation of Dr. Watson."

Worthy rose. "Well, then, Watson, shall we start by you showing me where it happened?"

"Of course," Father Fortis replied, moving toward the door. "At least that will get me away from the blasted printer problem. I think the computer is possessed."

Worthy walked around the desk and studied the computer screen. He hit a series of buttons and a new screen appeared. "It says that you've sent three documents to a different printer. That's probably the one out in your secretary's office." Worthy hit another button, and Father Fortis heard the paper jump in the printer next to him.

"Bless you, my friend. I am so in over my head here."

Worthy took Father Fortis by the arm. "You've got your printer. Now show me my crime scene."

Out in the hallway, Father Fortis pointed down a side corridor to another door. "We can take this shortcut to the altar area, or we can walk around to the narthex and come in that way."

"Is that shortcut door usually locked?"

"Yes. Always, in fact, except on Sunday morning."

"Then let's go the other way. I'm guessing that's the way the killer entered and probably left."

That the very hallway they were in had been used that fateful morning when Father Spiro was murdered was not a new thought to Father Fortis. In fact, he'd had a hard time thinking of anything else as he struggled to write a homily that morning. No doubt that's what the parishioners would also be thinking on Sunday, no matter what he said.

Worthy broke into his thoughts. "I'll need to interview your secretary next."

"Go gently, please. Mrs. Hazelton feels terrible that she wasn't here that morning."

"Perhaps she was lucky," Worthy replied.

"That's what I told her, but guilt isn't logical."

In the narthex, Father Fortis paused before the icon of Christ, crossed himself, and prayed for Father Spiro's soul, the church, and the killer.

As the two men moved through the doors into the sanctuary, Worthy said, "You'll have to explain a few things, Nick."

"What do you mean?"

"All this," Worthy said, gesturing toward the altar and to a side wall of glass icons set in floor-to-ceiling windows.

Father Fortis nodded. "Ah, my mistake. We're such good friends, Christopher, that I just assumed you'd be familiar with our churches. Ask whatever you want."

They walked down the center aisle of the darkened sanctuary to stand at the foot of the raised platform. In front of them, a row of candles flickered below the icons of Christ and the Virgin Mary.

"Actually, I was only at your monastery for that one case, and I think I was still smarting from my own problems at the time. When I look around this place, I realize that I've always known you were an Orthodox monk, but I never quite understood what that means. I do remember a time in my junior high school years when a Greek Church was on my paper route. One afternoon, I was walking by the church, and they must have had some service going on. I looked into a room full of smoke and candles burning beneath paintings just like these. I remember wondering if there could be any place more different than my dad's Baptist church."

"Ah, yes, my friend," Father Fortis said. "A lot of people find us very different. It's hard for many to accept that we Orthodox are every Christian's oldest relatives. No Christian group has avoided changing over the centuries, but because of a series of circumstances outside of our control and conscious choices, we Orthodox have changed the least."

"I thought that honor went to Catholics," Worthy said.

"In a sense, that is also correct. Pope John Paul II was right when we said that the Orthodox and the Catholic Churches represent the two lungs of the ancient Church. Of course, the Catholic Church changed quite a bit after Vatican II in the 1960s. The Orthodox Church might be considered the eastern lung and the Catholic Church the western lung. Does that help?"

"I never thought of being Baptist as being modern," Worthy replied.

"Maybe the difference would be better understood like this. The Protestant Reformation centered on each person's relationship to Christ. The Orthodox were mainly in Eastern Europe, the Middle East, and Russia at the time of the Reformation and were not directly affected. For us, Christian faith centers not so much on a person's relationship to Christ as on Christ's relationship with a people, with the Church. As a Baptist convert to Orthodoxy once expressed, 'We Orthodox don't focus on having Jesus in our hearts. We focus on desiring to be in Jesus' heart.' Does that help or just make things worse?"

"Don't worry about it, Nick. I promise that I'll attend services here at St. Cosmas, so maybe I'll have some more questions. Right now, I think we should focus on the murder scene. He died right there, didn't he?" Worthy pointed to the square of new carpeting.

"Yes, my friend. The carpet piece is just temporary, of course."

"Speaking selfishly, I'm glad they've waited to re-carpet the whole area," Worthy said as he knelt down, laying a folder next to him. It struck Father Fortis as odd to see his friend kneel as parishioners do, and not far from the icons before which confessions in the Orthodox Church generally occurred. But that, he knew, wasn't in the cards for Worthy. Large parts of Worthy's life had disintegrated with his divorce and then with the strain of Allyson's running away. Faith in God had been one of those casualties.

"What have you learned about Father Spiro?" Worthy asked.

"Not as much as I had hoped. Naturally, no one wants to speak ill of a dead priest, but I get the feeling his mind was slipping a bit."

"The file says he had some sort of spell on the Sunday before he died."

"A 'spell'? I guess you could call it that. I was told that he just stopped in his tracks during one of the processions. But there were earlier indications of some problem. It wasn't the first time he'd forgotten parts of the liturgy. And he'd missed a few meetings recently."

Worthy looked up from the carpet square to the rear of the sanctuary. "I was looking at a photocopy of his schedule for the day he died. There was an asterisk by the nine o'clock slot, but no explanation. And then there was nothing on the docket until six that night, when a land acquisition committee meeting was scheduled."

Fortis folded his arms across his wide chest and nodded sagely. "Oh, yes, Mrs. Hazelton told me about the asterisks. That was something Father Spiro had added recently, and she has no idea what they meant. Mr. Margolis, the head of the parish council, put it this way: being with Father Spiro was like driving an old classic car. The ride was smooth, very polished, and you could be lulled into thinking everything was fine. But suddenly the transmission would slip. The motor would keep right on humming, smooth as ever, but the car wasn't going anywhere."

Worthy rose from his knees. "Why is the church thinking about land acquisition?"

"Ah, that I do know about. The parish council president said that some in the parish are discussing quite seriously the possibility of moving. One reason is that this facility was built back in the 1960s, when the Greeks wanted to fit into America. So what you see here, this rectangle of a room, isn't traditional Orthodox architecture. That would be a more Byzantine design, with a dome, for example. As someone at the monastery who'd been here before told me, St. Cosmas looks more like a Methodist Church with icons. Of course, the ultimate decision about moving will be made by the metropolitan."

"And what is a metropolitan?" Worthy asked.

"Sorry. A metropolitan is the same as a bishop. He visits each parish in the diocese when it suits him, but he receives regular updates from each of his churches. I'm sure he's heard the arguments on both sides about St. Cosmas moving."

Father Fortis looked over his shoulder and pointed to the street outside. "Those in favor of moving have raised another argument, one that will now gain strength. That faction says this neighborhood is too dangerous. They're particularly worried about one of the projects nearby."

"I bet that's Suffolk," Worthy said. "Sherrod thinks the killer is from over there."

"That theory would have a lot of support around here."

"Hmm, yeah, maybe," Worthy said vaguely as he rose to his feet. "Do you have a few minutes to look over some photos of the body?"

"I do, but you know me and crime photos. I remember nearly fainting when you showed me the photos of Sister Anna in New Mexico."

"Let's take this front pew," Worthy said as he opened the folder he had been carrying. "I'll warn you; they're pretty gruesome, but you know I wouldn't ask if I didn't need some help figuring out Father Spiro."

"You always speak as if the victims are still living, Christopher."

"Yeah, I've been told that before. In some ways, they are alive for a lot of people. I know that's true for those who loved them."

"I would say that's true for the people of this parish," Father Fortis added.

Worthy held the photos in his hand. "When someone we love dies suddenly, and especially if they are killed, the most natural thing in the world is to believe that death cheated them. Everyone thinks about the future that won't be lived. Now, in Father Spiro's case, people might be thinking about him not being here on Sunday or not being in his office when they need him. Or, they might think about him being cheated out of his retirement years. To most people, unexpected death is this great thief."

"But isn't that true?"

"Only partially, Nick. The problem with seeing things that way is that it doesn't help one bit in solving the murder. In fact, it gets in the way of solving it."

Father Fortis sighed. "When my younger brother died in Vietnam, I felt the same way. Every year on his birthday, I realize I still do. I think about how old he would be and about how many nephews and nieces I'd have if he and his fiancée had married."

"But in a murder investigation, it's different," Worthy countered, "at least I hope it is. Yes, death interrupted an old priest's life. But for me, cruel as this sounds, that's simply a given. What I want to find out is what Father Spiro was worried about that day and what he was hoping would happen if he were still alive."

"Give me an example."

"Sure," Worthy said. "Was he looking forward to retirement or dreading it? Did he want St. Cosmas to move from this neighborhood or stay?"

"Ha, well, that may be a bit difficult. Father Spiro tended to contradict himself on almost every point."

"Then I need to understand why he contradicted himself so much. At bottom, I have to know why the victim gave death some sort of opening."

Father Fortis exhaled deeply. "I wouldn't share that thought with the victim's family and friends. It makes murder seem invited."

"If I do my job right, they won't even know I'm asking that question. Look, I'm not saying people want to be murdered. But most of the time, the victim did something to make it more likely."

"And you think Father Spiro can somehow still help you?"

A frown crossed Worthy's face. "Maybe, if I ask the right questions of those who knew him. It's this way, Nick. I need to know why Father Spiro came into the sanctuary early that morning, a half hour before his mysterious appointment. And if I don't know why he put an asterisk in his calendar, maybe I can determine if this priest was sleeping well in the days and weeks before or if he was seeing his doctor for some problem. And I especially want to know what caused that spell on Sunday."

"What if Father Spiro didn't tell anyone about any of that?"

"Then I hope something in his patterns will speak anyway," Worthy said. "Which is why I need you to take a look at these photos."

Father Fortis sighed. "Yes, of course."

He accepted the first one, a gruesome shot of an old man stretched out on the floor before them, blood oozing from his eyes and nose. "I will never understand how you live with this, Christopher," Father Fortis whispered.

Worthy didn't offer an explanation. Instead, he pointed to one feature in the photo. "Tell me why he was wearing a robe that morning."

Father Fortis studied the photo. "He's vested in a *rasa* and what we call the *epitrachelion*."

"Which is which?"

"The rasa is the robe, and the epitrachelion is the vestment piece that goes over the shoulders and down the front of the robe."

"Epitrachelion," Worthy repeated. "That's what strangled him. Is it usual for a priest to wear a get-up like this on a weekday?"

"Father Spiro was old school, or so I've been told. For them, the rasa is quite normal. You can see I have mine on. But the other, the epitrachelion, is perhaps suggestive."

"Suggestive of what, Nick?"

"It's usual for hearing confessions. But that doesn't quite fit. Yesterday, Mrs. Hazelton told me the pattern at St. Cosmas is to hear confessions on Thursdays."

"So either Father Spiro was a bit confused that Tuesday morning or—"

"Or he'd scheduled a special confession, off the radar screen," Father Fortis mused.

"Wouldn't it be nice if we could trust the old guy, Nick? Now, take a look at this next photo. Anything strike you about it?"

Father Fortis looked at a view of the body photographed from the feet upward. The legs dominated, the right one unnaturally bent beneath the other. "I don't know what to make of this, Christopher."

Worthy glanced up at the stain. "Nick, do you have one of those epitrachelions here?"

"Of course. I've stored several of mine behind the icon screen."

"Do you think there are some of Father Spiro's still back there?"

"Yes, I'm sure I saw quite a few when I hung mine up. Why?"

"Something's not right about this photo. Not the legs, but something else."

Father Fortis walked through the doors of the icon screen and bowed toward the altar before going toward a side room with a wardrobe closet. On the far left he found several epitrachelions, most well worn.

He returned to the sanctuary and laid five of them on the edge of the platform.

Worthy approached slowly. "Am I allowed to handle them?"

"Of course, my friend. But what are you looking for?"

"Watch." Worthy picked up each of the five and felt the fabric. Taking one, he lifted it to eye level before letting it fall to the carpet. He did the same with the others before returning to the pew, a smile on his lips.

"You look pleased," Father Fortis said.

Worthy picked up the photo. "The legs are what draw our attention, but the way the legs are crossed only tells us what we'd expect—that Father Spiro was already unconscious when he fell. He may have already been dead, in fact."

"So there's something else you see," Father Fortis said, studying the photo.

Worthy pointed next to the epitrachelion in the photo. "Look how it lies on his body. Straight as a die. Compare that with those I just dropped on the carpet. See, they're full of folds, just as we'd expect."

"Well, I'll be. Straight as a die, indeed," Father Fortis observed.

"From his shoulder right down the side of his body to his feet. It's almost rigid."

Father Fortis pulled on his beard. "That's not very likely, is it?"

"Nope."

Father Fortis looked at the first photo. It was the same. "So unless Father Spiro was wearing a particularly stiff epitrachelion that morning, the only other explanation is that someone straightened it."

"And after he fell. Probably after he died," Worthy offered.

"And who found him first?"

"The file says it was a Mrs. Filis who'd come to water the plants."

"Ah, yes, I know her."

"And she testified that she didn't touch the body," Worthy said.

Father Fortis scratched his head. "So that would mean it had to be the killer."

Worthy nodded. "Now ask yourself this, Nick. Why would somebody from the projects who'd come here to rob the place do something like that?"

Father Fortis studied the photo again. "I'm not sure why anyone would do that."

"Think about it, Nick. Don't assume the killer did it consciously."

Father Fortis sucked in a breath. "Good Lord. The killer did it because he knew Father Spiro."

"It was at least someone with an ingrained respect for the priesthood." Worthy walked up on the platform and bent down over the carpet square. "Whoever strangled Father Spiro that morning bent down right here, trying to figure out what to do next." Worthy looked up at the altar. "Maybe that's when he saw the altarpiece and took that to throw us off track."

Father Fortis leaned forward in the front pew. "And that's when he unknowingly straightened the vestment."

Worthy nodded, eying his friend. "I think you know what that probably means."

Father Fortis groaned, a sick feeling rising in his stomach. "If you're right," he muttered, "then the killer could be one of my parishioners."

CHAPTER THREE

———— ♦ ————

Every time Worthy uncovered a clue, he doubted it within the next forty-eight hours. The clue of the epitrachelion was no different. Just because Sherrod hadn't noticed it, Worthy reminded himself, didn't make the clue important.

The major flaw in his logic wasn't hard to find. The vestment's abnormal position on the body didn't necessarily mean the killer was a parishioner of St. Cosmas. Perhaps the killer was simply the neat type. Even worse, the straightening of the vestment might be like the missing altarpiece, a ploy by the killer to throw them off.

But after repeatedly sifting through the angles over the next two days, Worthy ended up believing in the discovery's importance. The old priest was dressed for a confession, though none was listed in his calendar. That anomaly suggested a parishioner and fit nicely with the clue of the rearranged vestment. If nothing else, the clue gave him an edge, something in his pocket when he met with his new partner at lunch.

Carnell Henderson's muteness in the captain's office troubled Worthy. Maybe Henderson's silence expressed his anger at being overlooked after Sherrod was pulled from the case. If so, Worthy could forget Betts' dream that he could mentor the man. Establishing a civil relationship would be hard enough.

He was surprised to find Henderson already seated at the Blue Bayou, a Cajun mom-and-pop eatery across town from the precinct. The place had been Worthy's choice. When they were first married, Worthy and Susan met there after she got off her shift at the hospital. In all those years, he'd never once seen another cop.

"Afternoon," Worthy said as he slid into the other side of the booth. He noticed a folder sitting on the table next to Henderson's glass.

Henderson looked up. "Hello."

"Thanks for coming."

"Thanks for the offer. What do you want me to call you, by the way? Are you the Lieutenant this, Lieutenant that type, or are you first names, last names, what?"

"Call me Chris, or Worthy. Not 'Lieutenant,' though. And you? Carnell, Henderson, or Hoops?"

"Definitely not Carnell. No one's called me that since grade school except my wife. Hoops would be fine."

"Basketball, then?" Worthy asked, looking at hands on his partner large enough to palm two basketballs. They also looked like they could do major damage in a fight.

Before Henderson could answer, the waitress approached the booth to pour Worthy a glass of water. "Haven't seen you in a ton of years," she said, smiling at him.

Worthy nodded. "Been busy, I guess."

"You gentlemen ready to order?" She rattled off the luncheon specials and warned them which dishes were extra spicy.

Both ordered the gumbo. The two sat in silence for a moment before Worthy repeated his question.

"Yeah, I used to play ball, a little bit in college. How about you? You're pretty tall."

"Just in high school. Baseball was more my sport."

Henderson nodded. "What position?"

"I'm a lefty, so I pitched."

"A southpaw, huh? I played outfield."

There was another silence, and Henderson swished his water glass.

Worthy studied the man across from him. Henderson had already been much more talkative than in Captain Betts' office, but his words had come out in staccato bursts.

Henderson cleared his throat. "How'd you find this place? You from the South?"

"I grew up partly in Kentucky, but I had a college summer job in a halfway house in Louisiana. A corrections job. If the guys behaved during the week, we took them into town on Saturday night for a movie and supper. Millersburg, Louisiana, had just the one restaurant. Anyway, the first time I tried the gumbo there, it burned a patch off my tongue big as a quarter."

Henderson laughed, a bit too loud, Worthy thought. "Some of my people are Caribbean, so there's no such thing as too hot. But I didn't know this place existed."

"Do me a favor and keep it that way," Worthy said.

"No problem."

The waitress brought their cokes as well as a basket of bread. Once they were alone again, Worthy said, "I thought I might start by asking if there's anything you'd like to tell me or ask me."

Henderson hurriedly buttered a piece of bread. "Like what?"

"Like if you're pissed that you're not in charge on this case. If so, I'd like to know up front. Not that I can change things, of course."

"Me, in charge? You the only one who hasn't heard about what happened?"

"About decking Pescatelli? That I heard."

"Here's what I learned from that mistake. If you lay out a fellow cop in locker room—in front of an entire shift, by the way—know that it's going to follow you to the grave. Hell, I'll never make promotion now."

"I'll be honest with you. If Spicer were still in charge, I'd say you're right."

Henderson munched on the bread, his jaw muscles flexing. "Spicer was one unforgiving prick. If he were still here, I'd be out of a job."

"So you timed your bout with Pescatelli just right. Maybe that means you're just lucky or maybe it means you're smart. That's how our new captain seems to see you. She thinks you have potential."

"She said that?"

"In so many words. By the way, I never heard why you hit Pescatelli."

"He only got about half of it out, but I'm pretty sure he was calling me a lazy, fucking nigger."

"So why'd he say that?"

"Because I'm not nine to five."

Worthy waited until the waitress had set down their plates and left. "What does that mean?" he asked.

"It means I'm the kind of guy who does my job, follows my leads, and tries to put it all together. I'm a plodder, but I plod on my own schedule." He paused before adding, "It's better for my family that way."

"How so? Your wife work?"

Henderson looked toward the bar. "That and we got a kid, so I'm helping out for a while. Pescatelli made a big deal of it on a day I wasn't in the mood. That's all."

"Knowing Sherrod, I'm surprised he didn't go at you for the same reason."

"Are you kidding? The way he rushes around, he barely noticed me."

"Which is not my style, by the way," Worthy said. "You called yourself a plodder. You've maybe heard that some of our colleagues find me too damn slow."

"But not in your career," Henderson said, lifting the folder.

"Oh? Is that what that is? Here I thought it might be case material."

"Thought I'd check you out before we got too lovey-dovey."

"And you found out what?"

"That until about seven years ago you were a real Barney Fife. Then you solve two—what's the word?—enigmas, that's it; two impossible cases. But you solve both of them within three months, and all of a sudden your picture is all over the papers. Hell, you get a few more gray hairs and they'll make you Captain."

"You must not be a very thorough reader."

"Oh, I read it all. Yeah, I found the setbacks, if that's what you're getting at. But from what I heard, all that was from around the time of your divorce. Am I right?"

Worthy sat back in the booth and considered his new partner. "Not bad for a plodder. And what would I find if I looked into your file?"

"You mean you haven't?"

"Nope."

"Nothing flashy like in yours. Until Pescatelli opened his trap, I didn't have any real problems." He wiped his face with a napkin. "But now I need something to happen, something good. Otherwise, I'm going to end up a security guard in some mall."

"And you think that good thing is solving this case. You still think the killer is from Suffolk?"

"Hell yes. I'll bet you a hundred bucks that altarpiece is over there right now. And if it is, I'll be the one to find it. Shit, Sherrod always brags about his goddamn informants, but I got family over there. Yeah, somebody there did it. See for yourself. I sent records on those three guys to you through interdepartmental mail."

"What if I told you things are a bit more complicated at the church than Sherrod thought?"

Henderson sneered. "I don't give a good goddamn what Sherrod thinks. The business about the church is all in your head."

Worthy pulled out the photos from his sports coat pocket. "Look at these."

"I already have."

Worthy put the telltale photo on top of the pile. "There's something not right about this one. Maybe you noticed."

Henderson's face sobered. "Noticed what? There were no prints or DNA."

Worthy pointed at the vestment. "So how did this part of the vestment, the part that killed the priest, end up so perfectly straight?"

Henderson studied the photo for a moment. "Well, I'll be damned. Still, what's it mean?"

"You think somebody from Suffolk would take the time to do that after he killed the old man?"

"Maybe. The guy, Bales, is a real wacko. I'm due to interview him again sometime tomorrow or the day after. But I sat in on Sherrod's first go-around with him. He's crazy enough to do anything. So I'm keeping my chips right where I said. You stay on at the church, and I'll work the Suffolk side. Winner takes all."

"No, winner doesn't take all. We both get the same credit or the same blame," Worthy corrected.

"Are you saying the next time I see your picture is in the papers, mine is going to be there, too?"

"I don't control the papers. I'm talking about what happens at the precinct."

Henderson studied his face. "Okay, then."

A cellphone beeped and Henderson pulled it out of his pocket. "Who? Yeah, he's here."

He passed the phone over to Worthy.

"You don't have a cellphone?" Henderson whispered.

"No. It's a long story," Worthy replied as he took the phone. "Which button do I push?"

Henderson laughed. "Just talk into it like a regular phone."

"This is Worthy."

"Christopher, Nick here. I was just calling your sergeant to find out where I could reach you. Look, I think I've found something. One of my parishioners, Mr. Bagios, is in my office. Mr. Bagios is the church photographer, and he's brought in some photos of Father Spiro taken about a week before he died. I think you should see them."

"Oh? What do they look like?"

"It's hard to describe over the phone. Can you drop by the church this afternoon?"

"Absolutely. Maybe I can get Henderson to come by, too."

"Who? Oh, right, your partner."

"See you in about thirty minutes."

Worthy handed back the phone.

"What was that about?" Henderson asked.

"Somebody at the church brought in photos of Father Spiro taken just before he died. Father Fortis thinks we should see them. I said you might stop by the church with me."

Henderson took a swig of his drink. "I heard."

"It'd give you a chance to meet the new priest."

Henderson looked down at his watch before pushing his plate away. "Sorry, I got to run."

For the first time, Worthy recognized the look Henderson had given him in Captain Betts' office. "Shouldn't take more than an hour," he added.

Henderson rose. "Like I said, I got to run. Thanks for the lunch."

FATHER FORTIS PICKED UP ONE OF the photos and studied Father Spiro's face. He must have been a striking man in his day, Father Fortis thought. His predecessor's long white hair and neatly trimmed beard made him look like a cross between an early Church Father and a Greek tycoon. But the eyes betrayed him, the heavy bags beneath pressing down on cheeks dotted with age spots. Something about the gaze suggested more than an old priest contemplating retirement.

"I hope I haven't done anything wrong," Mr. Bagios said, looking up from his chair as Father Fortis pulled on his beard.

"Wrong? No, not at all, Mr. Bagios. What makes you think that?"

The elderly photographer pleaded with open hands. "You see, I didn't develop the film right away because of his death. And I don't take digital. No, that is not true photography."

"No one can blame you for that, Mr. Bagios. And I'm sure you were as shocked as the rest of the parish."

"No, no, Father, it was also because of the other. I was the one who took photos at the funeral."

A macabre childhood memory flashed through Father Fortis' mind. It was his fifteenth birthday, that terrible day his grandfather and uncle, partners in the family fishing business, were laid out side by side in their coffins. It was unusual for bodies of drowned fishermen to be recovered, but the two had been dragged overboard in a malfunction of their nets. His birthday cake had sat untouched, candles unlit, in the middle of their dining room table until after the funeral. Every five dollar bill pressed into his hands by tearful aunts and cousins had burned him with guilt.

There were no birthday photos that year, but Father Fortis remembered as if it were yesterday the old photographer with the Rolleiflex who set up his tripod close to the casket of his grandfather, then that of his uncle. Flashbulb after flashbulb hit the floor of the old New Bedford church.

"Father Spiro still had relatives back in Greece, then?" Father Fortis asked.

"Oh, yes. I always take photos for those back home. I did the same for Theone, his wife, *presbytera,* when she died. May her memory be eternal."

Father Fortis appreciated the reference to home. For Mr. Bagios' generation, America would never replace Greece.

Father Fortis walked over to the window and looked out toward the parking lot. "How long had Father Spiro been widowed?"

"Five years, or was it six? Theone was a wonderful asset, as dear to us at St. Cosmas as Father Spiro, God rest their souls."

"How did Father Spiro take her death?"

Mr. Bagios sighed. "Not well. You see, Theone was sick for nearly a year before the end. Cancer of the pancreas." The photographer paused, seemingly lost in a memory.

"It's a wonder Father Spiro didn't retire then," Father Fortis mused, looking out the window for Worthy's car.

"Some people thought he would. His daughter lives out in California, somewhere sunny, but after Theone's forty-day memorial, Father announced to the community that he intended to stay on. That's when we knew we were his closest family."

Mrs. Hazelton knocked on the door. "Lieutenant Worthy is here, Father."

"Huh? I didn't see his car. Come in, Christopher. Where'd you park?"

"I drove in the back way."

"I didn't know there was a back way. Where's Sergeant Henderson?"

Worthy took a breath and released it slowly. "He couldn't make it."

Something wrong there, Father Fortis thought. Odd that he hadn't even met the sergeant yet. He'd heard from Mrs. Hazelton that he was African American and also that there was something about the man's silence that made her uneasy.

Introducing the photographer to Worthy, Father Fortis said, "Mr. Bagios was filling me in on Father Spiro, and he's been very helpful. I think his photos are as well."

Worthy took the first photo handed to him.

"As you can see, this one took Father Spiro completely by surprise," Father Fortis explained.

"More than surprise," Worthy said. "I'd say he's pretty angry."

Mr. Bagios wiped his mouth with a hand. "This is my fault. I wanted a candid shot of Father for the new church directory, and I asked Mrs. Hazelton to open the door for me."

Worthy tapped a finger on the edge of the photo. "So what we have is Father Spiro trying to block the shot with his hand. It also looks like he's trying to say something. What do you remember about this particular shot, Mr. Bagios?"

The old photographer cleared his throat, as if giving testimony in court. "I thought it was just, forgive me, a bit of his vanity. Father Spiro was a very good-looking man when he was younger."

"Did he say anything afterwards?" Father Fortis asked.

Mr. Bagios' face reddened. "Sorry, Father, I can't remember."

"What do you think, Nick?"

Father Fortis studied the photo more closely. Lines stretched from the old priest's mouth down toward his jowls, the neck a bundle of tight cords fighting beneath the sagging skin. A far cry from the man portrayed in the photo in the hallway. The old priest was also holding a pen in the hand. On the desk was an open notebook.

"My guess is he's saying a loud 'no,'" Father Fortis offered.

"Wait. Yes, now I remember," Mr. Bagios interrupted. "He told me I had to take another. That's why I shot the other two."

Worthy turned to the second and third photos, both nearly identical and far less interesting. Father Spiro sat officiously behind the desk, his face transformed by a big smile. The priest's hands were folded in front of him, the pen to the side.

"And did he talk to you after you took these others?" Worthy asked.

Mr. Bagios sat forward. "Yes, he did. He told me to be sure to give him that first one once it was developed."

"Did he say why?" Worthy asked.

"He said something about it being blurred, but I told him he was wrong. A professional photographer knows when a picture will turn out."

"It is indeed a good photo," Father Fortis said, nodding approvingly at his parishioner. Worthy positioned the three photos side by side on the desk. "You see something here, don't you, Nick? That's why you called me."

Father Fortis blushed. "As I'm sure you see yourself, Christopher, the book is missing from the second and third photos."

Worthy nodded.

"Well, I'll be," Mr. Bagios said. "Where'd it go?"

"And you didn't leave the room between the two shots?" Worthy asked.

"No, no. But I wasn't actually in the room for the first one. I was back in the doorway. It took me only a minute to come in here and set up for the other two."

Worthy scratched his head. "So did he drop it into his lap or do something else with it? And what kind of book are we talking about?"

Father Fortis scurried back to the desk and opened the center drawer. Pulling out a magnifying glass, he handed it to Worthy. "Father Spiro must have used this for the fine print."

Worthy bent over the first photo. "I'd say the book is one of those older types with leather at the corners. Ask the secretary to come in, will you, Nick?"

Mrs. Hazelton entered when buzzed and looked at the photo through the glass. "No, I'm sure I've never seen that book."

Worthy took the three photos and returned them to the folder. "I'm going to have these blown up back at the precinct. Maybe we'll find some lettering on the book. Meanwhile, Mrs. Hazelton, maybe you could look around the church. Wherever Father Spiro tended to store things—bookcases, storage cabinets, that sort of thing."

"But what's so important about the book?" Mr. Bagios asked. Mrs. Hazelton looked up as if she had the same thought.

Worthy pursed his lips. Father Fortis knew his friend was debating how much of his suspicions to disclose.

"I want to know what was on Father Spiro's mind in those last few weeks. Your photographs, Mr. Bagios, suggest that this missing book just might—I'm saying *might*—be important."

"Do you think it could have something to do with who killed him?" Mr. Bagios pressed.

Worthy shook his head. "I'd ask you not to say anything about the book, because I don't want to give any false hope. I'm just saying the book could help us know Father Spiro better."

Mr. Bagios nodded approvingly. Mrs. Hazelton's face seemed less tortured that it had since Father Fortis had arrived.

And that, dear people, Father Fortis thought, is the difference between my friend and Lieutenant Sherrod.

CHAPTER FOUR

———◆———

WORTHY TOOK THE ELEVATOR FROM THE lab up to his office, feeling pleased with the start to the case. Perhaps obstinacy as much as loyalty to his own methods had made him rebel at Sherrod's convenient robbery theory, but the clues of the vestment and the missing book seemed to justify his more careful approach.

The one nagging problem was Henderson. Outright opposition would be easier to work around than the confusing signals he got from his partner. But true to his word, Henderson had left the records of the three suspects from Suffolk in his mail slot. On an attached memo, Henderson had added his plan to conduct second interviews of the three, starting the next day.

Worthy found it telling that the times of the interviews weren't listed. *So we're both loners,* he thought. *That probably isn't a good sign.*

His thoughts were interrupted by a piece of paper taped to his door. Approaching, he saw it was a newspaper clipping, a piece from the morning *Detroit Free Press*, with the words "hot shit" scribbled across it in ink. He tore the article off the door and brought it to his desk.

DETROIT'S TOP COP CHASES PRIEST'S KILLER

A change in team in the Father Spiro George murder investigation has occurred after only two weeks.

A police memo obtained by this reporter has confirmed that Lt. Christopher Worthy, noted for his brilliant work on past "cold cases," has been assigned to lead the case following a teaching stint at the police academy. He replaces Lieutenant Phillip Sherrod, who has been transferred to another case.

Worthy yanked at his tie. He looked at the byline of the column, "Around Town," and found the reporter's name: Kenna McCarty. How the hell had a society writer gotten ahold of an internal departmental memo?

Worthy thought back to his lunch with Henderson. Was this the reason he'd made that crack about his photo not being next to Worthy's in the paper? But if Worthy had any question about who'd scribbled across the article, it was answered by Sherrod barging into his office.

Worthy, not bothering to get up, turned the article over. "Ah, Phil."

"Shut the fuck up," Sherrod spat out as he walked toward the desk, his finger pointing like a gun. "You think I'm just going to forget what you did to me yesterday?"

Worthy leaned back in his chair. "Exactly what is it you think I did?"

Sherrod's eyes narrowed as he took another step forward. "You bent me over and did me like a Texas sheep, and you did it in front of my new captain. Where the hell you get off pulling that shit?"

Worthy rose and looked over the desk at Sherrod. "And I'll ask you a question. Where do you get off talking to me like you're my captain?"

Sherrod looked up at the taller Worthy. "I'm talking about basic, fucking respect."

"Oh, really," Worthy said. "I asked a few questions about your approach, an approach which no one has abandoned." He lifted the Suffolk folder off his desk. "Henderson is interviewing those guys tomorrow. If you took my comments personally—"

"Wake the fuck up." Sherrod's face was beet red as spit flew out with his words. "Remember Milander and Autrey? Do you think they'll get their promotions now, after you grabbed their glory? You're a fucking parasite, Worthy, and everybody around here knows it. Not taking your comments personally, my fucking ass. Read the goddamn paper this morning!"

"Get out of here," Worthy ordered, jabbing his index finger at the door.

"First, you listen," he said, wagging his own finger in Worthy's face. "I watched you stand up there like Lindbergh flying fucking solo and take that commendation. You didn't even have the courtesy to mention Milander and Autrey, as if they'd done nothing on the case before they handed it to you. No, you just stood there with their cojones in your back pocket." Sherrod grabbed at his own crotch and wagged it toward Worthy.

Worthy could feel the heat suffusing his face as the anger boiled up. "I'm not going to ask you again. Get out of here," Worthy said, stepping around his desk.

A knock on the door was followed by the lab tech. "Here they are. Oh, sorry."

"No problem. The lieutenant was just leaving."

Sherrod stood in the open doorway and delivered his last shot down the echoing hallway. "Don't you ever forget whose case you're finishing. It's mine! Don't even try to cut my balls off. I won't go down like the others."

The lab tech's eyebrows arched upward as he turned back toward Worthy. "Nice guy," he whispered. "Is he always like that?"

"That, young man, is Lieutenant Phil Sherrod, one of our colleagues in this fine precinct."

"I'll remember that," the tech said, wide-eyed, as he dropped a folder on the desk before turning and departing.

Alone in his office, Worthy stood by his window and watched the cars streaming past on the freeway. Always a question of "balls," cutting them off, keeping score. Forget the victims and their families. Save face, the first rule of detection. *It's a wonder we catch anyone,* he thought.

Exhausted, Worthy returned to his desk and opened the folder left by the lab tech. Taking an eight-by-ten photo and enlarging it in one inch squares led to a lot of photos. Worthy sorted them into three piles—one of the priest's face, another of the desktop and book, and a third for the rest of the photo. At the back of the folder, he found a note from the new lab tech. "A speculation on the subject's mouth," the note read. "In my judgment, the subject is either forming the 'w' or the long 'o' sound. Happens to be one of my specialties. Alex. P.S. I was in one of your classes at the academy."

No wonder he's still eager, Worthy thought. *I'll give you six months. Then we'll see how willing you are to stick your neck out.*

Worthy picked up the phone and called Father Fortis. "Nick, do you have a minute?"

"Why not, my friend. This parish priest business is going to drive me insane. I mean, who gets anything done?"

"I can call back if you'd like."

"No, no, forgive my frustration. How can I help?"

"I'm looking at the photo enlargements of the victim right now."

"That was quick. I thought it might take a few days."

"It seems computers have taken over here."

"Don't talk to me about computers, my friend. Did you find out about the book?"

"I'm not sure. The angle of that first shot is pretty poor. I can tell that the book is open, but that's about it."

"Nothing about the words?"

"No. So that means we won't know much until we find it. But Nick, here's an easier question. One of our new lab techs said he thinks Father Spiro is saying something that begins with a 'w' or a long 'o.' I'm guessing, 'what the hell.' "

"No, I wouldn't think so, Christopher."

"You mean because he's a priest?"

Father Fortis laughed loudly. "I can tell that you've never visited a seminary. No, I'm just thinking that Father Spiro was Greek-born. Surprise any immigrant, and he'll probably use his first tongue."

Worthy exhaled. "Of course. I forgot about that. Okay, let's skip that for a moment. I did find something else on the other side of the desk—another book."

"Really? Is it in Greek?"

"No. It was lying to the side, and it's in all three of the photos."

"Which means that Father Spiro wasn't trying to hide it," Father Fortis said.

"Very good, Watson. Now, explain this. It's titled *Remaining Jewish in America.* Interesting, huh?"

Father Fortis didn't answer for a moment. "I was just checking here. No, it's not on the desk now, but I'll ask Mrs. Hazelton."

"Any idea why he'd have such a book?" Worthy asked.

"I have no idea. Hang on a minute. Here's Mrs. Hazelton."

Worthy gazed down at the enlargements of the priest's mouth while he waited. "So you were reading about Judaism," he whispered, "and you hid another book from us. How about a little help, old man?"

"Christopher? Were you talking to me?"

"No, no, Nick. What did she say?"

"It's good news," Father Fortis announced. "She knows the book. In fact, yes, here it is. Thank you so much, Mrs. Hazelton."

"What's it look like, Nick?"

"It's a hardcover. Ah, this is probably what you want to know. On the first page there's something handwritten. It says, 'From one Orthodox to another. Your friend, S. Milkin.' "

"That could be a help," Worthy said, as he wrote down the name. "Nick, does it look well-used?"

"I'm not sure what you mean. It looks like somebody has read it, if that's what you mean."

"Exactly." Worthy thought for a moment. "Try this, Nick. Hold the book up and let it fall on your desk."

"Really? Okay."

Worthy heard a thud as the book hit the desk. "Did it open to a page?"

"Yes, Page 123. Let's see. It's part of a chapter on ethics. The page has a list of righteous deeds for every Jew to do in daily life."

"Okay," Worthy said. "Now do the same thing again and tell me what you find."

He heard Nick's heavy breathing and then the thud of the book hitting the desk again. "It opened to Page 175, on kosher laws."

"Huh. Okay, a third time, Nick."

Again, the sound of the book hitting the desk before Father Fortis spoke. "It's back in the chapter on ethics, about two pages from the first time. Wait a minute. Yes, there's some pencil underlining as well."

"Really," Worthy licked his lips. "Read it to me."

"It says, 'He who stands by and lets evil happen to another, it is as if he committed the evil himself.' Hmm, wouldn't we like to know why he underlined that?"

Worthy scribbled the phrase down on the folder. "Maybe there's a way to find that out, Nick. Thanks."

Worthy hung up and studied his notes. "S. Milkin." He pulled down a city phone book and found four S. Milkins, with one, Sol A. Milkin, having two numbers—one on Conrad Street and one at Congregation Beth Israel. He turned back to the yellow pages under "Churches" before realizing his mistake. He flipped back to "Synagogues" and found Congregation Beth Israel's listing.

A secretary answered and said that yes, Rabbi Milkin was on staff there, though he was retired and served only part-time.

"Could you tell me if Congregation Beth Israel is an Orthodox synagogue?" he asked.

"We certainly are," the woman said proudly. "Would you like to know the times of our services?"

"No thank you," Worthy said. "I'd like to know when I could talk with Rabbi Milkin."

"Try him at home. That would be my suggestion."

Worthy called the other number, and after the fourth ring heard the scratchy voice of an old man. "Rabbi Milkin. How may I serve you?"

"Yes sir, this is Lieutenant Christopher Worthy of the Detroit Police Department. I understand you were a friend of Father Spiro George."

There was a moment of silence on the other end before the rabbi spoke. "Who did you say you were?"

Worthy explained again.

"How did you get this number?"

Worthy explained about finding the book with his name on the inside cover.

"Ah, yes, my poor friend Spiro. Such a tragedy. Perhaps I should have expected one day someone to call me."

"Oh? Why's that?"

"Because I know who killed him."

CHAPTER FIVE

———◆———

WORTHY HAD TAKEN UP RABBI MILKIN'S invitation to meet early that Friday afternoon before Sabbath services began at sunset. With Father Fortis in tow, he exited I-696 and drove northwest out of downtown toward Bloomfield Hills. With each block, the lawns were greener, the sidewalks newer, straighter, whiter. KFCs and Popeyes yielded to ethnic and health food options. Leaving the actual city limits, Worthy took note of the glaring contrasts as he had a thousand times before. Drugstores with actual windows stood beside gas stations with attendants who no longer hid in bullet-proof bubbles. Delis with white wrought-iron furniture and sun umbrellas snuggled up next to wine bars and florists, while women nonchalantly pushed strollers, unaware they were no more than two miles from crack houses.

Volvoland, Worthy thought. In Detroit, the drive from third world to first world was shorter than the time it took to finish a Big Mac and fries.

"Christopher," Father Fortis said, interrupting his thoughts, "I appreciate that you're letting me come along to meet this rabbi. But what did you mean on the phone when you said not to get my hopes up?"

Worthy fished out the last few french fries from the bag sitting between them. "I've met his type all too often. They want so badly to do something to catch their friend's killer that they begin to think of ways that they can. He's going to have a lot to say, but statistically his type is hardly ever that helpful."

"*Statistically?* Since when did that matter to you, Christopher? I mean, a rabbi and an Orthodox priest. Let me tell you, that's not a very common friendship."

"Two old guys. Who knows, maybe they met in a coffee shop."

"Ah," Father Fortis added, fingering his pectoral cross, "but don't forget this particular 'old guy' gave Father Spiro some very unexpected reading material."

They found the synagogue, a new building set low and unobtrusively within the residential neighborhood. On the façade, a stone-relief bush with copper flames bore the name CONGREGATION BETH ISRAEL in English below Hebrew lettering.

The two walked through the front doors and followed the sign down a hallway to the rabbi's offices. There, a man in his seventies with bushy white hair stood watering a fern. After introductions, the three went down the sunny hallway to an office.

The rabbi offered chairs to both visitors and then nodded in Worthy's direction. "I see you brought my book back," he said. "I've been wondering all day how to explain that. But just before you came, I realized something. How can you make sense of the book if you don't know how Spiro and I became friends?"

Rabbi Milkin paced the office, moving from his desk to the windows overlooking the snow-covered lawn outside. Before speaking, he took out a handkerchief and blew noisily into it. "Imagine," he said, pointing to the trees outside, "bare trees, and I'm still allergic. Spiro would have said it was penance for something."

"Leah, Leah!" he called loudly to the open door. "Make us some coffee, please." He turned to Father Fortis. "You're his replacement?"

"Temporary replacement, just until the metropolitan—the bishop—makes a decision."

"I'm glad you came along. You will maybe appreciate that our friendship was rare, yes?"

"I have wondered about that," Father Fortis replied.

"By chance, strictly by chance. It was at one of those Jewish-Christian conferences, over at Allgemein College." A look of disgust crossed the old man's face. "Two or three years ago, who can remember? We both found a way to leave the same session and found ourselves drinking coffee. We felt the same way about the conference. A few intellectuals agreeing that your Jesus was a simple rabbi. As if that would solve everything. Spiro told me he found the whole thing silly. I said he was right."

Father Fortis leaned back in his chair, realizing how right Worthy had been. Out of this man's respect for his dead friend, the rabbi would spare no detail.

"We started to meet every two or three weeks for lunch and to commiserate about the pressures of our line of work. Sometimes we'd talk theology, but Spiro's brand was too mystical for my blood. He was as bad as our Hasidic brothers and sisters," Rabbi Milkin said with a laugh.

"When was the last time you saw him?" Worthy asked.

"If I answer that, what will you know? Nothing."

The secretary came in with the three cups and a tray of cookies.

"Almond crescents," Rabbi Milkin said. "Spiro's favorite, right, Leah?"

"Bless his memory," the secretary added as she left the room.

The rabbi slowly munched a cookie while continuing to gaze at Father Fortis. "My family emigrated from Russia to Palestine, then here. We were driven out by Russian Orthodox Christians, so you will understand that it was a miracle for Spiro and me to find friendship. But even miracles are fragile."

He took a long sip from his cup as he stood by the window. "One night I couldn't sleep. I turned on the TV and heard one of those late night preachers. I thought he was funny, but then he said God didn't listen to the prayers of Jews. He said we weren't saved. And in that moment I was a boy back in Russia, waiting for someone to knock on my door in the middle of the night. I didn't sleep at all."

After a moment's pause, he continued. "The next day, I called Spiro and asked him to come here. He did. I told him what had happened. Then I demanded that he say the preacher had blasphemed. Do you know what he did, what my friend did?"

Father Fortis shook his head.

"He laughed and told me not to take the fundamentalists so seriously. I exploded and said something horrible. I said I knew what his liturgy—what *your* liturgy—calls us during your Holy Week."

Father Fortis looked down at his cup of coffee but didn't respond.

"You call us 'the synagogue of Satan.' Then I said it was people like him, like you, too," he added, nodding toward Father Fortis, "who'd killed my grandfather."

"When did you have this argument?" Worthy asked.

"Does it matter? Maybe a year ago, maybe a month or two more or less. The important thing is that four weeks ago, Spiro walked back into this office and asked for a cup of coffee. We embraced, I asked him to forgive me, and he asked me to forgive his people. We had some almond crescents and agreed to start meeting again. Like old times. But then someone killed him."

"How did he seem that last time? Mentally, I mean?" Worthy asked.

"He'd lost more hair, and he was a man very proud of his hair," the rabbi said. "I was surprised. I asked if he'd been ill. He said no. I told him to retire."

Father Fortis and Worthy waited patiently while the rabbi continued to stare out the window. "What did he say to that?" Worthy asked.

"Something strange. He asked if offering forgiveness could ever be wrong, if there were times when absolution gave evil too many chances."

Father Fortis remembered the underlined section of the book. "Did Father Spiro say why he wanted to know that?" he asked.

The rabbi shook his head. "May I show you something in the book, please?" After Worthy handed it to him, he opened it to a page before looking up. "This chapter discusses the limits of kindness, especially when faced with unrepentant evil." The rabbi took out his handkerchief again and blew into it. "I told him to read it and we'd talk about it the next time we met. But—"

Father Fortis struggled to understand the odd concept of a limit to kindness. And did that mean Father Spiro had done something he was ashamed of? Or was he concerned about someone else, someone in the parish?

Worthy rose from his chair. "Rabbi Milkin, your friend Father Spiro faltered during the service on his final Sunday. He stopped midway in one of the processions. And from what we can tell, he never explained why that happened."

Rabbit Milkin shrugged, looked out at the trees, and then laughed. "Maybe he had one of his mystical moments of illumination. What my Hasidic brothers call 'the veil of the visible world being pulled back.' I used to tell Father Spiro that he was too much like the Baal Shem Tov. Ah, I see you don't know that name. The Baal Shem Tov was the founder of modern Hasidism, the most mystical form of Judaism."

The rabbi took a pamphlet from off the desk and came around to hand it to Father Fortis. "This I want you to read. Maybe it is Spiro's legacy, something he wrote during your Lent for his church newsletter. He explains the ancient origins of the anti-Jewish language of your Holy Week liturgy, which didn't interest me at all, but then he writes something extraordinary. He tells his people the language of the liturgy must be changed. He laments how the language could promote anti-Semitism. Can you imagine?" The rabbi grabbed Father Fortis' arm, and tears welled up in the old man's eyes. "Your church is as tied to tradition as we are, yet Spiro was asking for this change. I will always cherish his memory, not just for friendship, but for his open heart."

As the three said goodbye at the door, Worthy asked a final question. "You said on the phone you thought you knew who killed Father Spiro. Who is that?"

"Why, I thought I made that plain. On his last visit, Spiro gave me the impression—not in exact words, but there are other words, are there not?— that he was searching for the courage to face someone, someone who he'd come to believe was evil. I believe he did that, and that person killed him. Yes, of this I am sure. Someone in his church killed Spiro."

WORTHY SAT IN HIS TINY KITCHEN Friday night and all Saturday morning, the file of Sherrod's three suspects open in front of him. But his attention was only moderately given to the fairly standard arrest sheets of Allen Lashad, Luther

Rimes, and Carl Bales. Rather, he kept looking at the phone that never rang. His daughter Allyson and he wouldn't be going to the cabin this weekend. *Was I a fool to think she'd ever agree?* he wondered.

In the years since the divorce, each had become an expert at keeping the other off balance. They seemed to be forever circling each other, but with different goals in mind. Worthy wanted nothing more than to find some grip that would offer hope of a future relationship. Allyson seemed intent on staying clear of her father, yet always close enough to train her sharp tongue on him. Allyson was an equal opportunity abuser, lashing out at her mother as well as her younger sister Amy, who shared the same household. They too had received the clear message that Allyson wanted a bubble of privacy around her. But with her father, Allyson expressed through her therapist her desire that he stay away entirely. When he did, she chastised him for caring so little about his family. Worthy had hoped that a weekend at the family cabin, just the two of them, would allow him to figure out what she really wanted from him in this last year before college.

"Not this weekend, maybe never," he said to his empty kitchen as the clock struck eleven.

He'd been unable to concentrate on the Suffolk file, finding more relief in replaying the rabbi's conviction from the afternoon before. "Someone in his church killed Spiro." He'd like to think Rabbi Milkin was right. That would account for the straightened vestment piece and perhaps be confirmed by the missing book, once found. *If found*, he corrected himself.

But there was a way of considering the rabbi's accusation that led him to totally dismiss it. What he'd hoped to gain from Rabbi Milkin was some sense of Father Spiro's state of mind in the weeks before he was killed. But all he'd really discovered was something of the rabbi's state of mind as he ruminated on his friend's murder. The man had leapt from Father Spiro's odd taste in theological reading to a certainty that the killer was a parishioner. The fact that this man was himself a clergyman—no doubt with a trunk full of his own stories of run-ins with members of his synagogue—made his accusation all the more suspect.

He closed the Suffolk file in frustration and did what he usually did when he couldn't see the way forward. He cleaned his apartment and watched TV until he was tired enough to go to bed.

He fell asleep sooner than usual, and so awoke the next morning with two hours to spare before the morning service at St. Cosmas, the Service of Divine Liturgy. Making himself scrambled eggs and toast, he sat down at his tiny kitchen table and retrieved the folder on the suspects.

Let's get this over with, he told himself. The first two, Allen Lashad and Luther Rimes, were exactly the types who would draw Sherrod's attention.

Both had been in and out of jail since they were juveniles. Now in their mid-twenties, both had been picked up only weeks before for questioning on break-ins in the neighborhood. Worthy found that suspicion logical. He could even see them being in the car of a gang drive-by. But strangling a priest? That seemed like something else, a jump to the big leagues.

The third, Carl Bales, was Sherrod and Henderson's favorite, and Worthy had to admit he was more interesting. Bales was twenty-two, with previous arrests for auto theft, possession of a controlled substance—crack cocaine—breaking and entering and aggravated assault, as well as a stint in a hardcore juvenile psychiatric facility for "impulse control issues." In two other important ways Bales was different from Lashad and Rimes. He was white and also a skinhead. He was connected with the White Crowns, a gang that had instigated a racial brawl during a concert at the fairgrounds two years before.

Worthy studied the vacant face in the photo and noted the SS tattoo on the side of Bales' neck. So why would a skinhead hang out in Suffolk? That should have gotten him dead a long time ago.

Worthy turned to the second page in Bales' file and noticed what must have caught Sherrod's attention. Bales had been involved in a prior incident over at the church when he was twenty. "Arrested for public disturbance at St. Cosmas Greek Festival, September, 2002," the record read. "Two months in juvenile detention."

Worthy closed the file. Bales had a previous beef with the church, sometimes hung out in Suffolk, and probably was robbing for drug money. Yes, a nut job like Bales might be capable of anything. But would he have straightened the priest's vestment after strangling him? Worthy closed the file and went into his bedroom for a sports coat. Just as he was heading out the door for St. Cosmas, the phone rang. For a moment, his heart leapt at the thought that Allyson had called to explain.

"Lieutenant Worthy? This is Kenna McCarthy," the voice on the line said.

His heart sank.

"Hello? Is anyone there?" the voice asked.

"Yes, I'm here. But I'm on my way out."

"Hmm, working on a Sunday morning. Very impressive, Lieutenant. But I only need two minutes of your time." Her voice was slippery, with a bit of laughter just below the surface, and despite his efforts, he couldn't help trying to picture her.

"Two minutes, then. Shoot."

"Someone told me you didn't enjoy my article. I don't get it."

Worthy thought back to all the people with whom he'd shared his complaint. He'd emailed Captain Betts and Henderson to ask what they knew about it, and he'd also vented a bit to Father Fortis. Had he said something about it to Sherrod when he'd barged into his office? "Let's just say I don't like your style of journalism," he said.

McKenna's laugh sounded metallic, forced. "Really. May I ask why?"

"If you want to waste one of the two minutes, sure. In one paragraph, you manage to single me out, ignore my partner, and crap on another officer. Why don't you stick with charity balls and fashion shows?"

There was a pause on the other end of the line. "My column always singles someone out. That's why people read it, and why most people I flatter call to thank me. But not you. Are you honestly telling me you don't want the limelight?"

"What I want is for you, and everyone else at your newspaper who has nothing better to write about, to remember something: a priest was strangled in his own church, right in front of the altar. My partner—whose name is Sergeant Carnell Henderson, by the way—and I would appreciate working this case without inane interference."

"In his own church in front of the altar," she repeated slowly. "That's well put, Lieutenant." Before Worthy could respond, she added, "Look, Lieutenant, I don't think we've gotten off to a very good start. How about letting me buy you lunch. Say tomorrow? I have something I think you'll find interesting."

Hadn't she heard him? "We have nothing to offer each other, ma'am," he said.

"Oh, Lieutenant, how wrong you are! And 'ma'am'? How old you do you think I am?"

She's not going to let go, he thought. *Probably her first real story outside those describing who wore what to what party.* "Okay. I can meet you for thirty minutes at noon tomorrow at Denny's on the south side, right off of I-75."

"Denny's? My, how elegant. But I'll be there."

WORTHY ARRIVED AT ST. COSMAS AT nine fifty-five, frustrated that the reporter had made him cut it so close. He'd wanted to observe people as they came in. Now it would be the congregation who would be watching him. He was consequently surprised to find only about fifteen mainly older people sitting silently in the sanctuary. Had he misunderstood Nick's instructions about the time? He walked heavily up to the balcony and sat in the front row.

But at ten o'clock precisely, bells rang outside and Father Fortis appeared in the doors in front of the altar. Worthy looked down on those below, remembering his childhood in other church balconies, when he'd hoped his father's sermon wouldn't be long, hoped his buddies would keep him company, and hoped his funny faces could force a smile from his mother in the choir loft. Now he was in a church balcony again, wondering if a killer could be sitting down below.

By fifteen minutes into this service, sixty people were present as Father Fortis started to process a silver-covered Bible down the side aisle. Worthy watched intently, aware that it was during one of these processions that Father Spiro had frozen up. Altar boys bearing candles and large circular golden medallions on staffs escorted Father Fortis toward the rear of the sanctuary, where the entire group disappeared from Worthy's view.

But Worthy could still hear his friend's baritone voice ringing in his ears. And he could clearly recall the reaction of those standing in their places below him, many of them closing their eyes as the melody continued. To his surprise, the hair on the back of his neck stood on end, even though the words were in Greek. And to his surprise, he asked himself something he should have wondered about a long time ago. How was it that Father Fortis—with such a voice and all his gifts with people—wasn't a parish priest? What had ever led his friend to become a monk?

The procession moved up the center aisle toward the altar, Father Fortis trailing with the silver book in hand. Once Father Fortis returned at the altar again, his actions were more understandable to Worthy. A laywoman read a passage from one of the epistles before Father Fortis opened the silver-bound book and read the gospel story of Zacchaeus. The homily was short and well-crafted, though Worthy wondered if his friend's concluding moral, "just as Zacchaeus, we need to come early to meet our Lord," was meant as a gentle reprimand to the fifty or so parishioners who trickled into the pews before the homily.

The guy is a natural, he thought, once again wondering what had led him to hide himself away in a monastery. Shortly after the homily had ended, the altar boys followed Father Fortis as he marched the same slow route around the sanctuary, this time holding aloft what Worthy assumed to be two communion chalices. *A second procession*, Worthy realized. Was this the point when Father Spiro had faltered? Of course, with Father Fortis there was no hitch. His massive friend, robed in the tent of his vestments, chanted in both Greek and English, and again Worthy felt a shiver pass through him.

The service ended with parishioners coming up the center aisle for communion. The congregation, now filling St. Cosmas, was hushed and seemed keenly alert as they stood to wait their turn. Worthy watched as Father Fortis smiled radiantly, spooning the contents of the chalice into the open mouths of all who came forward.

After the service, Worthy rose from his seat. A man behind him in the balcony tapped Worthy on the shoulder, and obviously assuming him to be a visitor, invited him to meet the priest and receive a piece of blessed bread.

Worthy joined the line and accepted the piece of bread from his friend. "Good of you to make it to the whole service, Christopher," Father Fortis said with a smile. Moving closer, he whispered, "Looking for suspects or trying to make sense of our service?"

"A bit of both," Worthy replied. "How come you never told me about your singing voice?"

"Yes, isn't it beautiful?" a woman next to him said.

Worthy noticed a catch at the corner of his friend's mouth, then a couple of rapid blinks. *Well, I'll be damned*, he thought. He'd never seen his friend at a loss for words. Nick was positively embarrassed by the compliment.

"Listen, Christopher," Father Fortis added quietly. "The parish council is having a brief meeting in a few minutes. Would you like to meet them?"

"Might be good. You'll be there?"

"Of course. They meet in the library, right next to my office. I'll be there in a couple of minutes."

Five members of the parish council were mingling in the room when Worthy entered and introduced himself. Another six straggled in over the next five. As Worthy expected, most offered Greek names, though he noted that two were as blond as he. Mr. Margolis, the council president, offered him a seat and passed the plate of donuts his way. From behind him, an older woman who introduced herself as Mrs. Filis brought him a cup of coffee.

Mrs. Filis. *Right*, he thought. She was the one who discovered Father Spiro's body. She looked about the old priest's age and spoke, unlike most of the others in the room, with an accent.

Worthy found it interesting that Mr. Margolis introduced the others by name and then by occupation. He learned that three of the members were lawyers, while another, Dr. Pappas, was a cardiologist. Would he be able to tell him about the old man's mental condition? Another member, David Sanderson—one of the blond men—worked at the city's blood bank, while several others were introduced as restaurant owners. Two worked at Allgemein College: a professor of literature named Dr. Stanos and a younger woman, Dr. Boras, a classics professor. Nearly all professionals, Worthy noted. None seemed particularly surprised to have a policeman among them.

Mr. Margolis tapped Worthy on the arm. "We understand you already know Father Fortis." His comment brought silence to the entire room.

"Yes, I've known Nick—Father Fortis—for a couple of years. We spent some time out in New Mexico about a year and a half ago."

"From the newspaper accounts, that must have been exciting," Mr. Sanderson said from across the table. Others around the table murmured their agreement.

"Police work is mainly desk detail, filling out papers and answering phones. But yes, that one had some excitement toward the end."

"And is it true that Father Fortis helped you in—"

Hello, everyone," Father Fortis said, bursting through the door. "I see you've met Lieutenant Worthy. And I see he already has a donut. Is there a chocolate éclair left? Ah, good."

The group laughed easily and joined with Mr. Margolis in expressing their appreciation for the Divine Liturgy. "Especially the beautiful chanting," Dr. Stanos added.

Father Fortis put his hands up. "I'm just happy we all got through it. My first time in quite a while, not counting when it's my turn at the altar at the monastery. But a crowd of twenty monks, half of them hard-of-hearing, is far different than several hundred customers."

Everyone looked toward Father Fortis, as if waiting for something. Finally, Mr. Margolis said in a stage whisper, "Father, we can't start until you offer an invocation."

Father Fortis put the half-eaten éclair down on a paper plate and rose from his chair. The rest of the room followed suit. "You'll have to forgive me for not knowing the ropes," he said. He offered a brief prayer, which ended with everyone crossing themselves before sitting down.

"I asked Lieutenant Worthy to attend our meeting for several reasons," Father Fortis began. "As most of you know, he has been put in charge of the case."

"What about the other lieutenant?" Dr. Boras asked.

"Lieutenant Sherrod," Dr. Pappas said. "Not what I would call a courteous man."

Again, murmurs of assent circulated around the table.

"George Bagios made a point of telling me this morning that we're in much better hands," Mr. Margolis said, sending a broad smile Worthy's way.

"You do understand that Lieutenant Sherrod wasn't removed from the case," Worthy quickly interjected. "He was needed on a federal matter."

"But can we be assured he won't be back?" Dr. Stanos asked.

"I think you can assume that, although Sergeant Henderson is still working on the case."

"The Black?" Mrs. Filis asked.

"Yes, yes, Irene," Dr. Pappas said hurriedly.

"Let's begin the meeting, then," Father Fortis said. "Mr. Margolis mentioned before liturgy that the council wants to begin planning for Father Spiro's forty-day memorial. Because of a conflict in Metropolitan Iakovos' schedule, he has asked that we have the memorial in two weeks, so that pushes things up a bit. We all know that the memorial must be handled with great care and dignity."

Mr. Margolis cleared his throat. "Something else has come up in the past few days, Father. A few members of the council and some in the parish itself are wondering about a more permanent memorial for Father Spiro. A plaque, perhaps."

"No, more than a plaque," Dr. Pappas objected.

"Perhaps a room dedicated to him, or some new icons," Mr. Sanderson offered.

"How soon are you talking about?" Father Fortis asked. "I don't think that's possible before the memorial service."

"Oh, no, Father," Mr. Margolis assured him. "We merely want to take a vote on it today and set up a subcommittee."

"Go right ahead, Mr. Margolis," Father Fortis said. "I view this as your meeting."

"Fine, Father. And we welcome your friend, Lieutenant Worthy. Let's start with the memorial."

Dr. Stanos cleared his throat. "I want to make a motion that Father Daniel Prendergast be invited this time."

"Hear, hear," Dr. Boras added. "It was shameful that he sat in one of the pews at the funeral. He should have been invited up to the altar."

"Why?" Mrs. Filis asked. "St. Cosmas has had many seminarians. Why is Deacon Daniel special?"

"Now, Irene, let's not be contrary," Dr. Pappas said with a weak laugh. "He's Father Daniel, not Deacon. For crying out loud, St. Cosmas ordained him."

Almost under her breath, Mrs. Filis said, "I must have missed that."

"And Father Daniel brought a lot of new people into the parish," Dr. Stanos added.

"Including me," Mr. Sanderson said, staring down at the table.

"I take it Father Daniel was also a convert?" Father Fortis asked.

"Oh, yes, Father," Mr. Margolis said. "He was here for nearly three years, right after seminary. Very progressive."

"In those two years, St. Cosmas moved ahead more than it had in the last fifteen to open our doors," said Dr. Boras.

"I assume you're talking about more English in the liturgy?" Father Fortis asked.

"Too fast. *Much* too fast, Father," Mrs. Filis said in a louder voice.

"He also started a class on Orthodoxy for those interested," Mr. Sanderson said, just as loudly. "That's how a number of us became interested in the faith."

"How did Father Spiro deal with all of this?" Father Fortis asked.

A few members of the parish council laughed.

"He spoke out for change, but only sometimes," Dr. Boras said.

"But for tradition, too," Mr. Margolis countered.

"In other words, Father Spiro was a bit hard to read on such matters. Especially toward the end," Dr. Pappas, the cardiologist, said.

"Such matters? Were there others?" Father Fortis asked the doctor.

"Let's be candid. We all loved Father Spiro, but he had his weaknesses, just like anyone else. Whether you agreed with Father Daniel or not, at least he offered a clear position. With Father Spiro, who could tell? One week he chanted the liturgy almost entirely in English, and a person thought, okay, here's the change we need. But the next week, it was nearly all in Greek."

"And that was when Father Daniel's face would turn bright red," Dr. Boras added.

"Yes, yes, I understand about the English. But what else?"

From the other end of the table, one of the lawyers spoke up. "There was the issue of whether the parish should move. Many of the parish said 'yes' very clearly. They want to get out before the value of the property goes down even further."

"Not to mention the safety issues," Mr. Sanderson said.

"Father Spiro couldn't stay focused on it, at least over the last couple months," the lawyer finished off.

Worthy listened quietly, aware that he was learning more about the victim's state of mind in five minutes that he had in the half hour with Rabbi Milkin.

"Where did this Father Daniel stand on the issue of moving?" Father Fortis asked.

"He definitely wanted St. Cosmas to stay right here," Dr. Boras said. "And even though I didn't agree with him, he made a strong case. He said we'd be abandoning the neighborhood just when her needs are greatest."

"We should be 'the church in the midst of the pain of the world,' " Dr. Stanos said. "Wasn't that how he put it?"

A few agreed, though Worthy could feel a new tension in the air.

"And when was it Father Daniel left St. Cosmas?" Father Fortis asked.

Mr. Margolis answered. "About a year ago. It was his choice, I should add. He was given permission by the archdiocese to start a new parish in East Lansing."

"A wise decision on the archbishop's part," Dr. Boras said. "Father Daniel was beating his head against a wall here, and he's certainly doing well with the university set over there."

Worthy could sense all eyes on him as he brought out a notepad and wrote down the young priest's name. The meeting moved to the matter of the more permanent memorial for Father Spiro, with the cardiologist, the two university professors, one of the restaurateurs, and two of the lawyers agreeing to serve on a planning committee.

That business finished, Father Fortis asked for the floor. "Before we leave,

I want to give Lieutenant Worthy a chance to ask any questions he might have for this group."

Worthy cast his eyes around the table. "First, I'll ask a very typical police question. Lieutenant Sherrod probably asked it already, but I don't see it in the file."

If these people are as bright as they seem, they'll see through that in a minute, Worthy thought. Sherrod had never asked the question he was going to ask, because he'd believed from the moment he heard the altarpiece was missing that he knew motive. "Can you think of anyone who might have had a grudge against Father Spiro, someone who'd maybe argued with him over the last few weeks."

The reaction in the room caught Worthy by surprise. First, one parish council laughed, then several more, until finally everyone in the room, including Mrs. Filis and even Father Fortis, were laughing.

Mr. Margolis tapped him on the shoulder. "We're laughing at ourselves, Lieutenant, not you. You see, we Greeks tend to argue. We argue at home, at work, but even more at church. We haven't done much today because we've been on our best behavior with Father Fortis and you."

"So you're saying Father Fortis may have argued with many people in the last month or so?"

"Oh, yes, including nearly all of us," Dr. Pappas confessed with a smile.

"I think what Lieutenant Worthy would like to know is whether there's anyone in the parish whose problems with Father Spiro had gotten out of hand," Father Fortis clarified.

"In the parish? Why are we talking about the parish?" Mr. Sanderson asked.

"That's the way I always begin a case," Worthy explained. "In an investigation such as this, my approach is to take the life of the victim very seriously. I want to know as much about Father Spiro as I can. Ever since I was assigned, I've been trying to understand what had Father Spiro worried or preoccupied. So, if anyone stands out as a person who might have been a particular concern to him, I need to know."

"But what does that have to do with the robbery?" another of the lawyers asked.

"The thief was from the projects, which is precisely why St. Cosmas needs to move," a restaurateur said.

"We're still pursuing that line of questioning," Worthy assured them. "To be more exact, Sergeant Henderson is doing that. He believes it will prove the most hopeful direction."

"And you don't agree?" Dr. Boras asked.

"Give me a few more days before I answer that. At least give me until we complete some interviews."

"Now I'm a bit confused," Dr. Stanos said. "Are there two separate investigations going on all of a sudden?"

Yes, these people do indeed like to argue, Worthy thought. They had met him only thirty minutes ago and had already taken off the gloves. How hard would they have been on the old priest? "There is only one investigation, and I'm in charge," he stated, looking around the room.

"But you just said that you're not looking into the projects," Mr. Sanderson added.

"I intend to look into everything. But I'm also trying not to narrow the investigation too early."

"That seems fair enough," Dr. Pappas said.

"So, back to Lieutenant Worthy's question," Father Fortis said. "Can you think of anyone who posed more than the usual challenge for Father Spiro?"

"Please understand that I'm not accusing anyone, but wouldn't you agree," Dr. Boras began, looking around the room sheepishly, "that Lloyd Hartunian might have been someone who troubled Father Spiro?"

"Lloyd Hartunian?" Dr. Stanos said. "Do you honestly consider him dangerous?"

The female professor shrugged and looked down.

"Now, now," Dr. Pappas said, "I think Lydia has a good point. I saw Hartunian corner Father after liturgy on more than one occasion. I'd say you should talk with him. Again, we're not accusing anyone, of course."

"You can find his address in the church directory," Mr. Margolis added, "though I'm not sure Mr. Hartunian's picture—and that of the woman he sometimes comes with—is in there. By the way, was he in church this morning?"

The restaurateur who'd advocated for the parish to move shook his head. "I was working the candle stand in the narthex, Lieutenant, and he didn't come through."

"Hartunian," Worthy repeated, jotting down the name. "There's just one more thing. Father Fortis brought it to my attention." He passed out the first of the photos, the one of Father Spiro caught off guard by the church photographer. "Mr. Bagios took this a few days before your priest's death."

Worthy studied the faces in the room as the photo was passed around the table. He caught a few grimaces, while others quickly looked away.

"You might have noticed a book on Father Spiro's desk in that photo. We'd like to find that book. Here's a close-up." He passed the enlargement around the room and watched as each person on the council studied the photo and shook his or her head.

"It looks like one of those old accounting books, but Father Spiro, bless his memory, was not a man who understood figures. Why is it so important?" Mr. Angelo, the oldest man in the room, asked.

"It may not be important at all," Worthy said, "but in the other photos taken by Mr. Bagios that day, the book is missing. We find that interesting."

"I guess we can assume the case isn't as close to being solved as we thought," Dr. Pappas said.

"It's somebody from the projects," Mr. Angelo muttered. Others began to talk with those next to them.

"One at a time, please," Dr. Pappas said. "The parish isn't going to want to hear that the investigation is starting over, Lieutenant."

"So don't tell them that," Worthy replied. "We're not starting over, just looking into everything. The book in the photo may mean nothing, but as I said, I don't want to narrow the investigation at this point. Father Fortis and I are just starting to get to know Father Spiro."

"God bless both of you on that front, Lieutenant," Mr. Margolis said. "Your task won't be easy. I don't believe I'm breaking any confidences when I say that many of us in this room were worried about dear Spiro. We'd tried for some months to have a candid discussion with him about retirement."

"Tried?" Father Fortis asked.

"Yes, tried. I went to see him privately only two weeks ago to broach the subject. He put me off, just as he had so many times before."

"He didn't want to retire?"

"That's what's so odd," Mr. Margolis said. "Six months ago, he approached me to talk about it. But when I brought it up recently, he changed the subject. Two weeks ago, he said he had some matters to settle. But then he had that embarrassing lapse during liturgy. How could we put it off any longer?"

"And he never offered an explanation for what happened that Sunday?" Father Fortis asked.

"I talked to him right after the liturgy," Dr. Stanos said. "He acted like nothing had happened."

Mr. Margolis, the parish council president, reached for his handkerchief and dabbed his brow. His voice was clouded with emotion when he spoke. "I just remembered what he said the last time we talked. He said he'd explain everything to the parish council at our next meeting. He said he would tell us in confidence. That would have been today."

"So, WHAT DO YOU THINK OF the council?" Father Fortis asked, taking a bite out of his hamburger.

"The parish council? Very bright, I'd say, and lots of people used to getting their way."

"Amen to that, my friend."

"I don't envy you, Nick. No wonder Father Spiro had bags under his eyes."

"We Greeks are fond of saying we treat everyone like family. The problem is we don't treat our families very well. Love, yes, but not respect."

"Which makes it all the more interesting that Father Spiro was holding off retirement," Worthy commented. "Mr. Margolis said the old man was waiting to finish something, but nobody in that room seemed to know what it was."

"And if the parish council doesn't know," Father Fortis mused, "who does?"

CHAPTER SIX

---◆---

Worthy drove to Denny's in a foul mood. Everyone who knew Father Spiro well had a vivid impression of him. It just wasn't the same impression. For some, like the majority on the parish council, the old priest was drifting into senility but couldn't see it, while others, such as Rabbi Milkin, saw him as an old knight intent on retirement after one final battle. Which view did the photos of Father Spiro and the missing leather-trimmed book support?

The rest of the Sunday afternoon hadn't gone any better. He'd called his old house to say he would stop by to see his daughters, but when he arrived he found Allyson again conveniently out. His ex-wife Susan had repeated the same tired words, that he had to be patient and not push her. In the end, he'd taken his younger daughter out for pizza and then sat alone in his apartment.

And now he had to face this McCarty woman over lunch on Monday. He remembered the standard mantra from training about not alienating the press, but this woman wasn't press. She was an intruder, a verbal paparazzo.

He walked into the diner precisely at noon and spotted a woman looking at him from a booth as if she knew him. She waved at him as some women can do, not embarrassed by standing out. Her dark auburn hair was pulled back to reveal the sculpted curves of her elegant cheekbones, and the large, oversized glasses, together with the business suit, completed the message—intelligent, attractive, on my way.

"So nice to meet you, Lieutenant," she said, looking him over before passing a piece of paper across the table. "That's a peace offering. It's an upbeat article about how St. Cosmas is moving ahead after their tragedy. You'll see that the investigation is mentioned just once."

"Where's that?"

She leaned over, pointing to a sentence in the fourth paragraph, the barest hint of perfume filling the space between them. "It's here. 'Mr. Margolis, the parish council president, said the presence of the new team has given the parish an assurance that everything possible is being done.'"

"I'd like you to strike that," he said, passing the paper back.

Kenna McCarty sat back in the booth and eyed him. "You know, Lieutenant, you don't seem to realize what a lucky man you are. You have friends in high places, and now you've been handed a very high-profile case."

"Let's not confuse my friends in the department with yours."

The waitress poured two cups of coffee and took their orders, then departed.

"What should I say?" she asked. "It's my job to make friends, and so, yes, I do see your superintendent sometimes at social gatherings."

"And I've only met him once," Worthy replied. "He wouldn't even know my name."

She smiled as she leaned forward as if to share a secret. "Oh, you and I both know that's not true. That one meeting you mention happened to be your last commendation for solving that monk's murder in Ohio."

Worthy felt his face burning. "What I don't understand is why your paper assigned a society writer to a murder investigation."

She took a sip of her coffee and offered a tight smile. "I'm past the society column, Lieutenant. I've been assigned to the city beat, and that covers everything."

"Sounds like a fancy way of saying the *Free Press* is downsizing."

"You know, Lieutenant, I'm going to let that pass. Why don't we change the subject until our food comes." She produced a small notebook from her purse. "I understand your older daughter is back home. How's that going?"

Worthy stared at his coffee and said nothing.

"That must have put quite a strain on your marriage."

"It might have, except I was already divorced," he said, not looking up.

She laughed. "Finally. Something makes sense about you. I should have guessed from your record that you'd have tired of the little wife and kiddies."

He looked up, his hatred of this woman settling his head. "Then you'd have guessed wrong. I wasn't the one who wanted the divorce."

Her tongue darted to the corner of her mouth. "So why'd she leave a guy like you?"

"And this is your proof you're not a society writer?"

She raised an eyebrow and studied his face. "You think you're being rude, Lieutenant, but I find you very compelling. Very believable. Frankly, most men I know, especially the married ones, hate marriage. My ex-husband did.

Of course, that didn't stop him hating it all over again with a twenty-two-year-old."

The food came, and Kenna McCarty let him eat in peace. She was holding something back, he knew, but she hid her cards well. When the waitress came to clear the table, she asked for another cup of coffee.

"Now, down to business," she said. "I have something to offer you on this case."

"If you have evidence, then you should have turned it over right away."

"Oh, give it a rest, Lieutenant. I have an offer, not evidence," she said, crumpling her napkin in her hand. "And it happens to be something Superintendent Livorno likes. In fact, he likes it very much. It's legal and benefits both your department and my paper."

"Sounds too good to be true."

"It *is* good. I want to shadow you during your investigation and write articles as we go. It will help readers understand the difficulties and challenges even the great Christopher Worthy has to deal with. Given the opinion polls, the police of this city need a human face."

"And I'm that face?"

"Superintendent Livorno thinks so."

"What about Henderson?"

"Who?"

"You see, that's my point," he said, leaning forward. "Forget about how crazy your scheme is, and I don't care if the FBI thinks it's a good idea. You'd contaminate the investigation just by being there. Witnesses would watch what they say or wouldn't say anything at all, not to mention what you'd think of the way we cops tend to talk about a case. But here's the worst part of all of this. All you'd do is isolate me in my own department, and I don't need help there. And I sure don't need to be turned into a media cartoon just to help your career."

"Henderson is your partner, right?" she asked.

"If you have to ask, then you already have your answer. You're going to have to cover this investigation the same way everyone else does. You can piece together your story from police updates and what comes out at trial."

"Tell me, Lieutenant, you find those stories based on what you call departmental 'updates' reliable?"

"Not particularly."

"That's my point," she said, both hands reaching across the table toward him. "If we get fifty percent of it right, which would be about average, that's fifty percent we get wrong. And what we get wrong usually makes you guys look bad. All I want to do is humanize your work. I want my readers to see the case through your eyes. All right, through your eyes and your partner's."

He scanned the diner, half expected to see Superintendent Livorno smiling at him. "No. Not a chance."

"Why you?" she said, shaking her head. "I thought from your record that you'd understand. Of course I'm trying to isolate you. That's what I'm trying to do in my own career. Creative work does that, Lieutenant. I guess I was stupid enough to think you'd see this for what it is—an opportunity to give your career a boost."

He snapped up the check when the waitress put it between them. "It's not my style to step over others."

She stabbed across the booth at him with her finger. "But that's exactly what you do, Lieutenant. Spare me the tender picture of your buddies throwing you a party after your last two cases here in Detroit, the ones they couldn't do diddly-squat with." Her voice was loud enough for those at neighboring tables to look their way. "Isn't your fondest desire on this case to win and make Sherrod look like a two-bit asshole?"

She smiled knowingly as she got up, gathered her things, and walked out. He sat alone for a minute with his coffee, feeling the quiet in the diner. Even the cashier seemed shocked into silence. *They probably think they just saw a wife walk out on her husband*, he thought.

As he finished his coffee, Worthy felt none too proud of himself. The truth was that the reporter, in trying to shine the spotlight on him, threatened him. The "previous successes" Kenna McCarty referenced had come at a steep price. His gift or specialty was closing cold cases, and that meant that when he succeeded, his police colleagues resented him even as the media lauded him. And when he failed miserably, as he had not long ago, his colleagues rejoiced.

Sherrod wasn't the only one who resented his notoriety. But his red face was the one that Worthy saw waiting for him regardless of the outcome of this case. *He'll hate me if I solve the case—his case—and he'll dance on my grave if I fail*, he thought.

CHAPTER SEVEN

———— ◆ ————

THE SAME MORNING, IN THE CHURCH'S office, Father Fortis was fighting off a headache as he tried, with Mrs. Hazelton's help, to make sense of the parish's finances.

"It looks like the parish can barely pay its bills," he said.

Mrs. Hazelton pointed at one of the columns. "And that's with the help of the fall festival."

"Oh, I know about festivals. My home parish was the same way. We'd open up the parking lot for gyros, baklava, and dancing and charge people from the city twenty dollars apiece. Everyone in the parish worked their fingers to the bone, but afterwards we could afford to fix the leaky roof."

"It's a huge deal at St. Cosmas. God help the parish if that weekend is rained out. And yelling and screaming? I can say that because even though I work here, I'm not part of the parish."

"Really? Do you attend elsewhere, Mrs. Hazelton?"

"Methodist all my life, Father. I hope that isn't a problem."

"Not at all. I suspect it might be the best thing in a parish like this."

"I like to think so. I hear all the stories, but who am I going to tell? Widowed, you see, so I only tell my cat."

"Any stories I should know about?" Father Fortis asked.

The secretary crossed her arms over her slight frame. "No, I don't think so. You should start fresh here, Father. Besides, most of what I hear is just gossip. Of course, if there's something specific that you've heard, I might have a thought or two about that."

He leaned back in the chair and pulled at his beard. "I confess I am a bit curious about this business of the church moving."

"Oh, that. Well," she said, adjusting her glasses, "I think there's been a truce on that for a few months."

"Meaning it was a war before that?"

"I'm not Greek, Father, and I don't mean to offend," she said.

"I take your point, and no offense taken. Lots of yelling on that too, I suspect."

"Of course. Within the council as well as the congregation, from what I understand. But then there was that embarrassing piece in the paper."

"Oh? What was that?"

"Well," she said in a whisper, "it seems that someone sent a flyer out to the entire parish asking members to consider buying the homes in this neighborhood. Or at least on the west side of St. Cosmas."

"Why there?"

"The projects are only five blocks over that way," she said with a dramatic sweep of her arm as if they had a clear view. "The article claimed some members were trying to create a buffer zone."

"I see. And that was sent out by someone who doesn't want the church to move."

"Of course, but how did they get our mailing list, Father?"

"Ah, yes, that is interesting. Someone on the parish council, perhaps?"

"That, or someone who served on it recently. It was a very up-to-date list."

"And what did Father Spiro say?"

"Privately—I mean, in this room—he was livid. He said it made the church look racist."

"You'll have to explain that to me, Mrs. Hazelton."

"Call me Bernice, Father. You see, if people in the parish bought up the homes around the church, then no more projects could move in."

"Yes, indeed. That does sound a bit racist."

"Folks over in Suffolk were pretty mad, which hurt the parish."

Father Fortis sat back in his chair. "How?"

"It all goes back to the festival, Father. Parishioners do the cooking and baking, but who do you think they hire to do the nasty jobs, like clean-up of the grounds?"

He smiled and shook his head in wonder. "You are a wealth of information, Bernice."

The secretary glowed. "Just so you don't take me for a gossip."

He raised his hands in protest, as if it was the furthest thought from his mind. "Not in the least."

The phone rang out in Mrs. Hazelton's office, causing her to scamper through the door. In a moment, his own phone buzzed. "Dr. Pappas' office for you, Father."

He pushed a button and heard a female voice say from the other end of the line. "Father Fortis, please."

"I'm here," he said.

"One moment, please."

The tune "*Guantanamera*" barely got through the first bars when the music suddenly stopped. "Father Fortis?"

"Yes. Is that you, Doctor?"

"Listen, Father, I thought of something this morning, right in the middle of surgery, in fact. You might want to pass it along to your policeman friend."

"Oh, yes?"

"It's like this. I wasn't Father Spiro's physician of record, but I have the name of someone who knew his medical condition pretty well. Maybe better than anyone. I'm talking about Maria Siametes, a nurse from the parish who happened to be the best friend of Father Spiro's deceased wife. They were from the same village, I believe. Anyway, she told me she brought a hot meal to him once a week and checked to make sure he'd been taking his medications. She looked after him, you might say. I thought you might want to talk to her."

Father Fortis read between the lines. A widowed priest was prohibited by canon law from remarrying, but there was usually some woman in the parish who watched over him. "I see your point," Father Fortis said. "Where can she be reached?"

"Ah, good question. Let me think. I believe she stays with Athena Portis, out in Grosse Pointe. She's Athena's private nurse. I'd try there."

Father Fortis hung up and asked Mrs. Hazelton to try to reach Worthy at his office. The cardiologist seemed to be one of the real powers on the parish council, no matter what office he held officially. Hadn't others on the council tended to give way to his comments at yesterday's meeting?

When Mrs. Hazelton buzzed, he told Worthy the doctor's suggestion.

"Grosse Pointe, huh? You have time to go out there with me, Nick?"

"I'm trying to figure out the parish finances. Besides, you don't need me, my friend."

"Think about it, Nick. You said she was from the priest's village. What if she doesn't speak English? I mean, what if I can't understand her?"

"I said she was from his wife's village, but I take your point."

"Besides, you could probably use some time away from the church. Trust me. From my days growing up in a parsonage, I can assure you that church finances are always a mess."

"You can stop now, Christopher. You've made the sale."

IT WAS IN FACT A BEAUTIFUL ride and a welcome relief from St. Cosmas. The more he felt the stresses of the parish, the more he wondered how Father Spiro had coped with the job. Even the hour set aside that morning for his private prayers before hearing confessions had done little to raise his spirits. The three older members who'd come to speak with him had mainly complained of feeling unloved by family members or burdened by health worries.

He rolled down the window and took a deep breath of winter air. Having grown up in Baltimore, he'd hoped to smell a salt breeze, but then he remembered that the Great Lakes were freshwater. Out in the bay, he could see the portable shacks of people ice-fishing. On the other side of the road, mansions peeked out from behind iron fences and snow-covered spruce and pine. "Quite a neighborhood, my friend."

"Not where homicide usually takes me, Nick. I think I've been up here only once, when Susan and I were invited to a cocktail party at the superintendent's home. Once was enough."

Father Fortis gazed at the addresses flying by and checked the number on the note in his lap. "It's hard to believe people who live in these places have the same kind of problems we do."

"Do they? I can think of a number of problems I wouldn't have with this kind of money."

"But can you imagine the other problems they have because of it? No, my friend, the people hiding behind these walls are usually the only ones who know the truth."

Worthy looked over and gave the priest a puzzled look.

"I'm talking about the fact that these people are usually far unhappier than the rest of us who envy them."

"Yet we envy them, nonetheless."

"Indeed we do, Christopher. Jesus said you cannot serve both God and mammon. But every one of us believes we'd be the exception."

Worthy looked out at the frozen bay. "I heard my dad preach on that, at least once a year. But I also saw how he counted the pennies. Ministers don't have a lot of mammon to tempt them."

"Nor monks, but greed knows no social class. We had to drop our cable TV contract at the monastery, you know, because of that. People said it wasn't good for us to see so much sex, but the sex wasn't the problem. It was the commercials. Life's a race. Don't be left behind. All those reminders of discontent made us irritable. We began to resent the retreatants, especially the ones who drove up in the big cars. And then we noticed we were having these silly disagreements among ourselves about wanting more recognition."

"And cutting off cable solved that?"

" 'Solved' is probably too strong a word. But yes, it helped, especially when we began to watch more PBS. It was as if a fog cleared, and we remembered the vows we'd taken." He rechecked the address on the sheet of paper in his lap and pointed to an open gate. "There's the place."

They drove through two pillars and down a winding driveway. Gardens with cypresses and replica classical statuary greeted them and led them toward a cluster of buildings, all in white stucco.

When the car drew to a halt, Father Fortis undid his seatbelt with a sigh of relief and took a deep breath. "Take away the snow and cold and just leave this architecture, and we could be in Greece. I wonder what Mr. Portis did in his life to get all this." He pulled himself out of the front seat and looked back through the cypresses to the frozen lake. "My guess is he started in this country like they all did, washing pots and pans in some uncle's restaurant or shining shoes until he could get on his feet. Greek men dream big, like this place, and they work like dogs to get that dream. Of course, they also tend to die in their sixties. And here we see what Mr. Portis left his widow—cypresses and a view of a body of water, a scene she saw for free back in the old country."

"You're starting to depress me, Nick. You need to get back to that monastery."

"Do me a favor, and tell the metropolitan that."

A housekeeper answered the bell and ushered them into a vestibule, which stood at the foot of a massive staircase made of honey-colored wood. Father Fortis followed Worthy as they were shown into a parlor overlooking the lake.

The two had barely sat down when a woman in starched white walked into the room. The slender, black-haired woman in her late fifties or early sixties introduced herself as Mrs. Siametes, gave Worthy a slight bow, and kissed Father Fortis' hand. She said something in Greek to the priest.

"Christopher, Mrs. Siametes tells me her employer would like to welcome me personally. I'll be just a minute. Enjoy the view."

Mrs. Siametes led Father Fortis down a hallway lined with paintings of Greek villages and into a small dark room. Two kneelers fronted onto a table covered with icons. Candles gave off small circles of light in the chapel, nearly obscuring the old woman in the wheelchair. When he sat down in the chair next to her, the old woman struggled to kiss his hand. He noticed half of her body was motionless.

"Mrs. Portis and I are from the same village in Crete," Mrs. Siametes said in a halting voice.

The old woman nodded vigorously.

"I knew that you and presbytera, the priest's wife, were," Father Fortis said, "but I didn't know about Mrs. Portis."

"Just the three of us in all of Detroit from our small village in Greece. When I first came, Mrs. Portis found me work in a hospital, but I couldn't do the English very good. So I took care of the old people at church. Now I take care of her."

"Would she like me to say a prayer?" he asked.

The pressure of the old woman's hand on his was her answer.

"She can hear you, but she cannot talk since the stroke," Mrs. Siametes explained.

He offered a prayer and looked up to see Mrs. Portis, with her one good hand, following him as he made the sign of the cross over her.

"She'll be okay in here," Mrs. Siametes said. "She spends most of her day in front of the icons."

"She prays for Father Spiro?"

Mrs. Siametes shook her head quickly and escorted him from the room. "She doesn't know what happened," she whispered. "She thinks he's gone back to Greece. I know I should tell her the truth, but it would kill her. And she doesn't have much time left."

"You did the right thing, my dear," Father Fortis said.

Back in the parlor, Father Fortis sat down while Mrs. Siametes remained standing.

"Dr. Pappas told us you would be the one to ask about Father Spiro's health, my dear."

"The doctor is a brilliant man. His family is from Athens, not Crete. Many of those on the council are from Athens or Thessaloniki. Big city people. They do well here." She paused, then said, "I've made some coffee and cookies. My *Kourabiedes* are famous, Father."

"Greek butter cookies, my friend," he explained to Worthy. "I don't see how we can refuse."

She returned with a tray. She poured a small cup and handed it to Father Fortis, then did the same for Worthy. Father Fortis noticed the woman had brought an old cracked cup for herself.

"These are delicious, my dear. I've been losing weight in this city, but these should keep me from being blown away into the lake."

Mrs. Siametes smiled broadly as she took one of her own cookies, but then her face sobered. "I took care of presbytera, Father Spiro's wife," she said. "It was a very long, slow death. That kind of cancer is so awful."

"When was that?" Father Fortis asked.

"Six years ago, I think."

"And I understand you looked in on Father Spiro after she died."

"He didn't take care of himself. I even did his laundry out here."

"Can you tell us about his mental capabilities toward the end?" Worthy asked. "Could he perhaps have had the beginning of Alzheimer's?"

Mrs. Siametes shook her head. "No, not that. Some people in the parish told me that's what he had, but that was just gossip. They wanted him out."

"But he was having problems of some sort," Worthy prompted.

"He was under a great strain," she said hurriedly.

A second vote for Rabbi Milkin's perspective, Father Fortis thought. "Would you have any idea what those burdens were, my dear?"

Mrs. Siametes put down her cup and offered a simple "no."

"You never asked him?"

"Yes, of course. I said, 'What's the matter, Father?' I could see he was losing weight, and his hair was thinning. But he only smiled at me. He said being a priest is always hard, but being an old priest is even harder. I asked him what he meant. He shook his head and said it would all be settled soon."

"But you do know about his faltering during the service on his last Sunday?" Worthy pressed.

"I was there. I saw it." She looked down at her hands. "It was like he was hit by something. No, that's not the way to say it." She looked up pleadingly at Father Fortis.

"Like he was struck by something?" he suggested.

"Yes, that's the word. He stopped, maybe for a minute. We were worried, but I know for a fact he had no spell."

"How can you be so sure?" Worthy asked.

"I work with old people. When they forget their words, they start over. It's like they drop something. Back they go to pick it up before they go on. I see this all the time."

"And Father Spiro?" Father Fortis asked.

"He picked up where he left off," Mrs. Siametes said.

"In mid-sentence?" Father Fortis asked.

"Yes, yes, that is what I mean."

Father Fortis considered the nurse's point. This was new. But was the nurse right?

"I saw his eyes. He was like a man thinking about something, like he figured something out. His voice was stronger after that. Do you understand me, Father?"

"Yes, my dear, I think I do." What Father Fortis realized was that people interpreted Father Spiro's mysterious faltering on the basis of how they already saw him. For most, he was slipping into senility. For a few, he was courageously bearing a burden, maybe figuring something out.

So what, Father Spiro, really happened that morning?

CHAPTER EIGHT

———◆———

A FTER TWO DAYS OF SEARCHING FRUITLESSLY for the missing book at both the church and Father Spiro's home, Worthy awoke on Thursday morning with Henderson on his mind. That should have been a warning. But over breakfast, he thought the day looked bright with promise. He thought he finally understood why Henderson always avoided St. Cosmas. Driving back from visiting Mrs. Portis and Mrs. Siametes, Father Fortis had told him about the church's real estate campaign the year before. The crazy notion to create a buffer between Suffolk and the church brought back something Henderson had said at the restaurant about having relatives in Suffolk. No wonder he wanted nothing to do with St. Cosmas.

Once Worthy got that out in the open and explained how Father Spiro had nixed the whole idea, maybe he could bring Henderson into the loop of developments at St. Cosmas. As even that parish council member had observed, it was looking more like there were two completely separate investigations going on. And other than setting up another interview with Carl Bales and talking with contacts over at Suffolk projects, Henderson's activities were unknown.

But that was Henderson's problem, not his. With Mrs. Siametes' input, Worthy was more certain than ever that Father Spiro's mind wasn't slipping, but actively engaged in dealing with something worrisome. Rabbi Milkin's bizarre testimony had supported that, and Mr. Bagios' photo could be viewed as supporting that interpretation as well.

The two clues still tantalizing Worthy remained the missing book and the faltering in the liturgy. Now Mrs. Siametes had given him the prospect that Father Spiro had understood something in that bizarre moment. If that were true, how likely was it that his death two days later was a coincidence?

Worthy figured that the clues of the faltering in the service and the missing book should be enough to bring Henderson back to St. Cosmas. So today, after Henderson finally conducted the interview with Bales, the two would have time to compare notes. Maybe then they could finally begin to work together, whether that meant at St. Cosmas or at Suffolk.

"Maybe this is what mentoring feels like," he said to his reflection in the mirror as he tied his tie. The phone rang.

"Worthy?"

He recognized the voice of Hubert, the precinct desk sergeant. "Yeah, Hubie. What's up?"

"Thought you'd like to know. I just got the paperwork on an assault and break-in last night at St. Michael's."

"How's that my business … wait a minute. Is that the Catholic church a couple of blocks from St. Cosmas?"

"Three blocks down the street. Somebody hit a nun over the head with a brick. She's okay. But guess what they stole?"

"Don't tell me … something off the altar."

"You got it. The report in front of me makes it look like the same damn kind of thing. Hell, what's the market for something like that? Fifty bucks?"

Shit, Worthy thought. *What's this supposed to mean?* "Hubie, make sure Henderson knows about this. In fact, if you see him, tell him I'm on my way."

"I already saw him. Not in the conversing mood. The prick blew me off on his way to the interview tank. The guy's got one big problem."

"Listen, Hubie. Keep that bit about Henderson to yourself, okay? I'll talk to him later."

Worthy crawled through morning traffic toward the Catholic church. A second break-in, three blocks away, with a similar object taken. Henderson should be thrilled. *Hell*, he thought, *Sherrod will throw a party.*

All his certainty from just a half hour before was gone. If Father Spiro had been killed in a botched robbery, then the photo, the missing book, and the faltering in the liturgy meant nothing. Had he simply been fooled by a senile old man?

He pulled up to St. Michael's thirty minutes later. The church couldn't have been more different from St. Cosmas. The mahogany wood and wall surrounding St. Cosmas, along with its glass icons in the side windows, had been designed to isolate worshipers from the outside world. St. Michael's was futuristic by comparison. The Catholic facility was new, built with just enough pale brick to support the massive windows on three sides. Drivers passing by had full view of the narthex, and through the glass doors, the golden Franciscan cross suspended above the altar.

Walking to the side door, Worthy noticed the construction trailers with their piles of building materials. St. Michael's couldn't be more than ten years old, yet the church was obviously adding on. *And*, Worthy thought, *staying in the neighborhood.*

As soon as he came into the sunny hallway, Worthy found his path blocked by a nun who introduced herself as Sister Margaret. Her habit was the modern sort, the knee-length skirt and plain blouse suggesting a life of practical duties. Over her one ear was a thick bandage.

Offering his ID, Worthy added his condolences for the attack.

"Sweet Mother of God," she said, pushing his comment away. "Don't you go telling me to head back to the rectory. It was only a bump! A couple of stitches. It's not as if it's the first time we've been robbed, you know."

"But I bet you don't often get hit on the head with a brick."

The nun gripped the crucifix around her neck as she assessed Worthy. With a shrug, she turned and headed down a hallway. "I'll show you where they got in. It's the third broken window this year, but an old lady gets hit on the noggin and you'd have thought we'd been attacked by the Irish Protestant militia."

"What did they take before?" Worthy asked.

"Until this time, always the petty cash."

Rounding a corner, they came to an area lit by construction safety lamps. "I thought the other cops were all we'd see, so I've let the boys do some sweeping up. The window people are coming any minute to replace the glass."

Worthy looked at the empty frame near the door handle and saw the dusting powder on the handle. *No prints there*, he thought. Same use of gloves. But this time it had been an evening break-in.

"How'd you happen to be here, Sister?" he asked, still bent down to look at the floor.

"I came over to say the rosary, like I do every night. Some kids did it, that's all. That's what I figure."

Worthy straightened up. "You don't think it could be connected with what happened at the Greek church?"

"Mind if I sit down?" Sister Margaret asked. "I feel like a tour guide." She drew up a folding chair. "The last cop said the same thing. He said the newspapers were sure going to see it that way. I'll tell you just what I told him. Look, I'm not strangled. It was just boys." The nun leaned forward in the chair, punctuating her words with the crucifix, the silver feet of Christ thrusting at Worthy.

The one unavoidable point—the fact that an altar object had been stolen in each case—pounded in Worthy's head like a hammer. But if both break-ins had been done by the same guys, why was the nun barely wounded while Father Spiro had been brutally strangled?

"Let me tell you," the nun continued, "that other cop didn't want to hear my opinion. He said he was working the other case and knew they were connected. No doubt in his mind, he said. And Lord, was his face beet-red."

So Hubie, the precinct desk sergeant, had been wrong. Henderson had already been here by the time he got to the station. *Good work*, he thought.

"The poor guy was just itching to cuss me out," the nun continued. "I told him he'd better watch his Irish temper."

Irish? Face beet-red? Worthy felt the blood drain from his face as he stared at the nun. "Sister, what was this guy's name?"

Sister Margaret shrugged. "I can't remember, but it started with an S, I think. It's not like he went by the book, you know. He didn't even bother to stop by the office first. One of the pre-school teachers said there was someone crawling around by the broken window. So I came down to sort things out, and he was right where you are, measuring angles and writing notes."

"Was he a short guy, balding, with a little mustache?" Worthy asked, feeling light-headed.

"That's the guy! Sherman or Sherwood."

"Sherrod."

"That's it. Oh, he gave me a time. Questions, questions, questions. Everything I'd already told the other officers. But no, that wasn't good enough for this one."

Worthy felt himself swaying on his feet. "No, I bet not." He saw stars begin to dance in the corner of his eyes as he leaned back on the door.

"I finally had to get back to the office," the nun said. "But he went out to his car and came back in. And guess what he wanted to know?"

"What?"

"He showed me a brick and asked if it was like the one that hit me. Can you imagine? As if I noticed that! He said he bet it was like the one the first cops had found. I suppose he was right in the end."

"What was he getting at?" Worthy asked, more to himself than the nun.

"Ack! He finally told me it was about our construction stuff out back. For the school addition, you see."

"And …?"

"He showed me the brick, said it was a different color entirely. Said it was even a different kind of brick. He said it came from somewhere else, and he thought he knew where." The nun threw up her hands. "That's when I gave up. I told him to come back if he had a question I could answer."

Worthy looked out toward the construction site, to the stack of bricks not more than thirty yards away.

He felt Sister Margaret's hand on his arm. "You okay, son?"

FROM THE CORNER OF HIS EYE, Worthy saw Hubie's slight wave but walked right on by toward Captain Betts' office. *Later,* Worthy thought. He paused before the captain's door to catch his breath. He wanted to be calm, but determined, with his new superior. There was no way he had to put up with Sherrod doing a back-door on this case.

He knocked and heard his captain invite him in.

"News gets around quickly, I see," Captain Betts said, looking up from her desk.

"So he's already been in. The guy's got a lot of nerve."

"Nerve? That's one way to put it. I'd say stupidity in your partner's case."

Worthy stopped in the middle of the room. "Henderson? What are we talking about?"

"I'm talking about the stupid-ass thing that happened this morning. And where were you, by the way?"

Exactly where was I expected to be? Worthy thought. "I was over at St. Michael's to look into the break-in. It's down the street from St. Cosmas."

She curtly waved him to a seat. "You honestly haven't heard? I don't know whether that's supposed to make me feel better or worse. Your partner had a meltdown, Lieutenant."

"What? Are you saying he slugged somebody again?"

"Did he ever! He tore into his witness right in the middle of an interview. Some guy named Bales, must be all of a hundred and thirty pounds. He's over at the county hospital now. We got it all on tape."

Worthy sat down heavily in the chair. "Just when I thought I understood him."

"I don't think the guy understands himself, but why am I wasting my time telling you? From what I hear, you two hardly know each other."

Should he tell her he'd tried? Should he explain how he'd invited Henderson over to the church, but had been rebuffed? And how well could two cops get to know each other when one insists on working his own hours?

"You were here, Captain, when we divided the two angles on this case," he explained. "Henderson stayed with the robbery theory, connected with the projects. I had the church angle. I didn't know there was a problem with that."

"Well, guess again, Lieutenant," she said. "Ever thought about you two working together on both angles?"

I did, he thought, *but about a day too late.* "Where's Henderson now?"

"I sent him home, since he had absolutely no desire to explain himself. I have to find out what the procedure is in Detroit in a case like this. Not exactly something I had to deal with before."

He rose to leave.

"Not just yet, Lieutenant," she said. "I want you to see the damage. Let's go down to the interview room."

They entered the room where Henderson had been with Bales less than an hour before. On the floor and also on the table there were pools of the blood. He sat down heavily next to his new captain.

As the tape of Henderson's interview with Bales rolled, Worthy tried to connect the pale face staring into the camera with the photo in the case file. Bales had shaved his head even closer since last year. The kid sat with his head bobbing and both hands drumming on the table as if he were listening to music. Henderson had to repeat most of his questions before Bales would focus, and even then, the skinhead's responses where barely audible over the banging on the table.

"It doesn't take a genius to see the interview isn't going well," the captain commented. "But if you can pick out Henderson's voice, you can tell there's no clue he's losing control at this point." Captain Betts paused. "Until just about here," she said, turning up the volume.

The skinhead had stopped hitting the table and was staring across at Henderson. In a rush, Bales leapt to his feet and yelled, "Morning's darkness is coming for real niggers!" An even louder drum roll on the table followed, accompanied by his leaning across the table to sneer at Henderson.

Worthy waited for the explosion. But Henderson stayed seated, calmly writing down Bales' response before moving to the next question.

Bales seemed confused by Henderson's even response as he remained leaning over the table. Slowly, like a bird, he lowered his head and whispered something in Henderson's ear. Henderson reared back as if he'd been spit on, then shot up to grab the kid's neck, catching Bales' momentum and yanking him completely over the table. The camera caught only bits of the next ten seconds, with Henderson's words, "you fucking cocksucker" and "I'm going to kill you, you fucking prick" coming through loud and clear. After what seemed interminable minutes of flying bodies, the tape showed someone rushing into the field of vision and pulling Henderson off. But the viewer— any lawyer, any jury—had clearly witnessed Bales' head being slammed on the table by Henderson, over and over again.

Captain Betts turned off the machine. "I'll say this. It isn't any better the third time."

"What did Bales say right before all hell broke loose?" Worthy asked.

"That's what Henderson won't tell us. And the kid is in no shape to talk."

Worthy looked down at the blood on the table as he waited for his new captain to release him.

"So you and I have a decision to make, Lieutenant Worthy," Captain Betts said, squaring to face him. "I have another cop itching to get back onto this case and—"

"Look, Sherrod has no business—"

"Don't interrupt me, Lieutenant. Yes, Sherrod says he wants back on the case. He's almost done with the feds, but I gave the job to you and Henderson. So do I pull you both, or stick my neck out and stay with you?"

"Wait a minute, Captain. Why do I go down with Henderson? You knew when you put me on this case that the guy's got problems."

"I put you with him to help with that, but you haven't done a damn thing. I thought you'd at least try, but Sherrod could have done what you've done. I meant you two to be a team. I meant you to work together."

No, Worthy thought, *you meant me to babysit. And the little kid you gave me to watch threw a tantrum.*

"So, Lieutenant Worthy, you decide. Are you going to work this case with Henderson, or do I send it back to Sherrod?"

Worthy nodded up toward the blank screen. "You don't think the review board is going to recommend charges?"

"They'll take their time, unless the media gets ahold of the story. So I recommend the two of you solving this case as quickly as you can. And that means you work with each other, do you understand me? You both work the projects, and you both work the church."

"And if Henderson won't?"

"He will if he isn't completely crazy."

Worthy shrugged. "This is a mistake, Captain."

"Then it's mine to make. It may be my first here, but it won't be my last."

"And Bales? What do we do with him?"

Captain Betts gazed back down at the table. "Right, right. I don't want him seeing Henderson. I guess that means you and I will do the interview—when Bales gets out of the hospital, that is. Now, I suggest you go visit Henderson and see if he'll talk to you. And by the way, I'm going to need better updates. I know my predecessor was obsessed with them, but don't paint me with the same brush. I don't need them every day, but I think it's in your best interest to keep me informed."

Worthy looked down, but nodded.

Captain Betts got to her feet. "Not a very good day, Lieutenant, for either of us. Another break-in and assault at a nearby church, and now your partner has done his best to throw his career away. You get to try to talk some sense into him, and I get to explain my decision to Sherrod. Want to trade?"

Chapter Nine

———◆———

To Worthy's surprise, Henderson lived in one of Detroit's newly gentrified and racially mixed neighborhoods. A tall woman, who would have been striking if she hadn't been crying, let him in. A boy of about ten sat on a couch staring at a cartoon show.

After the awkward introduction, the woman led Worthy down a hallway to a study where Henderson was stretched out in a La-Z-Boy, an arm over his face. The woman stood helplessly for a moment before closing the door behind her.

Henderson looked out from under his arm and pinned Worthy with a stare. "Am I fired?"

"Who knows? You might be arrested before the day is out," Worthy answered. "Can I sit down?" When Henderson covered his eyes again without answering, Worthy sat down anyway in the desk chair. Glancing around the room, he noted photos of athletes, mainly basketball players, along with two diplomas.

"I saw the tape. So, what did he say that set you off?" Worthy asked.

"Not important now."

"The captain thinks it is. She also thinks it was partially my fault for not being there."

Henderson peeked out at him. "What'd you say?"

"Nothing."

"Hell, I was already pulling away when that other guy came in. The tape should show that."

"You must be thinking of another tape. The one I saw had you about ready to kill him. Was it the racist shit?"

"Fine, sure, why not."

Worthy waited for something more, an explanation perhaps. "So, that's all you're going to tell me?"

"What's it matter? They'll fire my black ass, and then you can work the case by yourself."

"That's not what the captain wants," Worthy said.

"But it's what you want."

"It's not my call. The captain demands we work it together from here on out. That is, if you still want your job."

Henderson took his arm away and looked up at the ceiling. "I got a son and a wife who's between jobs. Sure, I want the job."

"Then you have to come with me to the church as well as the projects. Agreed?"

Henderson exhaled slowly, still focusing on the ceiling. "Not a problem."

Worthy didn't find the comment convincing. "How about telling me what you got from the other two Suffolk guys."

Henderson leaned forward and stared at the floor. For a moment, Worthy thought he was going to tell him to forget it, to have him tell the new captain he was through.

"Their alibis check out, but they both cut Bales loose," Henderson began slowly. "They won't say more than they know the guy, and I got the feeling there's no love lost. So when Bales came in loaded, I wasn't surprised. All I got out of him in between all that banging on the table was that he'd seen his probation officer the afternoon of the murder. I already knew about that. Then he claimed that he'd slept late that entire morning. So if he killed the old guy, he showed up on schedule with his probation officer that afternoon. It's possible."

"But you'd have thought he'd split town, right?"

"If he wasn't such a crazy fuck, yeah. But who knows what he was thinking?"

"Maybe beneath all that bizarre stuff Bales is pretty smart. After all, he knew how to rattle your cage."

Henderson's head shot up, and for a moment Worthy thought he was going to jump him. "Leave that be," he whispered.

"Okay … for now, at least. The review board won't let it go, however. But then you already know that."

Henderson's hands were tightly clasped, his attention back on the carpet. "You said we're going to work together. What do I get to do?"

"I had Father Fortis put a message in the church newsletter. That should reach people today. It asks anyone who came to see the victim in the two weeks prior to call the parish office."

"Somehow, I don't think the killer is going to call," Henderson said.

"I'd settle for people telling us what the old man was like toward the end. Right now, I'm trying to decide between two different pictures. There's a senile old man and then there's a faithful priest working to solve some problem."

"So, like I said, what's my part in all that?"

"You're going to follow up on every response we get. And while you're waiting for the phone to ring, I want you to look in every nook and cranny for a missing book."

"A missing book?"

"Something the old priest hid two or three days before he died. I'll show you a picture of it."

Henderson sat silently for a moment before nodding. "Okay. I'm ready when you are."

A knock on the door was followed by the woman looking in. Henderson stood and walked toward her.

"Worthy, you met my wife, Sulla? Sulla, this is Worthy, my partner. He tells me I still got a job, at least for a while."

She threw her arms around her husband. "Oh, baby," she murmured, choking back a sob.

Henderson patted her on the back. "Hey, it's okay, it's okay. What'd you need, babe?"

"Can you watch Jamie? I have to get to the pharmacy."

"Now?"

"I think I better. Can you do it? I'll be back in less than an hour."

Worthy felt a cloud in the room as Henderson's wife pulled away, and the two looked at each other.

As soon as his wife left, Henderson walked to the window and turned his back on Worthy. "I got to take care of some things here. I'll meet you at the church at nine tomorrow morning. No, tomorrow's Saturday. I'll be there on Monday. That is, if that's okay with you."

The guy has some nerve, Worthy thought, as he studied the large shoulders of his partner. He'd come within an inch of losing his job and his wife had said she only needed an hour, but he was going to take the rest of the weekend off. The cooperative partner of only minutes before was gone. The other Henderson—the guy who'd tried to bash in Bales' head—was back.

THURSDAY MORNING FOUND WORTHY SCRATCHING HIS head and trying to believe what he was hearing over the phone. "This weekend?" he asked.

"I had some plans that just fell through," Allyson said, a defensive edge to her voice. "Do you want to go to the cabin or not?"

He thought of Sherrod horning in on the case, of Henderson's meltdown.

Then he thought of all the things that he should be doing over the next two days, beginning with interviewing Lloyd Hartunian, the name that had surfaced in the parish council meeting. There was also the unfinished interview with Carl Bales as well as any responses to the plea in the church newsletter.

He started to tell Allyson the trip was simply not possible, but then he stopped. Given Bales' nasty head wounds, how likely was it that the skinhead would be released from the hospital before Monday? And hadn't Mrs. Hazelton assured him the church mailing wouldn't reach most people until early next week? That left the interview with Lloyd Hartunian as well as the need to alert the robbery division to be on the lookout for altarpieces.

Most crucial of all, hadn't Henderson's mess created a kind of calm after the storm? Captain Betts had asked them to work together on everything, and Henderson had made it clear he wasn't coming in until Monday.

"This weekend it is, then," he said.

"Jeez, it took you long enough to decide," Allyson said. "You know, we don't have to do this."

"Sorry," he said, "this weekend is fine, perfect in fact. When can we leave?"

"I'm out of school by four o'clock tomorrow. So, I'll be ready by five. Okay?"

She'd only need an hour to get ready? This from the girl who could make him wait a half hour just to go out for pizza?

"Like I said. It's perfect."

He called Father Fortis to explain why he wouldn't be in church on Sunday.

"Blessings on you, Christopher. Yes, by all means, don't worry about Sunday. I can't tell you how glad your news makes me."

"Hard to figure, isn't it? But it's not the best time to leave town."

"It probably never will be. There's just one problem from this end. Can you do something with me Friday afternoon before you leave?"

Worthy paused. There was no way that he'd risk being late to pick up Allyson. "Yeah. Maybe, I mean. What is it?"

"I got a call from Lloyd Hartunian about an hour ago. He asked me to stop by and see him after three thirty today. He claims he has something he wants to tell me as a priest."

"Maybe he'll confess to killing Father Spiro," Worthy joked.

"Oh, if only it could be so easy. Anyway, I know you were planning to interview him and thought we might do it together."

"Actually, that was the one thing on my list I felt guilty about leaving undone, Nick. But now I'm thinking his seeing only you might work out even better. What's Hartunian going to think if he's expecting you to call and a cop comes along?"

"I suppose you're right. I just hope I don't foul things up."

"You'll be fine, Nick, but before I leave town, I wanted to ask you if you heard about the break-in at St. Michael's."

"The Catholic Church? Both Mr. Margolis and Dr. Pappas called me about it this morning. They want to know if that proves ours was a robbery after all."

"Nick, ever think the timing on that break-in is a bit convenient?"

"How do you mean?"

"I'm probably simply frustrated, but here we are just starting to figure some things out on Father Spiro—like maybe he wasn't a nutcase after all— and this happens. If I didn't know better, I'd accuse Sherrod."

"Sherrod? Oh yes, your predecessor."

"Who wants to be my successor," Worthy added.

"I don't follow."

"It doesn't matter."

"You sound tired, my friend."

"Well, between my partner beating up on a witness two hours ago and now Ally giving me my first real chance to spend time with her in nearly four years, I guess I am."

"Good Lord! Henderson beat up on somebody?"

"Long story, Nick. I'll tell you Monday."

"I know this won't be easy, my friend, but try to let the case go this weekend. You have more important things to attend to."

"I'm not so sure about that. You don't take weekends off when you're in charge of a homicide investigation. And based on past experience, the time with Ally might be a bust."

He had an urge to ask his friend to keep him in his prayers, but that he could no longer do. Yet he had to admit that Father Fortis was right. With Hartunian thinking he was simply talking with the new priest, Worthy would find out more than if he did the interview himself. So, yes, he could devote his attention to Allyson. What did a father say to a daughter he'd been estranged from for nearly four years?

"And Christopher," Father Fortis said, "please don't feel you need to respond to this, but I want you to know you'll both be in my prayers."

THE FOLLOWING AFTERNOON, AN OBESE WOMAN opened the door and squinted at Father Fortis. At the same moment, Father Fortis found himself overpowered by the fetid smells of decay and cats.

The woman turned and called back into the dimly lit house. "Lloyd, dear, the new priest is here. Shall I let him in?"

Before Father Fortis could puzzle over the odd question, a voice called back, "Well, of course, Sylvia. Bring him into the parlor."

Father Fortis followed the woman down a hallway lined with stacks of newspapers, yellowish brown at the bottom shading toward white at the top. The parlor itself was dark except for an island of light from two old floor lamps positioned next to each other. A similarly obese man stood in front of an overstuffed chair, his hands first in his pockets, then reaching to smooth back his oily hair. Lloyd Hartunian wore a flannel shirt with a string tie cinched to the top. His outfit was completed by black, wide-framed glasses precariously perched on his nose. Father Fortis had the feeling he'd walked into a *New Yorker* cartoon.

"It's so nice of you to come right over, Father," Hartunian said, giggling as he rocked back and forth on his feet.

"Not a problem," Father Fortis replied. "I want to meet as many parishioners as I can."

Hartunian plopped down in the chair and motioned Father Fortis toward a couch. Father Fortis looked down on three cats who clearly had no intention of moving.

"Sylvie, be a dear and move Franny and Zooey."

The woman did as she was told, then sat on the armrest of Hartunian's chair. As Father Fortis sat down on the couch, he noticed a newspaper on the side table. The headline read GREEK ORTHODOX PRIEST FOUND STRANGLED. Why did he have the odd feeling the paper had been put there intentionally?

Hartunian's eyes were trained on the floor as he offered his visitor a cup of coffee. Father Fortis declined, not wanting to even imagine the taste of coffee brewed around so many cats and bowls of cat food.

"And how do you like St. Cosmas, Father? I understand you're a monk. My, my, what a big change that must be for you."

The woman stroked Hartunian's hair. Who was she? Wife, probably, but she looked enough like Hartunian to be a sister. Her skin, like his, was so bloated by obesity that age was impossible to estimate.

"Yes, St. Cosmas is a big change for me," Father Fortis replied. "And a big challenge, especially when we consider what a tremendous ordeal everyone has been through."

Hartunian nodded, his eyes still on the floor. "But your voice is so lovely. Such a waste to hide that away in a monastery."

"So you were in church last Sunday?"

"Just at the end. Problems with my teeth, don't you know. Bleeding gums."

"I'm sorry."

"Diabetes, you see. Sylvie and I both have it." Again, an odd smile beamed on Hartunian's face. "But I wanted to comment on what you just said, Father, about St. Cosmas' ordeal. You may not know this, but the parish has been going through an ordeal for some time. Very disconcerting over the past few months, what with deacons being transferred and then Father Spiro becoming so … ill, I guess one must say."

That's one thing to be thankful for, Father Fortis thought. For some reason, Hartunian wanted to talk about Father Spiro as much as Father Fortis wanted him to.

"I take it from your comment that you knew Father Spiro well, Mr. Hartunian."

The smile continued to play at the corner of Hartunian's mouth. Sylvia sighed deeply.

"I have no desire to speak ill of the dead, especially when I parted with him in a state of disagreement." Hartunian reached up and took Sylvia's hand. "And I think you're being a bit coy with me, Father Fortis. That busybody, Mrs. Hazelton, must have told you your predecessor and I had a disagreement two weeks before he died. And then three weeks before that. I don't make a secret of any of it."

"Actually, Mrs. Hazelton never mentioned it."

Hartunian looked disappointed. "I'm surprised."

"Could I ask what you spoke about?"

"Well, Father, I believe that's protected by confidential privilege," Hartunian said with the same smile. He tilted his head back to push up his sagging glasses, causing Sylvia to shift her weight on the armrest.

Why this teasing game? Father Fortis wondered. "No, of course you don't have to tell me. It's just that people have described Father Spiro so differently, and it would help if I understood him."

"Differently? How so?"

"Some saw him as burdened with parish cares, I guess you might say. Others saw him as perhaps losing touch with reality."

Hartunian burst out in an overzealous laugh, causing two of the cats to slink farther away. "Sylvie, shall I tell our visitor what I thought of Father Spiro?"

"Oh, Lloyd," Sylvia giggled as she stroked his neck.

"Well, to put it succinctly, the parish was near a veritable rupturing, and I blame Father Spiro. Crisis was imminent. My word, there was this embarrassing article in the paper, and Father Spiro was in geriatric la-la land. The same thing happened to my dear grandfather, didn't it, Sylvie? So I know what I'm talking about. Classic symptoms, Father."

"Such as?"

"There was that terrible display his last Sunday. Surely, you heard about that."

"Of course."

"But even before that. Well, what can I say? The parish was flying in all directions, and what did Father Spiro do with his time? He had confabs with rabbis and maybe imams for all we know."

Sylvia's swollen hand moved to her mouth to cover a giggle.

How did Hartunian know about that? "Was that what you disagreed about?" Father Fortis asked.

Hartunian removed his glasses and began cleaning them on his shirt. "We disagreed about a whole variety of things. Where should I start? Perhaps I should begin when I came into the Orthodox Church three years ago. That was when Deacon Daniel was on staff as well."

"Isn't he Father Daniel?" Father Fortis asked.

"Technically true, Father. Yes, all ordained, and so they sent him on his way. With my blessing, I might add."

"You didn't like Father Daniel?"

Hartunian moved his attention to the ceiling. "I'd say on his behalf that he did his best to cover up Father Spiro's missteps. But Father Daniel had too much of an agenda. He thought he was St. Paul bringing in the Gentiles, if you take my meaning."

"Converts, I assume," Father Fortis said. "But aren't you a convert, Mr. Hartunian?"

Hartunian sat up straight in the chair. "My grandfather was half-Greek, and the rest of my family is Armenian. Deacon Daniel's crowd is an entirely different breed. Some are quite devout, but others are simply embarrassing. They can't even follow the liturgy, Father."

"And Father Daniel?"

"He pushed for English all the time, even though his Greek was passable."

"And you raised your objections with Father Spiro?" Father Fortis asked.

One of the cats jumped back up in Hartunian's lap. Hartunian stroked her neck in time with how Sylvia was stroking his. "Naturally, I did. I wasn't going to stand by and see Orthodoxy divorced from her Hellenic base, was I, Sylvie?"

The woman shook her head adamantly.

"There must have been something else, though," Father Fortis said. "Father Daniel left St. Cosmas long before your last conversation with Father Spiro."

"Of course, and I'm happy to tell you about that, Father. In fact," he said, fingering the bow of his glasses, "you may be able to help me. You see, I asked Father Spiro for the smallest of favors. I work at a church supply store downtown, Blitzen's. You may have heard of it. Ask that busybody Mrs. Hazelton. Anyway, I've been there for, oh, so many years. I asked Father Spiro to speak with the owner about a promotion, one I richly deserve. I have seniority, you know. Well, it didn't seem Father Spiro did anything, even after

I repeatedly spoke with him about it. As I said, his mind was slipping badly."

So, is this the real reason Hartunian called me out here? Father Fortis wondered. *To help him get a promotion?* No, that wouldn't explain the cat and mouse game he was playing. Hartunian had invited him to his house to find out how much he and the police knew about his relationship with Father Spiro.

"About your promotion, Mr. Hartunian," he protested, "you must realize I know few in this city—outside the parish, I mean."

"Does that mean you refuse my request?"

There was an edge to Hartunian's voice, and Father Fortis saw the odd man before him in a new light. Could Hartunian be the killer? It would be the question Worthy would ask him. And what would he say? Two answers came to mind at the same time. Yes, indeed, a man this bizarre could do anything. And no, this guy wasn't capable of planning such a crime, much less carrying it out. So it took Father Fortis a few seconds to see the request from another angle. Wouldn't Worthy want to talk with Hartunian's boss, if for no other reason than to find out if Hartunian had been at work that fateful Tuesday morning?

Father Fortis rose from the couch, longing to return to sunshine and clean air. His movement caused the cat on Hartunian's lap to fly off in alarm. "Mr. Hartunian, the promotion isn't in my hands, but I can promise you that I'll personally speak with your boss as soon as possible."

CHAPTER TEN

———◆———

ALL MORNING FRIDAY AT THE PRECINCT, Worthy tried to stay as busy with minutiae as possible. Yet, there was no way he could avoid thinking of the weekend ahead at the cabin with Allyson. With so much that could go wrong, he chastised himself for not settling for a less risky situation. But he knew that there were no amount of movies to watch or pizzas to eat that would salvage their relationship before Allyson went away to college. A weekend at the cabin, just the two of them, was a risk. Time, however, was running out.

Allyson made the drive up to the cabin nearly stress free by putting on her headphones and then falling asleep. So it wasn't until they arrived and Worthy was unpacking the car that Allyson had a chance to show him what she needed from him in terms of distance. She dropped her suitcase in her room, and although it was already dark, immediately headed down to the shore of the lake. Worthy turned on the power and waited to hear the furnace fire up. Having already closed down the cabin for the winter, he'd brought the necessary bottled water they'd need for the weekend. They could thaw buckets of snow by the furnace to use to flush the toilets.

After he started a fire in the wood stove to warm the cabin, he meandered into the fish room, the tiny space at the front so named by Allyson as a grade-schooler for the rods and tackle boxes it housed. From there, he was able to watch his daughter as she stood on shore, gazing out at the lake. How many years had it been since he'd seen this sight?

The cabin was about the only family item to survive the divorce intact. In the final divorce papers, the cabin and property were listed as remaining in both Susan's and his names, a kind of joint custody. The cabin was already old when they found it, having been built in the thirties by a local trapper and hunter. After a year of weekend trips to scout properties, Susan and he had found the place near Petoskey when Allyson was six and Amy only one. At the foot of the pier, Worthy had taught his daughters to fish and swim, and after that, Allyson had always seemed to linger near or in the water—in the summer swimming to the raft he'd built or fishing for bluegills, in the winter clearing the snow on the lake to ice skate. Later, Allyson had graduated to lifeguarding at a camp across the lake. Susan and Amy, on the other hand, had preferred gardening, or whatever passed for that in their losing battle with the deer.

Worthy jolted from his seat when Allyson turned and started up the path to the cabin. But he risked another look at his daughter as she strode up the way. She was clearly a woman. Gone was her bounding up the steps he'd built from old railway ties. She walked slowly and confidently, as if she knew she no longer needed to hurry. Then again, he thought, maybe she realized there was nothing waiting for her in the cabin to make her hurry.

He was on the stairs leading up to his second-floor room when she came into the cabin through the side door. He'd been stopped, as always, by the old photos and drawings by the girls taped to the walls. Nothing from the days of their marriage had been removed, even the picture of Susan and him mugging in the water when Allyson was already a teenager.

In the weeks following the separation, he'd come to the cabin as much as he could. Perhaps that had been as much to be with the family pictures as to escape his tiny apartment. He would study the photos of Susan and the girls for hours, as if they held some answer for him. "You've been here before," they seemed to whisper in that first year. "Find the key, and you could be here again."

He closed the door of his room behind him and breathed in the musty smell. Over the bed, a smallmouth bass would forever writhe in the taxidermist's pose. He'd caught it the summer before the divorce, the summer Susan first seemed to withdraw. When, two months later, Susan had shocked him with her request for a divorce, he'd thought back and realized Susan had been pulling away earlier than that, maybe even the previous winter. But he'd been busy at work, and it wasn't until they were at the cabin that summer that he finally began to wonder and worry. He probably should have asked her then, but the cabin had never seemed the right place to argue. And when they'd returned to the city, he'd been pulled into a particularly horrifying case—the rape and murder of an inner-city teenager. Things between Susan and him had seemed more normal. They weren't, but as the investigation stirred up racial allegations in the newspapers, he just hadn't noticed.

He heard Allyson below him in the kitchen opening one of the cookie boxes they'd bought at the store. He wondered how much she remembered from that last summer when the photos on the wall still made sense. He sat on the bed and listened to the unfamiliar sound of someone else in the cabin. It must be over four years since she's been here. Susan had told him that she'd tried to get Allyson to come up with her and Amy, but Allyson had always said she had to work. Maybe that was the real reason, or maybe it was just an excuse. In the fall of that same year, Allyson had run away.

Always that persistent question: why had she run away, and where had she gone? He was a detective and she was a great mystery to him, as big a mystery as his divorce. So many questions, but were they the right ones? Wouldn't it be better to focus on the immediate question of why his daughter had agreed to come to the cabin? What did she want, and what part was he supposed to play?

They both retired early on Friday night, and on Saturday morning, they slept in before putting on cross-country skis for a lap around the lake. They skied hard, as if they both realized pushing themselves would make conversation more difficult. The only topic Ally raised was which of the neighbors had sold their places since she'd last been there. But as they took off their skis at the cabin, she offered the smallest of smiles as she said, "I can't believe I remember how to do that."

It was a moment he'd thought might never happen again, maybe because he had once foolishly thought it would always happen. When buying the old place, he'd attacked its sagging roof and leaky windows with a certainty that it would stay in the family. And now he wanted to find some way to say that again, to tell Allyson that she would return here with her children. He wanted her to know that, just as he was doing at that moment, she too would kneel to feed the fire while her children played board games on the rickety card table. More than anything, he wanted her to know that when he and whatever pain he had caused were gone, this cabin was the one place that would always know her.

But he didn't say anything, not then or when they were checking the mouse traps. What he hoped she would realize about the cabin might not be even close to what she'd remember. For all he knew, she saw the photos in the cabin as all lies. For all he knew, what they'd had as a family was what she had tried to run away from.

"Should we make bacon and eggs for supper?" she asked from the kitchen.

He waited to hear if the word "Dad" would end that question, but when it did not, he replied, "Ah, give me a minute to think about it."

The thought of sitting across from Allyson in the silent cabin suddenly made him nervous. He knew how easily a careless word on his part could destroy the uneasy truce between them.

"How about we go to the Outpost?" he asked as he rose from his knees. "I know it's not Friday, but they still probably have the fish fry."

She stood in the doorway between the living room and the kitchen, hands on hips, as if she were ten. "Oh, gee, I haven't been to the Outpost since forever. I'll have to change."

He stood awkwardly, feeling giddy in the near normalcy of the moment. "You look fine." And then before he could stop himself, he blurted out, "I think Rick's off in the Army, if that's who you're thinking about."

That second seemed eternal to Worthy.

"Rick! That goof?" she said, as she returned into the kitchen. "I must have been insane to like him. Actually, I think I was thirteen, and everybody's insane when they're thirteen."

He took a deep breath as she ran upstairs. She hadn't freaked out. "I bet they'll still remember you down there. The girl who'd ride her bike down to the Outpost every day for a Coke."

"Proves my point," came the voice from overhead. "Thirteen and totally insane. Just like Amy's getting to be."

He stacked some logs to the side of the fireplace for later in the evening. Maybe they'd rent a movie at the gas station and cap off a better day than he could have hoped for. Father Fortis would think it was an answer to a prayer. For him, it was just an answer.

From her room upstairs, Allyson called out, "Give me a minute and then I'll be ready."

He came to the foot of the stairs and called up, "How about me? You sure you don't mind being seen with me in this old sweater?"

"Nobody would recognize you in anything else. Mom used to say your old clothes were like your uniform up here."

"I suppose. I found this particular sweater in one of the trunks when we bought the place. Must be forty to fifty years old. I couldn't believe it fit."

Allyson snickered. "And you haven't taken it off up here since."

"Fine, I'll go in my regular costume. Who's going to be looking at me, anyway?"

"Yeah, right, as if they don't always swamp you at the Outpost."

"Swamp me?"

"Sure. Mom always said you were like a celebrity up here."

"Oh, I don't know. I haven't been to eat there in … in more than a year, I guess. Bet you five bucks you get all the attention," he said as they walked to the car. "Look, it's Ricky's old girlfriend."

But he'd have lost the bet. The patrons that night in the bar and restaurant were the older set, the retirees still spry enough to endure the cold winters. One after another, they came over to his table on their way out to greet him, say when they'd last seen his photo in the Detroit papers, and leave him to introduce Allyson over and over again.

"You're Allyson? Why, I almost didn't recognize you." The old man took off his duck hat and swept back a strand of hair over his bald spot. "Your hair sure has grown since last summer."

"Actually, I haven't been up here for four years."

"No, I'm sure it wasn't that long ago."

The old-timer's wife stepped forward. Her sweatshirt, fanning out at the hips, showed faded photos below a logo: "Ask me about my grandchildren." Without waiting for Allyson to answer, the woman turned her attention to Worthy. "We still can't believe it about you and Susan. Just so sorry. We all say how much we miss seeing you both here together."

"I appreciate that," Worthy said. He felt an urge to say that though the past five years had been hard they were all doing okay, but he stopped. Allyson wouldn't understand the kind of lies adults told.

"So it's just the two of you up for the weekend?" the woman continued. "My, my, Allyson, you're looking so much like your mother. I suppose you get that all the time. And now you're having a little father-and-daughter time together? Well, well, well. Norbert, isn't that sweet?"

That was the problem with not telling lies, Worthy thought. People like this old woman could smell the scent of hard truth. Worthy felt panic rise in his stomach as the woman eyed Allyson, preparing for her next attack.

"Yes, just the two of us," Allyson said in a voice loud enough for the entire room to hear. "We were hoping for some peace and quiet."

The piece of fish stuck in Worthy's throat, forcing him to cough and cough again. Norbert hit him between his shoulder blades, then donned his cap before escorting his wife toward the door.

The other patrons silently pondered their food. In a few seconds, the waitress was standing by their table. "Do you want your check, then?" She'd already begun to tally the bill.

"Want anything else, Ally?"

"Not unless they serve liquor to minors here," she murmured, looking down. "Let's just go."

He handed his plate to the waitress. "I'll have some more fish."

Raising her eyebrows, the waitress walked the plate back to the kitchen.

"I don't think you'll be confused with the sweet lifeguard anymore."

"I'm not sorry," she said.

He took a swig of his beer. "I don't know why you should be. She had it coming. Other people are just wishing they could say things like that."

"No, most of them think your daughter is a bitch."

"So order some dessert and show them you don't care."

"Why are we the only ones talking in here?" she whispered. "That doesn't bother you?"

He shrugged and pondered the question. "My folks raised us to be nice in public, no matter what anyone said or did. Don't you remember what your grandmother always says? 'If you can't say anything nice—'"

"'Then don't say anything at all,'" Allyson finished.

"But I realized that was just my father's way of keeping his job. With him being a minister, he couldn't afford having what he called sassy-mouthed kids. As a cop, I learned pretty quickly being nice doesn't always work."

"My Dad, the sassy detective. That's how you make people confess?"

He basked in his daughter's interest and her occasional smile. "No, unlike on TV, it pays to be polite to witnesses, even suspects. But some of the other guys in the precinct are another matter."

"That why you never have a partner?"

"Who said I don't?"

"Mom told me once. She said you like to work alone."

The waitress put the plate of fried fish in front of him. "And my daughter would like dessert."

"What'll it be, sweetie?"

"A chocolate shake. Just a small one."

"One small shake coming up."

Worthy squeezed lemon over the fish. "I wouldn't say I prefer working alone. I just seem to do better that way."

Allyson balled up a napkin. "Wouldn't a good partner help you find the killer quicker?"

Worthy put his fork down. "It did in New Mexico. They gave me a good partner. Actually, two of them, if you count Father Nick. And I had some local help. She was very good."

"She?"

Worthy nodded.

"Let me get this straight. You had a woman for a partner, and it worked?"

"There was a rough spot or two, but yes. Does that surprise you?"

Her eyes were boring into his. "What kind of rough spot?"

Why is she so interested? he wondered. "Two people working on a case don't always see the clues the same way. I made some assumptions, kind of jumped ahead of her at one or two points, and she thought I was all wrong."

"Let me guess. In the end you were right."

"Not really. It turned out we both were partly right. Also partly wrong."

Allyson leaned forward. "Was she cute?"

He took a sip of his beer. "It wasn't something I paid a lot of attention to. I guess you could say she was cute, but I'd say we became good friends."

"So you had a partner in New Mexico, and you got along okay. So why doesn't that happen in Detroit? Why is it always just your picture in the papers?"

"Look, Ally, I don't write the news. And besides, I do have a partner on the case I've got now. The only question is whether he'll stay on it."

"Is it a murder?"

Worthy nodded. "A priest was strangled about three weeks ago."

"I heard about that."

"Actually, it's a takeover case. That means I got somebody else's case."

"The first guy screwed up?"

"No, he was just pulled away to work on something else."

"Oh, a big case like this. Boy, I bet he loves you."

"No, we've known each other too long for that. He pretty much told me he hopes I fall on my face, except he didn't say 'face.' I wonder when she's going to bring your shake."

"It's her way of telling me she doesn't like me."

"Nah. She's just busy," Worthy said.

"You know who she is, don't you?"

"No."

"Ricky's older sister. I think her name's Tammy. We hated each other."

"You going to let her know you remember her?"

"No, Dad. Anyway, back to you."

Back to me? Where did this sudden interest in his career come from?

"What did you mean when you said your new partner may not stay on the case?" Allyson continued. "Cops get to do that?"

"No, cops can't do that. But he's had some problems lately. Real explosive type, the kind who slugs people he shouldn't. They might have to pull him."

"Won't that cost him his job?"

"Probably."

Tammy brought the shake and set it down with a straw.

"I'll take the check when you're ready," Worthy said.

Allyson took a long sip and grimaced.

"What is it?" Worthy asked.

"It's vanilla. I asked for chocolate."

"Want me to call her back?"

"No, I don't want to give her the satisfaction." Allyson took the straw out and drank from the glass before looking back at her father. "Anything you can do to help?"

"Who're we talking about?"

"Your partner."

Worthy tried to make sense of the worried look on his daughter's face. He'd understood Captain Betts' concern, but why would Allyson care? "You're not the first to ask me that, but I can't see how," he said. "I mean, look at it this way. Somebody strangled a priest in front of his own altar in broad daylight. In this country, a priest or minister is like a symbol of goodness. If they get killed, people get really scared. And they should be. The media will roast us if whoever did it gets away with it. That's what I'm paid to prevent. My partner's problems are just distractions."

Allyson looked down at the half-empty glass. "That's what he is, a distraction?"

"Look, I'm not saying his problems aren't important. In fact, I told my captain the man probably needs professional help. But that's not my job."

Allyson pushed away the half-empty glass and rose from the table. "Let's get out of here," she said, looking past him.

"What's the matter?" he asked, still seated.

"Nothing. Can we just go?"

He could see tears in the corners of her eyes. "Don't do this again, Ally. Tell me what's the matter."

"It's always just that one thing for you, isn't it? To find your killer. The rest of us? Well …."

Worthy watched her walk toward the door, her hands in her pockets. There it was again, that sense he'd failed some test. What had he said?

THE FOLLOWING MONDAY MORNING, WORTHY'S BREAKFAST was interrupted by a phone call from Father Fortis.

"Christopher, did I wake you?"

"No, Nick, just finishing breakfast. After that, I'm headed over to see you. I want to hear about Hartunian."

"Fine, fine, my friend, but did you see the morning paper?"

He stopped chewing. Had something happened when he was up north with Allyson? No, he reasoned, if that had happened he'd have found a message when he got home. "I haven't opened it yet."

"I'm truly sorry, my friend. It's not fair at all, I must say."

Worthy opened his front door and picked up the paper on the mat before returning to the phone. "Come on, Nick, just spit it out."

"It's a small piece. Maybe people won't read it. By someone named Kenna McCarty."

Worthy groaned. "What page, Nick?"

"First section, Page twenty-three, left hand side."

Worthy opened the paper and saw the headline: ANOTHER ROBBERY.

VACATION TIME? He leaned against the door frame. Anger mixed with confusion. How'd she know about that?

"Christopher, are you there?"

"Yeah, I see it," he said as he scanned the small column.

> The break-in late Thursday night, early Friday morning at St. Michael's Catholic Church may have struck many readers as too much of a coincidence. Just two blocks away from St. Cosmas Greek Orthodox Church, where Father Spiro George was found strangled three weeks ago, St. Michael's also had an altarpiece stolen.
>
> That should send the investigative team off like a pack of bloodhounds, right? Wrong. This reporter learned that Lieutenant Christopher Worthy, in charge of the case, left town only hours later on a family weekend vacation.
>
> Let's hope the robbers/killers also take weekends off.

"This is my fault, Christopher."

Worthy found his car keys, leaving his breakfast unfinished. "How do you figure, Nick?"

"She called here yesterday. I happened to be in the office, working with your partner. She asked some questions about the robberies, then wanted to know where she could reach you. And I guess that's when my big mouth got you in trouble."

"Forget about that. Are you telling me Henderson was there yesterday?"

"Yes, he sat in the back during liturgy. He asked if he could see me in the afternoon. He wanted to hear what I thought about the case. He's here this morning, by the way."

"Doing what?" Worthy said, trying to cradle the phone with his shoulder while he tied his shoes.

"Looking for the missing book. Isn't that what you told him to do?"

"Not in so many words, Nick, but he'd surprise me no matter what he did. I'll be there in thirty minutes."

"Don't you have to go in to the precinct? I mean, shouldn't you explain?"

"Not now, I don't. I'll leave my boss a message where she can reach me. That writer is just paying me back."

"For what?"

"For *not* doing her a favor. Something impossible. Look, I'll see you soon."

WORTHY'S BRAIN DRIFTED BETWEEN TWO QUESTIONS as he drove through morning traffic. The first was: what's the worst thing that could happen? Possible answers ranged from Captain Betts bawling him out on the mild end of the scale, to the superintendent butting in, to being dismissed from the case. He imagined Sherrod making an appointment with anyone who would see him before the day was out.

The second question absorbing his attention was: do I wish I hadn't gone to the cabin with Allyson? Their weekend never recovered after the incident at the restaurant. She'd listened to her headphones the entire way home. But the first part of the weekend was worth it to him. In the old place, the two of them had found an old way of being together. Who knew if he'd somehow destroyed that possibility again, but for the first time since the separation, Allyson and he had been almost together.

As he pulled the car into the church parking lot, he admitted that had he known the society reporter was out to get him, he'd still have left town.

Father Fortis came around his desk to greet him. "I beg your forgiveness, my friend. It's been eating away at me all morning. And each phone call is salt in the wound."

"From parish council members, I take it?"

"Others, too. Whoever said newspaper readership is down? Things okay at work?"

"I left a message I'd be in after lunch. My boss will call me here if she decides things can't wait."

"What can I say, my friend? It's just what my abbot has told me for twenty years. A monk who can't control his tongue is like a serpent."

"Let it go, Nick. The woman trapped you. How were you to know? Anyway, where's Henderson?"

"Somewhere in the church. Mrs. Hazelton has decided she quite likes him. She started to call him the eager-beaver type."

"Oh, does she? I think I should go back to bed and start the day all over again."

Moving to the window, Father Fortis gave Worthy a puzzled look. "Don't you want him here?"

"I don't know. We're supposed to work together, so I guess this is as close as it's going to get—same place, same time. That sort of togetherness."

"Sit down, my friend. The more important question is how was your time with Allyson?"

Worthy dropped into a chair and scratched at his forehead. "Half of it was excellent, half of it terrible."

"Which came first?"

"Unfortunately, the excellent part."

"Will you have another chance?"

"We can hope," Worthy said, fearing how Allyson might react to the story in the newspaper. "Nothing much else to say about it. What happened with Hartunian?"

He listened to Father Fortis' review of the strange meeting. When Father Fortis asked him at the end if it sounded to him like Hartunian might be a killer, Worthy shrugged his shoulders.

"It sounds more like he wanted your attention. He reminds me of the type who hope they're suspects."

"Really? Some people want that?"

"Absolutely. Nothing bothers them more than when we find the real killer. Up to then, they get the satisfaction of looking out their windows to see if their house is being watched. He'll probably call to see you again."

"I think you're right, my friend. And that fits with the way he badgered Father Spiro. So, you definitely believe he couldn't have done it."

"I wouldn't completely rule it out. Attention-seekers live with mountains of frustration. You see, they never get enough, and if Hartunian thought Father Spiro was preventing him getting something he'd set his heart on, like this promotion, then yes, he could have done it. I'll bet he fantasized about it more than once. So we'll have that talk with his boss. In fact, it will probably make me look like I'm doing my job."

"But you are doing your job, Christopher."

"I'm talking from my boss' perspective."

Father Fortis groaned. "If I'd just kept my mouth shut—"

The phone buzzer interrupted them. "Father, Mrs. Theodora Nichols is here to see you. She's a member of the parish."

"I didn't know I had an appointment."

"She's come about your note in the newsletter. The one about those who spoke with Father Spiro in the last weeks?"

"Oh? Just a minute." Father Fortis relayed the message to Worthy. "Would you like to hear this?"

"Why not? That is, if she agrees." Worthy's entire world had seemed upside down since his fight with Allyson on Saturday. His daughter seemed as concerned about Henderson as his captain. On top of that, Kenna McCarty probably had the superintendent on the phone right now. Maybe this woman would bring his mind back to the one person who really mattered—Father Spiro.

A short, dark-haired woman in her thirties with a two-year-old in one hand and a canvas bag in the other came into the office. She smiled tentatively at Father Fortis before stooping to kiss his hand, then peered questioningly at Worthy.

"Please sit down, Mrs. Nichols. May I call you Theodora?"

Mrs. Nichols nodded with a small smile.

"And let me move some chairs back so your son can play on the floor."

"Thank you, Father. This is Andrew."

Father Fortis bent down and patted the toddler's head. "What a beautiful name. It happens to be my middle name as well, at least the English form. Theodora," he said, straightening up, "this is a friend of mine, Lieutenant Christopher Worthy."

The woman's eyes grew large at Worthy's title. "Are you a policeman?"

"That's right, Mrs. Nichols. I'm in charge of the investigation." He wondered how long that would be true.

"Oh, I didn't realize I'd have to speak to a policeman, Father. I'm not sure my husband would have agreed."

The two-year-old yanked on Worthy's pant leg. Worthy reached down to pull gently on the pacifier. "I know what this is," he said, smiling. The child laughed and sucked harder, having obviously played the game before.

The woman sat on the edge of her chair and rested her hands in her lap. "Bill said I could talk to you, Father, but he said I wasn't supposed to bother the police."

"My dear, I've known Lieutenant Worthy for some time, and I can assure you that you can trust him with whatever you want to tell me. I assume it's about Father Spiro."

She nodded and looked down as the child continued to pull on Worthy's pant leg. "Andy, do you want some Cheerios and juice?" She opened the bag and put a small plastic bowl and covered cup on the floor next to her. "I'll clean up what he spills."

"Don't even think about it, my dear. Mrs. Hazelton said you've come because of my notice in the newsletter."

"That's right, Father," she said, giving Worthy another look. "We got it Saturday in the mail. I thought about speaking to you after church, but … well, I didn't make it yesterday."

"I'm just glad you came in this morning."

"And I promise that if it doesn't have anything to do with my investigation," Worthy said, "I'll completely ignore it."

"I can't believe it could have anything to do with Father's … his death, but then maybe I'm hoping it doesn't," she said, tears starting down her cheek.

Father Fortis handed the woman a tissue from a box on his desk. "But I can see it's important to you, my dear. I assume it's something you talked about with Father Spiro."

Both men waited as the woman wiped at her tears. "I came the first time back almost a year ago, in February. I remember it was about St. Valentine's Day. I just wanted to talk … to talk to someone." Her hands squeezed the tissue in her lap. "It was about my husband—his work, actually. I could see that something had been bothering him, but he wouldn't talk about it."

"Where does he work?" Father Fortis asked.

"Oh, I'm sorry. He teaches physics at Allgemein. He's in his third year."

"Oh, a college professor."

Theodora Nichols grimaced slightly, as if the compliment had somehow hurt her.

"When he finally sat me down to talk about it, I couldn't make any sense of it. He told me he was having trouble with one of his students, a woman. I immediately thought *affair* and started to cry." She looked over at Worthy. "Are you married, Lieutenant?"

Worthy was surprised by the question and stammered a bit as he said he was recently divorced.

"I'm sorry," Theodora Nichols said, sniffling. "That's what I imagined was coming for me. I thought Bill was going to tell me he'd fallen in love with this woman. I call her a woman because she's an older student, not just some girl in her early twenties."

"But I take it from what you're saying that that wasn't the problem," Father Fortis coaxed.

"No, at least not on his side. He promised me there was nothing romantic. She was one of his students who just began hanging around the department, working on lab projects with him. He said the whole thing started to make him uncomfortable back at the end of the fall semester. I remember really crying then, because that's when I first noticed the change in him … in us, really. He'd been so happy at Allgemein, so hopeful this was where he belonged."

"Did he speak to the woman—I mean, to warn her off?" Father Fortis asked.

Mrs. Nichols dabbed at her eyes and nose. "He tried to put up some barriers, like not going into the lab when he saw her in there, but she just showed up at his office hours."

"Did he talk with his dean?" Worthy asked.

"Oh yes, but that was a disaster. When he asked the dean to remove her from his class, the dean turned everything around on him. He asked Bill what he'd done to encourage her."

"Not very helpful, my dear."

"It shook Bill. And then he found out this woman is the wife of an older faculty member, someone in the sociology department, I think. Bill thought the dean was too scared to call her in."

"And that's when you came to see Father Spiro?"

"Yes, that was the first time, and he was wonderful. He listened to me, and I probably wasn't making much sense at the time. I mean, I still wasn't sure

Bill hadn't done something with this woman. I know it's not right to distrust your husband, but I couldn't help wondering."

The woman's worry brought Worthy back to the memory of his own face in the bathroom mirror, the night after Susan asked for a separation. Was there another man? Had she found something she'd failed to get from him? But it hadn't been that for him. Never during the separation or the divorce had he ever sensed there had been another. She just got tired of him.

"Theodora, what did Father Spiro do when you told him this?" Father Fortis asked.

"He took me into the sanctuary, and I knelt in front of the Christ icon. He prayed for my family, for Bill, for Andy and me, and our protection. I cried. He was very good, like a grandfather, really."

Worthy tried to picture the woman in this office telling her woes to Father Spiro. Could this explain the panicked look in the priest's eyes when he'd been caught by the photographer? Was this the kind of thing he kept secreted away in the missing book? Lloyd Hartunian didn't seem the kind of problem the priest would bother to hide. But he might have been more careful with accusations against a college faculty wife. And if so, that raised an old question for him.

"Did Father Spiro seem mentally sound to you, Mrs. Nichols?" he asked.

"Huh?" she said, looking over at him. "Yes, why do you ask? Oh, I know. You're thinking about what happened on that last Sunday. No, he was fine."

"And you came to see him again?" Father Fortis asked.

Mrs. Nichols fought down a sob and shook her head. "The woman seemed to know Bill was in a bind. It was as if the dean suspected him, and Bill's not near to getting tenure. She started leaving him notes. Then by the end of the spring semester, I started getting phone calls at home. The person would just hang up. But I knew who it was."

"I think if I were in your husband's shoes, I'd have been pretty scared," Worthy said.

"Oh, Bill was a basket case until summer arrived. We spent the summer with my folks in Connecticut, and Bill was able to relax. The woman left us alone. But when August arrived, the Bill I'd been so worried about in the spring was back. Even before we came back to Detroit, I'd find him out of bed in the middle of the night, just curled up on the couch. I knew things were bad when just before we came back here, he started talking about applying for other jobs. Jobs in physics are very tight. I mean, there are hundreds of applicants for every opening. And like I said, we both thought Allgemein was wonderful."

"Tell us about the second visit to see Father Spiro, my dear. When was it?"

"I guess it was in September, maybe early October. Is that important?"

"Maybe not," Worthy said. "Please go on."

Mrs. Nichols glanced back at Andrew, who was looking at a cloth book upside down. She offered a weak smile at her son before continuing. "I would have come back to see Father earlier, but Bill freaked out after the first visit. You see, I didn't tell him beforehand. He said I was weak to come, like when I call my mom every week."

The two men waited. Finally she went on, "I hope Andy doesn't remember what I was like during those weeks. I'd sit in the kitchen every day and cry for hours. I thought I was going to go crazy, but I was even more worried about Bill. How can one sick person be allowed to destroy our lives, all we've worked for?"

"You hadn't met this other woman yet?" Worthy asked.

Mrs. Nichols blew her nose. "I still haven't. I began to wish her dead, though. That's when I came back to see Father Spiro."

"And what did he say?" Father Fortis asked.

She gave a brief laugh over her tears. "He told us to screen our calls, not pick up when she called. It was so obvious, but when you're scared, you don't think of those things. Then Father Spiro volunteered to talk with the dean."

"Theodora, do you know if he did that?"

"I don't know. Maybe, but I don't think so. I told him Bill wouldn't like it. Bill can be a bit proud."

February and then maybe late September, Worthy thought. Father Fortis' note in the newsletter had specified those who'd spoken to Father Spiro in the two weeks before his death.

"Something went wrong, I take it," he said. "Something that brought you back to Father Spiro."

"Yes," Mrs. Nichols said, rocking back and forth in the chair. "In November—I know it was before Thanksgiving—the woman came into Bill's office, all matter-of-fact, and asked him to read a draft of her project. He lied and said he had a department meeting in five minutes, but she said that would be enough time."

Mrs. Nichols put her hand over her mouth and stifled another sob. "At the bottom of the last page she'd written him a note. It said," she stammered, "it said, 'I know you're avoiding me' and then below that was 'Would you believe, Bill, that I tried to kill my husband four nights ago?' Bill said when he looked up from the page, the woman was just staring at him."

"Good heavens," Father Fortis exclaimed.

"Bill said he pushed the pages back toward her and told her he didn't want anything to do with her. He said he hated her and that she was driving him crazy. She just laughed."

"That's when you came back here, my dear?"

"That's when we both came in, Bill and I," she said. "I know I should have been grateful for that, but it felt horrible. It was the second week of December, and it was like Bill had given up. Bill is a true scientist, Father, and doesn't have a high regard for religion."

"But he came with you. That strikes me as significant," Father Fortis said.

Mrs. Nichols nodded. "Our meeting went better than I'd hoped. I guess Bill so desperately needed to talk to someone that he forgot Father Spiro was a priest."

"Did Father Spiro promise to do anything?" Worthy asked. He could imagine the old priest realizing that the Nichols' crisis was escalating. Had he decided to intervene in some way? Had a woman willing to kill her husband decided instead to turn her wrath on the meddling priest?

"He told us to both go see the dean and report what the woman had written. He wanted me to go with Bill so the university would know Bill wasn't covering up something. He said the university had to take responsibility, and he expected they would. He also asked us to trust him."

"What did he mean by that?" Worthy asked.

"He wanted to know what the woman's name was. I'm pretty sure he said he'd keep it in a safe place," she added.

Worthy looked at Father Fortis. That was it. The book must have been where he kept names and matters he didn't want others to find. But why keep it at all? Then Worthy thought he understood. No doubt the old man was forgetting things. The book was his memory bank.

"And so you told him the name," Worthy said. "I'm going to ask you to do the same with us."

Mrs. Nichols nodded as if she'd been expecting the request. "Peggy Hagarty. Bill asked him what he planned to do with it. Father said part of his vocation was dealing with evil."

Worthy's heart skipped a beat. "That's the way he put it? Dealing with evil?"

"Yes, I think so."

Too close to the chapter in the Jewish book and Rabbi Milkin's comments to be coincidence, he thought.

"Anything else, my dear?"

"He told Bill he intended to do something harmless to everyone but the woman. He intended to pray for her by name. I remember Bill laughed, and Father laughed too. It was like he knew Bill wasn't mocking him."

He did more than pray for her, Worthy thought. At least after he talked it out with the rabbi.

"Bill and I slept better that night than we had in weeks. Strange, isn't it? That's what I remember."

"So when did the two of you go in to see the dean?" Worthy prompted.

"The next day. Bill laid it all out and mentioned he might be getting a lawyer. The dean suddenly seemed more understanding and said he'd arrange a meeting with the college lawyer that afternoon. We walked out with the dean's assurance, in writing, that Mrs. Hagarty would be barred from his classes."

Tears flowed freely down her cheeks. "It felt so clean. Bill took Andy and me out to some kid's restaurant. The food was terrible, but Andy liked the puppet show." She shook her head and gave a weak smile. "Bill felt so good that he talked about staying at Allgemein."

"And that was all before the Christmas holidays, Theodora?" Father Fortis asked.

Mrs. Nichols nodded and cried softly. "We thought with the semester ending that the problem was over. We'd have the holidays, and then Bill wouldn't have to see her again. But," she said, then paused to collect herself, "but then we got a call from Andy's nursery school right after New Year's. He goes there two mornings a week. They said someone had broken into the school and vandalized the kids' finger paintings. I couldn't make any sense of it until the secretary said the person had only vandalized his."

He looked down at her son. "It still didn't make any sense," she added, and Worthy could see that she believed that. "How can you vandalize a finger painting? But they asked us to come in, and we did. When we got there, a policeman was waiting for us. I want to show you what we had to look at."

She reached into her bag, pulled out a folded piece of art paper, and handed it to Father Fortis, who spread it out on his desk. Worthy stood and looked down at the swirly shapes and the designs. At the top, someone had written "Die" in ink and underneath had drawn a crescent moon with a star in it.

"How odd," Father Fortis said. "Terrifying and odd."

"The secretary at the school told the policeman that she'd seen a woman come into the school the afternoon before. She thought she was a mother who'd come back to get something. She also said she thought she saw the woman talking and making gestures, as if someone else was in the room."

"You're saying it was Mrs. Hagarty," Father Fortis asked.

"They didn't have a good enough description, but I was sure. That was two weeks ago."

"And so you came back here," Worthy said.

Mrs. Nichols' shoulders sagged. "Yes. That was just a day before Father was killed. He was interested in the moon and stars in the drawing. He asked if there were any dots placed around the stars. I didn't know, and then he died. But I looked this morning. He was right."

"I don't follow," Worthy said.

"It's an old witchcraft sign," Father Fortis said. "How did Father Spiro react to what you said?"

"He volunteered to call a lawyer from the church. Bill said the college had already done that, but Father Spiro insisted. He said we needed an independent one. I don't know if he did that before he died," she whispered.

"What are your plans now, my dear?"

"We've got boxes all over the house. You see, we're leaving. We're going to live with my folks for a while."

There was motive here, Worthy thought. And with that he could explore the question of opportunity. But there was one question he still needed to ask.

"Mrs. Nichols, you said you were in church that last Sunday. What did you make of Father Spiro's problem?"

"I didn't understand it at all. Andy was fussy, and we'd been in and out of the service to the cry room. All I remember is feeling so sorry for Father. His face went white just before he stopped, then his face turned red when he started to chant again. I thought he must have been terribly embarrassed."

"Could you tell if he was looking at you?"

"At me? I don't think so. Why?"

"It's nothing."

A silence followed, a silence Worthy had come to understand well over his career. It was the silence that followed a witness having said everything that she or he had come to say. It was the silence of someone who suddenly felt empty and was not used to the feeling. It was the silence of a child who had turned over a problem to an adult and now wanted to think of something else.

Worthy thanked the woman for coming, as did Father Fortis, who asked that she call him if there was anything he could do.

As Worthy walked Theodora Nichols to the door, he could feel his mind beginning to race. He gave her his card and asked when the Nichols planned to move. He knew he needed time to put the pieces in order before he asked the couple to return to St. Cosmas to confirm his suspicions. But what she had told him made him feel better about the case than he had since the altarpiece was stolen from St. Michael's. And he finally had a clue to the case that was important enough to help him forget the chasm that had opened up again between Allyson and him.

He watched the Nichols' car drive away from the church before returning to the office. As he reentered the secretary's office, he was surprised to see Henderson waiting for him. The secretary handed him a note, saying Captain Betts had called and asked him to return her call as soon as possible.

No question what that's about, he thought. But with Theodora Nichols' testimony, he finally had something he could use to push back on Sherrod's robbery theory.

He looked up from the note, expecting to see Henderson's mask of boredom; instead he saw a shy smile on his partner's face. Henderson stepped forward, and like Santa at a Christmas party, brought something out from behind his back. It was the missing book with the leather corners.

CHAPTER ELEVEN

———◆———

WORTHY WALKED BRISKLY TOWARD CAPTAIN BETTS' office, the book tucked securely under his arm. He noticed as he passed that Hubie, the precinct desk sergeant, kept his eyes down. Several others, however, gave him knowing looks. He could guess what they thought they knew.

What he knew, and they didn't, was that Henderson had found the missing book. While the discovery posed an initial problem of it being in Greek, how big a problem would that be for Father Fortis, who was fluent in Greek?

The story of the book's discovery was incredible, as much for what it said about Henderson as the book itself. Mrs. Hazelton had already checked, to use her words, "everywhere, absolutely everywhere," but Henderson had found it within an hour of looking.

He had begun by inspecting the men's bathroom, believing that Father Spiro might have not simply hidden the book, but hidden it especially from his secretary, the one person who knew best his haunts and habits. But when he'd found nothing there, Mrs. Hazelton had admitted that there was another area in the church that was off limits to her.

"She told me that she was never allowed to go into the altar area," Henderson had told Worthy after the discovery. "And she sure didn't want me in there without the new priest's permission, but I went right in. I didn't find anything important for the first half hour. But then I noticed this small niche in the back of the altar."

"Ah, that's where relics are housed," Father Fortis had explained to both of them while Worthy was still at the church, sharing that every altar contained relics of one or more saints. Addressing Henderson, Father Fortis had said,

"I'm quite sure if you had asked my permission to open that, I would have refused."

"Good thing I don't always follow the rules," Henderson said, glancing knowingly at Worthy.

Worthy had paused before Captain Betts' door, feeling confident of the importance of the find, when the door opened from within. He stood face to face with Sherrod. For a second or two, Sherrod looked embarrassed before a cocky grin appeared on his face. As he passed by Worthy, he left a whispered, "You're making this way too easy" in his wake.

"Come in, Lieutenant, and shut the door behind you," Captain Betts said. She stood behind her desk, peering at him over her half glasses.

Little wonder why Sherrod is here, Worthy thought. He gripped the book in his hand. *This case isn't over yet.*

"Lieutenant Worthy, we need to pow-wow. When we first met, you seemed agreeable—mainly, that is—to what I asked. But whenever you leave my office, things seem to go haywire."

Worthy decided to wait until his captain had finished her tirade before speaking. The nasty taste left by McCarty's article couldn't stand up to Henderson's discovery. And in addition to that, Mrs. Nichols had offered more evidence that Father Spiro was not going senile but was preoccupied with serious issues in the parish.

Captain Betts shook her head. "It seems that my predecessor didn't give me the full scoop on you. He told me about your finer points and added a bit about your loner tendencies, but he didn't prepare me for this. Do you remember what we talked about last Friday?"

"Sure. We agreed that I was to go talk to Henderson, and that from now on the two of us are to work this case together. When we're at the projects, we're both there. Same with the church."

"Did I miss something in our little talk—say, about your right to take time off without permission?" She pointed down at an open newspaper on her desk. "I mean, for God's sake, this stunt of yours. Are you this stupid, or do you want to lose this case?"

"I didn't pull any stunt. The reporter did it to make me look bad."

"Well, she sure as hell succeeded." Betts paused a moment to gaze again at the damaging article. "If you'd gotten the phone calls I have this morning, Lieutenant, you'd know that when one of us looks bad, we all do."

Try that out on Sherrod, Worthy thought.

"Look, I met with that reporter last week," he said. "She asked for something impossible, and she didn't like it when I said no."

"A reporter well regarded by Superintendent Livorno, I might add."

"She made that perfectly clear. But it was still a stupid request."

Captain Betts removed her glasses and let them dangle. "And it didn't cross your mind that the best, not to mention most respectful, thing to do would be to run that by me? If what she asked was so stupid, I could have backed you up, or did you just assume that I'd side with Livorno?"

Worthy's jaw dropped. "To be honest, I never thought about telling you."

For a moment, Betts just stared at him. "That's quite a revelation, Lieutenant. No wonder your colleagues accuse you of being a loner."

Worthy could sense color rising on his face as he heard Captain Betts echo Allyson's comment.

"Now, is it true what's in the column, that you spent the weekend at your cabin?"

"I spent the weekend with my daughter, someone who hasn't had much time for me since my divorce. And I only did that after I made sure everything was covered."

"Explain everything being covered, Lieutenant."

"Okay. On Friday, I met with Henderson and worked out the new arrangement." Worthy paused and decided not to explain that the empty weekend was Henderson's choice. "With Bales in the hospital, the only thing we could have done over the weekend was interview a person of interest from the church. But then Father Fortis, the priest, said this person asked to see him."

"Are you telling me that you asked the priest to cover for you?"

Worthy didn't know whether to panic or laugh when he understood how low her trust in him had sunk.

"No, of course not, but we both thought that my tagging along would make our person of interest clam up."

Betts studied him for a moment. "Go on."

"It turns out that the guy did spill some things to the priest. Nothing that's going to break the case right away, but Henderson and I are going to follow up on it."

"And that's enough to put you in a good mood?"

"No, but this is." He handed the book across her desk.

Opening it, she looked up. "What is it? It's all in another language."

"It's in Greek," he said and explained the trail from the photo to the book's recovery.

"I take it this is the missing book that you mentioned in one of your emails. Where'd you find it?"

"Henderson found it."

Betts' eyebrows shot up. "Really?"

She's thawing, Worthy thought. "I'd never have found it, but he looked somewhere I'd have missed."

"Are you telling me that Sherrod forgot to check it?"

Worthy was in a magnanimous mood. "Sherrod and I both missed it. Even the secretary never thought of looking there."

She opened the book again and turned the pages. "But how do you know it's important? Are you telling me you read Greek?"

"No, but the new priest does. And I'm betting that all the recent sensitive problems at the church are listed in there. As you can see, the dates cover the last four months." Worthy decided to go out on a limb. "In a few days, we should know what was troubling the priest at the end."

"And the projects?" Captain Betts asked.

"I'll interview Bales with you whenever he's ready."

The captain closed the book and leaned back in her chair. "There are a lot of 'ifs' in your theory, but I think I understand your good mood. Now, help me recover my own good mood. Are you saying Henderson is working out?"

"Like I said, he found the book. So yes, I guess he is working out." Worthy stood. "Any way that I can stop bumping into Sherrod every time I come in here?"

"He works here too, Lieutenant. And that makes him one of my officers."

Worthy reached over and retrieved the book. "He's poaching, Captain. He'd already been over to the Catholic church."

"And he found something."

"I know about the brick."

Betts gave Worthy a sharp look. "But do you know it's from an old construction site behind the Suffolk projects?" She paused before continuing, "And Sherrod's not your only problem. There are some higher-ups who are asking if your investigation has any direction."

"Well, what does this prove?" Worthy posed, raising the book.

"Okay, but that could mean nothing. Part of your reputation, Lieutenant, is that you tend to complicate matters. People are wondering if that's what is happening again here."

Worthy could feel his face redden. "Okay, I'll make you a deal. After we interview Bales, if you still believe he could be behind this crime, then I'll charge him. Detroit can have its quick result, the newspapers will be happy, and we'll let the courts decide if we've got the right guy. But if Bales doesn't fit, which I don't believe he does, then you send Sherrod the hell back to Siberia, and let me investigate the case my way."

The room was silent for a moment. In a calmer voice, he added, "You and I both know that most murders aren't simple. I don't 'complicate' cases for the fun of it. I simply recognize when they're not simple, and most of the time," he added, "I solve them."

He strode to the door, knowing that the interview with Bales would reveal
to both of them if he'd just been bluffing.

AT THE END OF A LONG Tuesday, filled with hours checking and rechecking
the details of the coming memorial service while at the same time trying
to make sense of the book that Father Spiro had hidden, Father Fortis felt
hung over from the cumulative fatigue. And he needed to be alert, given the
group already gathered down the hall in the library. He hoped Mr. Margolis
would take charge and not count on him to lead the memorial subcommittee
meeting.

It wasn't that the translation of the journal itself was proving difficult. As
an immigrant, Father Spiro had not surprisingly lapsed into archaic words,
but Father Fortis' vacations with his family in Greece served him in good
stead. And the book was proving fascinating. It was, as both Worthy and he
had hoped, Father Spiro's confidential journal and contained material that the
priest wanted protected. Best of all, a quick review of the dates provided by
Mrs. Nichols revealed exact matches with the journal.

What was frustrating, however, was the total absence of names in the
journal. Instead, Father Spiro had used a puzzling code for each entry, four
different Greek letters that carried no obvious meaning.

Also troubling Father Fortis had been Worthy's final comment when he
dropped the book by that morning. "No one in the parish is to know that
we found the book. It's too bad that even Mrs. Hazelton knows about it."
That meant that Father Fortis would have to deliver a bald-faced lie to the
parish council waiting for him down the hall. He was indeed in a unique and
demanding position at St. Cosmas. He was a monk trying to be a good priest
to a community that was grieving over a terrible tragedy. But he was also a
type of detective, one who needed to remember that these same parishioners
were all suspects.

As he walked down the hallway to the meeting, it struck him that the
double life he found himself in had been Father Spiro's predicament as well.
The translated bits of the journal proved that the old man had borne several
heavy burdens in secret, while in public view he functioned as St. Cosmas'
presbyter, or priest. No wonder the man had been losing his hair.

"Ah, Father, good," Mr. Margolis said as he came into the library. "I think
we can now get started."

Father Fortis took the chair at the head of the table and gazed around
the room. Next to Mr. Margolis were the two professors, Dr. Stanos and Dr.
Boras. They were a tag team, he thought, and it was clear who was the leader.
Across the table sat Dr. Pappas—straight from the hospital, given the name

tag pinned to his lapel. "Chief cardiologist," Father Fortis read. Next to him sat Mr. Sanderson, an accountant and a convert, if he remembered correctly. At the far end, sitting by himself, was the outspoken restaurateur, Mr. Angelo.

After offering the prayer, Father Fortis turned the meeting over to Mr. Margolis. "I'll contribute where I can, but of course I didn't really know Father Spiro."

"Of course, Father," Mr. Margolis said before thanking those present for being so prompt. "And I'm sure we all want the same thing, something fitting for our dear Father Spiro."

"Something with dignity," Dr. Boras inserted.

"That's assumed," Dr. Pappas said with an indulgent smile.

"Of course, of course," Mr. Margolis added. "I'd suggest that we begin by making a list of ideas. You should know that the women's group has suggested a nice granite stone for our memorial garden."

The restaurateur cleared his throat. "And what would we do with a hunk of granite when we move?" Answering his own question, he added, "Here's what I suggest. I say we announce next Sunday that we're going to move the church in his honor. We've been arguing about it for too long—is the neighborhood safe, can't we add on here—but all that is past. It took our own beloved priest getting strangled in our very sanctuary, our temple, to show us that we've waited far too long."

Mr. Sanderson spoke. "Mr. Angelo, moving the church, even if the parish agreed on it, is years away. The reality is that the parish hasn't even found an appropriate plot of vacant land."

The restaurateur countered with a gnomic, "Reality is what reality is."

"A very Buddhist perspective, Jimmy," Dr. Stanos said with a laugh. "But—"

Dr. Pappas interrupted. "Look, Jimmy, tonight is not the night to fight about land and moving the parish. I propose a plaque. A nice bronze one with Father Spiro's likeness etched into it. And if we move, we can take that with us."

"How much money are we talking about?" Dr. Stanos asked.

"Cost-wise? A few thousand. No more, I'd think," Mr. Sanderson, the accountant, offered.

Dr. Stanos smiled across the table. "Mike, here I am a mere college professor saying this to a cardiologist—a Chevy talking to a Mercedes—but a few thousand dollars sounds cheap."

The comment was met by loud laughter from Dr. Boras, but Father Fortis sensed something else in the room. Dr. Pappas was being challenged by Stanos, with Dr. Boras backing him up.

"I'll have you know, John, that it's a two-year-old Mercedes," Dr. Pappas countered with his own laugh. "I take it that you and Lydia have another suggestion. I thought I saw you huddling out in the parking lot."

"Well, actually, Lydia and I," Dr. Stanos said, nodding deferentially to the woman next to him, "do have a suggestion. Some of you remember that the two of us had been working for about a year with Father Spiro on an icon exhibit and lecture over at the college. We'd like the committee to consider going forward with that, which is already in our budget, but using the event to announce an annual lecture series in Father's honor. We could title it, 'Hellenic Culture and Orthodoxy in the Modern World.' "

"It's a golden opportunity to make a connection between St. Cosmas and the college. And it would be a lasting connection," Dr. Boras added, "one that would carry on if the parish were ever to move."

"A lecture series?" Dr. Pappas questioned. "Father was a wonderful man, but hardly a scholar. I'm not sure that he even finished college."

"Yes, he did!" the restaurateur insisted. "In Thessaloniki."

"Well, taking a few courses for priests back in the old country hardly makes someone an intellectual—"

The restaurateur sat forward, his fist pounding the table top. "Who's talking about an intellectual? No offense, professors, but what good are they anyway? Father had wisdom."

Dr. Pappas' eyebrows arched knowingly toward the academics.

"Father Spiro clearly had gifts of ministry, even if he wasn't well educated in the American sense," Dr. Stanos said. "But the truth is that Orthodoxy in America is too passive, too easily intimidated. We hunch over with an inferiority complex. Do you know that Greeks are near the top, percentage-wise, among those who pursue higher education? Let me tell you after twenty-five years in the academy that few see us that way. A lecture series would be our chance to show our faith and culture in a public and positive light."

"So you're proposing a lecture every year?" Mr. Sanderson asked.

"Two hours of high-brow talk with baklava and Greek coffee afterwards," Dr. Pappas joked.

The restaurateur hooted from the other end. "I can just see our old-timers sitting through a lecture."

Dr. Boras leaned forward. "The lecture would, of course, be open to the parish, but its primary purpose would be to attract faculty and students."

The deliberations of the committee continued with little being decided. Father Fortis found himself viewing the group in light of Worthy's comment about suspects. Power flowed back and forth in the room, and the jockeying for influence soon prompted Mr. Margolis to raise his voice. But could any of them have killed Father Spiro? Mr. Margolis himself had admitted to disagreeing with the old priest, fighting with him, most recently over the issue of retirement. But was that a motive for murder?

Jimmy Angelo, the restaurateur, was clearly the angry type, as many restaurant owners were, in Father Fortis' experience. Working six days of week without a vacation for thirty years could do that to a person. But Mr. Angelo's prickly reaction to Dr. Pappas had passed quickly. He was quick to anger, but also quick to let it go.

Dr. Stanos? The professor obviously knew Father Spiro well and was bold enough to challenge Dr. Pappas' supremacy on the council. And he was willing to use the tragedy for his own faintly shielded advantage at the college. But the same could be said for Dr. Boras.

Michael Sanderson was harder to read. A convert under Father Daniel, he'd enough support within the parish to get elected to the council. Quite a feat for a recent member, much less a non-Greek.

Finally, what about Dr. Pappas, the Mercedes-driving cardiologist? He was the power behind the council and obviously didn't hold much respect for Father Spiro. But it had been Father Fortis' experience that many physicians held little respect for anyone beyond other physicians. Disdain might be typical of doctors, but that was hardly a basis for murder. And what would have been Pappas' motive?

"Father Fortis, can you tell us?" Mr. Margolis asked.

"Hmm? I'm sorry, it's been a long day. What have you decided?"

"About the memorial? We've decided to bring the three suggestions back to the parish council."

"Three? I heard a plaque and the lecture series."

"The women's group proposed the memorial stone."

"Oh, yes, right. Well, that sounds fine," he said, rubbing his forehead. "Shall we close with prayer?"

"Just a minute, Father," Mr. Margolis said. "We want to know if you have an update. About the investigation, I mean. We've all had parishioners call us, first about the break-in at St. Michael's, and then about the article in the paper. Will Lieutenant Worthy remain with us?"

"Of course. Why not?" he replied shortly. "You may tell this to whomever asks you: that reporter was not ethical. I for one won't speak with her again."

"Come now, Father," Dr. Pappas said. "The reporter made a valid point. I know Lieutenant Worthy is your friend, but to take the entire weekend off?"

"He didn't take it off," Father Fortis snapped. "Sorry, I'm just a bit tired. Lieutenant Worthy had an opportunity to spend two days with his daughter, who had previously refused his overtures. You see, he's been through a painful divorce." As soon as the last line came out, he regretted the pleading tone of it.

"I for one hope that he does stay on," Dr. Stanos added, much to Father

Fortis' relief. "I appreciate his independence, his willingness to follow his own trail and let his partner follow his own. It's the kind of initiative that I appreciate in my students."

"If we see it in our students," Dr. Boras added.

Dr. Pappas ignored her comment and spoke directly to Dr. Stanos. "But it doesn't take an intellectual to see that the two robberies are amazingly similar, John."

The doctor likes to have the last word, Father Fortis thought as he invited those present for a second time to rise for the closing prayer.

"One last thing, Father. Have you heard any more about that book?" Mr. Sanderson asked. "You know, the one in the photo? Did the police ever find it?"

Father Fortis looked over the parish council members to the Christ icon on the wall The severe face gazed down at him, waiting to hear his response. Was it fair to pray for the courage to lie?

"As far as I know, they are no longer interested in the book. I guess every case, from what they tell me, has clues that seem promising but then don't pan out." Seeing that Mr. Sanderson wasn't finished, he hastened to add, "Now, please join me as we pray. Our Father, who art in heaven …."

CHAPTER TWELVE

———◆———

FATHER FORTIS TOOK A LONG SWALLOW of morning coffee in an attempt to clear his groggy head. Across from him at the diner, Worthy was eagerly attacking his bacon and eggs.

"Sorry, Nick, about your staying up all night translating this," Worthy said, motioning toward the book.

"I'll be better after a couple of cups of this stuff. Plus, the good news is that I'd say it was worth it." Father Fortis yawned as he opened the book to extract his pages of translation. "As we thought, the book is a type of diary, a confessional diary, to be more exact, Christopher. Father Spiro begins the document with a prayer asking for forgiveness for having to keep it. And then he explains that he resorted to the diary because he was afraid of forgetting."

Worthy frowned. "So, he admits to having mental lapses. Perhaps the first stages of Alzheimer's?"

"Listen, Christopher. After only two weeks at St. Cosmas, I can confirm that forgetting the details of leading a parish is easy to do. I take the diary to be a type of insurance—he didn't want to let these people down. I don't think he ever expected anyone else to read it. In fact, that's the way he ends the opening prayer." He turned the first page. "Here it is. 'May God keep prying eyes from ever finding this.' "

"That would explain his anger in that first photo," Worthy said.

"And why he hid the book before Mr. Bagios could take the other photos." Father Fortis took another swallow of coffee. "I must admit, my friend, that this prayer caused me to search my own soul. Do I really have the right to violate his wishes? But, in the end, I believe he would want us to use it. And not just to catch his killer. No, I think he'd be worried that the killer might not be through."

"Always our fear, Nick. But does he actually talk about a killer in the diary?"

Father Fortis held up his hand. "Not in so many words. And I need to share the bad news. Father Spiro took another precaution, just in case someone did find the book. He never used any names."

Worthy sat back and sighed. "Oh, that's great."

"On the other hand, he does use a sort of code to identify people. A four-letter code. The only problem is that I can't make any sense of it."

"I guess it was too much to hope that the book would do our work for us."

"It's more like a layer on an onion, my friend. But a very important layer."

Worthy pushed his plate aside. "Show me what you mean."

Father Fortis turned the book over and pointed to four letters. "I can't always tell if the letters are English or Greek letters transliterated into English. But you can see that he's written PABA."

Worthy stared at the words. "I guess we should be grateful that he dated the entries."

"Yes, indeed, and the mysterious code at least stays consistent. What I mean is, Father Spiro used the same four letters whenever someone came back to see him."

"So, in a nutshell, what kind of secrets was he keeping?"

Father Fortis flipped two pages and pointed to an entry at the top. "This one begins with the code MRAG, and it's in the diary twice. It's from someone in the parish who wanted Father Spiro to help with a work problem."

"Lloyd Hartunian?"

"That's my assumption too, Christopher. The date fits. Translated, it says, 'Wants me to talk to boss. Wants a miracle. Thinks I can clear the way.' "

Worthy picked up a strip of bacon and munched on it. "And the second entry?"

Father Fortis turned toward the back of the diary. "This one was from three weeks ago. Same code, as you can see. It reads, 'Totally unreasonable. Has neither backing nor ability. Very angry, but she's right.' "

"*She*? Either that woman he lives with, or maybe his boss."

"I can't imagine the woman at the house ever contradicting him," Father Fortis said.

"Okay, that's easy to check out. We can interview his boss together."

Father Fortis nodded. "Just say when."

"I'm interviewing Bales tomorrow. Why don't you call the store and find out when Hartunian has his day off? I don't want him to know we're looking into him."

"Good thinking. Who is this Bales again, by the way?"

"The guy who Sherrod thinks killed the priest. He's also the guy Henderson beat to a pulp."

"Oh, I see."

Worthy wiped his hands with a napkin. "Let's move on to the next person. By the way, how many people are coded in here?"

"About eight, by my count, but I think there's only three worth talking about. The second one is coded as NISP. He's listed more than anyone else in the diary."

"MRAG, now NISP," Worthy repeated. "I don't imagine they mean anything together?"

"Not that I can think of. Besides, this is a very different kind of problem. The first visit was back on May thirteenth. It reads, 'Mother's idea he's here. Believes God hates him. It began before Christmas. Won't say why.' "

Father Fortis began turning pages when Worthy stopped him. "It. What's the 'it' mean? Wait a minute, Nick. Does that sound like a kid to you?"

"Possibly, though it could be a grown man still tied to his mother. I've seen that before."

"Right. Okay, go ahead."

"The next entry from NISP is dated over two months later, July seventeenth. It reads, "Came back. Told Mother he will stop coming to church. Asked questions about damnation. Effeminate. Wonder if he could harm self?' "

"Sounds sexual," Worthy offered.

"Exactly right. Listen to the third entry."

"Dated when?" Worthy asked.

"Sorry. It's November nineteenth."

"Quite a gap of time. Wait a minute," Worthy said, holding up his hand. "That's Amy's birthday, and it was on a Tuesday. I thought you said that Father Spiro scheduled his confessions on Thursday."

"You're right, my friend. I'd forgotten. So this was a special confession."

"Maybe like the one on the morning he was killed," Worthy added. "What's it say?"

"Oddly, it seems a rehash of the second. The person says he still wants to quit church. Angry that God would reject what I've translated as 'his kind.' "

"That's getting clearer, isn't it?" Worthy said.

"And now I come to the last entry from NISP, January third, just a few days before Father Spiro was strangled. Let me read it to you exactly. 'Says he loves the man. I asked if trapped. He says his own fault. Can't take Eucharist. But no previous history. Won't name man. Do I know him?' "

"So the boy—I'm leaning toward NISP being a boy—had something happen. A sexual experience?"

"Or perhaps *almost* a sexual experience?" Father Fortis suggested.

"But would a teenage boy kill a priest? He might, if he thought the priest was going to expose him. And that might explain why this boy, if he is the killer, straightened the vestment."

Father Fortis shook his head, which only seemed to unleash a throbbing pain over his left eye. "But that doesn't make sense. Father Spiro knew about the problem after the third visit, and the boy came back. He trusted his priest. And if the boy killed him, wouldn't he be a candidate for suicide?"

Worthy shrugged. "Maybe. The boy could have done it, but it's not likely. Anything more from the last entry?"

"It reads, 'Won't give name. I must know him. Blames self. Man said he's NISP's biggest fan. Evil not simple here.'"

"'Evil not simple here,'" Worthy repeated. "Well, that's right out of the rabbi's book."

Father Fortis took another sip of coffee. His eyelids were turning into sandpaper. "What I don't understand, my friend, is what he means by 'I must know him.' Does he mean that he needs to get to know him, to break this relationship up, or does he mean that he already knows him?"

"If he was worried about his memory, maybe the old man means he should be able to figure out who he is," Worthy offered. "You said those entries are about Person and Problem Number Two. And the third?"

Father Fortis yawned again and signaled for the waitress to refill his cup. "Decaf this time, please."

"You sure you won't have something to eat?" Worthy asked.

"I couldn't keep it down, not with this headache coming on. I'll be fine after a nap. No, let's go on to the last one. This is obviously a woman, coded as IOAG. Again, I have no idea what that means, but I think you'll recognize her. The first entry is dated February of last year. '"Infidelity? Husband lying? Harassment? Only she is Orthodox.'"

"Okay, that's Mrs. Nichols. Why'd you keep her to the end?"

"For several reasons. But in case my brain was foggy at five this morning when I got to her, I'll let you decide if she's the most important or not. Her second visit was in May, just as she told us the other day. It reads, 'Advised screening their calls. Where is husband? Trap. Evil closing in. He can't see it.'"

"That 'evil closing in' line. I'm betting that comes from the Jewish book as well," Worthy suggested.

"That's why I'm glad you're here. I was too exhausted this morning to make that connection. The language is pretty strong, isn't it? It's as if Father Spiro were battling forces, not problems."

"Where do things go after that?"

"Well, as we know, she came back, this time with her husband. 'Both here,'" he writes. 'Must contact college. If they won't, I must. Will pray, but do more? Might pay price.' "

Father Fortis looked up from his notes. "Do you hear that, Christopher? He said 'might pay price.' You have to admit that sounds ominous."

"Maybe, although we don't know if he actually followed through on contacting the college. It's worth a visit over there, though, to find out. Okay, Nick, don't keep me guessing. What's about her last entry?"

"It's from the day before his death."

"What? That doesn't make sense."

"Ah, patience, my friend. No, she didn't see Father Spiro that day, but I'll think you'll figure it out. Here goes. 'Face so sad. Alone, going to cry room. Evil paralyzes good people. Child terrorized. A wish that cannot be.' "

Father Fortis studied his friend's face. "Don't you see it, Christopher? The cry room is only used on Sundays. He's talking about seeing her in church the day before."

Worthy looked up, his brow furrowed. "I have no idea what a cry room is."

"It's a room just off to the left of the narthex as you come in from outside. It's where parents with young children can go and still watch the service. There is usually one-way glass, as I remember."

Worthy closed his eyes. "You say off the narthex, but they can see things in the sanctuary? Hmm. Okay, I get it." He opened his eyes and leaned forward on the table, nearly spilling his water. "He'd have passed by it on the procession." He threw his head back. "That's it! Yes, maybe that's what happened."

Father Fortis laughed, overcome with fatigue. "Help a sleepy man out, my friend. It's all a bit fuzzy."

"Mrs. Nichols told us she was there; she said she saw him. I think we know what she meant, and better than that, we may finally know what really happened to Father Spiro during that last service. Now do you see it?"

"Not as clearly as you do, Christopher."

Worthy walked his first two fingers across the table. "It's like this, Nick. Father Spiro processed to the end of the left aisle—that's what people have told us, right?—and just when he turned the corner, wouldn't he have been standing right in front of—"

"The cry room! Good Lord, How extraordinary!" Father Fortis boomed. Patrons at nearby tables looked over in alarm. "But wait a minute, Christopher," he added in a quieter voice. "It's only those in the cry room who can see out."

Worthy's eyes were flashing, and a grin covered his face. "Not if it's like the glass we used to have in the interview room. You can just manage to see through it, if you get close enough."

His headache forgotten for the moment, Father Fortis strained to understand his friend's point. "But I still don't see why he stopped."

"If he was close enough to the glass, he could have seen her face, Nick! He saw her sad face, just as he wrote in the diary. Here's what I think happened. When he saw her face, he finally decided what he had to do. He wasn't going to wait on the college to act for the Nicholses at all. He was going to contact Peggy Hagarty himself."

Father Fortis shook his head. "So Mrs. Siametes and Rabbi Milkin were right after all. Father Spiro didn't falter because he was ill but because his mind was suddenly clear." He paused before adding, "That would mean he must have called the Hagarty woman on Sunday and asked to meet with her."

"Or Monday, but in any case, she came," Worthy whispered excitedly, "on Tuesday morning."

"When she killed him," Father Fortis finished the thought. He remembered the photos of the dead priest, the blood oozing from eyes and nose. *This must be one very powerful woman*, he thought.

THAT AFTERNOON, WORTHY PACED HIS OFFICE, caught between what he desired and what was possible. He wanted to be to be at the college, putting some hard questions to the dean about Dr. Nichols and Peggy Hagarty. But he hadn't been able to get an appointment until the following morning. Short of that, he wanted to bring Mrs. Nichols back to St. Cosmas, to have her sit in the sanctuary and confirm what he strongly believed happened that last Sunday morning. But Father Fortis, perhaps wisely, thought the woman had been through enough for one day.

Finally, he desperately wanted to talk with Allyson, to find some way to clear the air between them, but she was working at the mall after school today. So that would have to wait.

With the Bales interview scheduled for the next morning, he was left with what seemed another pointless task, to talk with Lloyd Hartunian's boss. He was to meet Father Fortis at Blitzen's Church Supply House in an hour, after his friend had finished the bulletin for next Sunday services. Lloyd Hartunian and Carl Bales, two red herrings who got attention simply by being crazy, he mused. By noon tomorrow, he comforted himself, both men would be off the list.

This was the antsy time on a case, the part that he resented the most. They'd found the center piece of the puzzle, and he could feel his mind clicking at a higher speed, so fast that he forgot about food, sleep, everything but trying to put the last pieces in place.

He thought back on the path that had brought them to this point. There was the clue of the vestment, the odd photos of the victim in his office,

Rabbi Milkin's rambling, Mrs. Nichols' painful story, and finally Henderson's discovery of the missing diary.

In other words, the trail had been a complicated one, after all. He would love to point that out to Captain Betts. Sherrod had taken the easy path, running like a rabbit after the missing altarpiece. And he'd like to tell Allyson that they wouldn't be at the closing stages of the case if he'd dropped everything to deal with his partner's puzzle. Whatever Henderson's problems were, they had nothing to do with solving the case.

He straightened his tie and headed out to the parking lot. *Only one more day*, he told himself, and that knowledge should have warmed his heart. So why did he have the odd feeling that he was hurrying to escape something?

Blitzen's Church Supply Store remained a landmark in downtown Detroit. Nestled between a shoe repair shop and a high-price parking lot, Blitzen served mainly the Catholic parishes of the diocese. Statues fit for sanctuaries jostled for space in the window with those of St. Francis more suitable for gardens. Like most people from Detroit, Worthy had passed the place a thousand times, but this was the first time he'd had a reason to stop in.

To his surprise, Father Fortis had arrived ahead of him. Since when was Father Fortis early for anything? The priest was talking with an older lady, at least in her seventies, who introduced herself as Mary Blitzen.

"Gentlemen, my office is back here," she said, leading them at a crisp clip toward the back of the store. "And Father, I can't be calling you 'Father' all day. I hope you understand. Priests come through here faster than flies. So what will it be?"

Father Fortis smiled. "Please call me Nick."

"And I'm Mary, a good Catholic name," she said. "I suppose we'll call you," she said, eyeing Worthy, "Lieutenant."

Worthy was about to offer his first name, but she kept right on going, "Sit down, gentlemen, and pardon the mess. Inventory time. Nick, shut the door, will you? So tell me, how do you like St. Cosmas?"

"Challenging, under the circumstances," Father Fortis replied.

"They're an ornery bunch, if you ask me. People from the Mediterranean like to argue, know what I mean? I always felt sorry for the priests over there, like that young one, Deacon Daniel. Don't let them run you out too, Nick. I like the looks of you." She looked at Father Fortis as if she did, and Worthy didn't miss the color rising in his cheeks.

"Not to worry, Mary. You see, I'm a monk. I'm the equivalent of a loaner car, really. Once the metropolitan, the bishop—"

"Sweet Lord, don't get me going on bishops, Nick. They wouldn't know the meaning of time if they were sitting on death row. But enough twiddle-twaddle. Now let's get back to your phone call. I've been racking my brain all morning. You tell me you're the new priest at St. Cosmas, and then you ask to see me when Lloyd isn't working. And as if that's not juicy enough, you bring a detective."

Taking the cue from Father Fortis' look, Worthy launched in, "We're checking through all those who may have had disagreements with Father Spiro before he died."

Mrs. Blitzen sat back in her chair and hooted. "Oh, now I know what this is about. Why, that crazy fool."

"Father Spiro came to see you, then," Father Fortis said.

"Oh, yes. I liked Spiro. Unlike most priests, he knew the difference between a business call and a pastoral one. Within five minutes, he understood my position perfectly on the matter."

"And what matter was that exactly?" Worthy asked.

"You don't know? Hartunian wanted to buy me out. Imagine! Just goes to show you what goes through that addled brain of his. You see, everyone knows that I'm thinking of retirement, and my kids are grown and on their own. Hell, some of my grandkids are grown. Anyway, they all grew up working here, which is another way of saying that they hate this place like a prison. Can't really blame them," she said, looking around her at the boxes and stacks of bills on the desk.

"And so when Father Spiro came to put in a good word—"

"Can't put in a good word for someone you've carried along out of pity for fifteen years. Lloyd could no more run this store than—wait a minute, you think he could have killed Spiro?" Again, she threw back her head and laughed.

A knock on the door preceded the face of a frightened-looking young woman. "Mrs. Blitzen, someone's here from St. Barnabas. They want to bring back a box of candles. You know, the kind in the glass jars. They say they won't stay lit."

"Well, did you take a look at them?" the owner asked.

"Yes, ma'am. Some look in pretty bad shape."

"Then tell them to go to hell. And leave us alone, Marge."

The door closed. "Trying to return used candles. And I wonder why Lloyd, that feeble-brained idiot, is the only one who wants to buy this place. Now, where were we?"

"You were laughing at the idea of Hartunian as a suspect," Worthy prompted.

She laughed again. "Indeed I was. The poor fool has eccentricities out the wazoo, if they still use that term. Look, if he was going to kill somebody, he'd have killed me ten years ago. I don't suffer fools gladly. I may keep them on, but I sure as hell let them know what's what."

Worthy had already heard what he was hoping for, but he followed through on the rest of the questions. "Has Lloyd Hartunian acted any differently around here in the last three weeks?"

"Well, Lieutenant, unless I haven't made myself clear, Lloyd always acts a bit different. That's his saving grace. He's so pathetic that sometimes—only sometimes, mind you—I almost feel bad about yelling at him. You see, Lloyd wears this goofy smile all the time. You never know what he's thinking, and let me tell you, I don't want to know. But I can tell you this: he'd have given that church a full refund for those candles. And what the hell would we do with half-burnt candles?"

"And how about Tuesday morning, January ninth? Did he work that day?" Worthy asked.

Mrs. Blitzen opened a drawer and brought out a strong box. "Lieutenant, you're like a terrier I had once. You won't let the bone go. Come to think of it," she said, glancing up, "I think I recognize your face. You're in the papers, right?"

"All too recently, ma'am," he said.

"So you must be a good terrier. Okay, here it is. On January ninth, Lloyd came into work at noon. Is that important?"

Worthy wrote it down even as he dismissed it. Hartunian may have had opportunity, but Mrs. Blitzen's view made perfect sense to him. Unless Hartunian was totally crazy, his anger should have been aimed at his boss, not Father Spiro. And Hartunian hardly seemed the type to execute a murder this clever, not to mention take an altarpiece for insurance.

Worthy looked over at Father Fortis. "Anything else, Nick?"

Father Fortis pulled on his beard for a moment. "I don't think so. Well, maybe just a question out of curiosity. Probably none of my business," he said, rising from his chair. "Who is the Sylvie woman I met at his house? Is it a sister, his wife, perhaps?"

Mrs. Blitzen looked up for a moment, a look of shock on her face. Then she laughed so long and so hard that she ended up coughing.

"Sweet Jesus," she said, still sputtering. "I thought for a minute you were pulling my leg. You honestly don't know who she is?"

"No. Should I?"

"Well, hell, they look like two peas in a pod, don't they? Sylvie is Lloyd's mother."

Chapter Thirteen

---◆---

B Y THE TIME WORTHY ARRIVED AT the precinct's interview room the next morning, a uniformed colleague had already escorted in Carl Bales. Worthy looked at the kid's heavily bandaged head, a testimony to Henderson's physical strength. Bales was looking down at the table, his arms folded across his chest as he slumped in the chair. *Maybe he's asleep or still medicated*, Worthy thought, as he sat down on the other side of the interview table. At that moment, Captain Betts entered the room.

Worthy turned on the tape recorder. "It is one p.m., February ninth. Lieutenant Worthy and Captain Betts present to interview Carl Bales." He paused and looked over at his superior. "Do you want to start?"

"Lead on, Lieutenant."

"Mr. Bales, how did you hurt your head?"

Bales didn't respond. In a louder voice, Worthy repeated the question. This time, Bales opened his eyes slightly and looked from Worthy to Betts before closing them again. "A cop asked me the same thing when I was coming in here."

I bet Sherrod did, Worthy thought, though deciding he didn't need to look over at his captain.

"So, how did you hurt it?"

"I must've fallen down or something," he said with a yawn. "Probably happened when I was locked up. Yes, that's it. It's police neglect."

He doesn't even remember, Worthy thought. Not that that would help Henderson. The tape alone could damn his partner.

"Could it have been in a fight, Mr. Bales?" Captain Betts asked.

Bales scratched at a place on the side of his head where the bandage met his scalp. "Was it? You guys throw me in with niggers and let them wail on me?"

"I understand you hang around Suffolk projects a lot. Could it have happened over there?" Worthy asked.

"Fuck, no," Bales said, as he stared at Worthy. "It was here. I want a white fucking jail."

"You were in a hospital, not a jail, Mr. Bales," Captain Betts said. "And you're here for questioning."

He smiled broadly, revealing a large gap in his teeth on the left side. "You know what I'd do with 'em?"

"With whom?" Betts asked.

"The niggers. I'd cut off their thumbs and pricks. And I'd start with the thumbs. Know why?"

"Why don't you tell us?" Worthy asked. This was the guy who Sherrod thought was smart enough to don gloves, strangle the priest, straighten the vestment, and afterwards tell no one.

Bales held up his own hand. "You slice off the thumb, and they can't use a gun. See? And then I'd cut off their dicks. Watch the whole fucking race disappear." He leaned back in his chair and nodded. "Let me tell you, I think about these things."

Worthy heard a sigh from Betts and tried not to smile. *Be as loose in the head as you want*, Bales, he thought. *Leave no doubt.*

"I don't imagine you shared any of these ideas with Lashad and Rimes."

"Who?"

"Your friends. They're black, yet you seem to hang out with them."

"Shi-it. I'd leave those two homeys be. They'd get all the pussy they wanted." He paused. "Got a smoke?"

Betts handed Bales a cigarette and lit it for him. The cigarette trembled in Bales' mouth as he took a long drag then exhaled a smoke ring. Without warning, he bounded from his chair and jumped for the ring, sucking it in a second time.

"Sit down, Mr. Bales," Worthy ordered.

Bales leaned back on two legs and laughed. "So why am I here again?"

The guy's waking up, Worthy thought. *Let's see what he knows.* "Did you hear about the murder of a priest over at St. Cosmas Church?"

Bales looked puzzled. "Did that happen last night? Because I was with my girl last night. At least, I think I was."

"No, the murder occurred a month ago."

Bales looked down and beat the table like a drum. "Was that the one where they cut the priest's fingers off and stole the holy water?"

Worthy continued to take notes, as if Bales was making perfect sense. "No, this priest was strangled. It's just that in our records we see that you had that previous incident at the church."

"Huh?" Bales said, squinting at Worthy.

"You know," Worthy reminded him, "the time you were arrested in the church during the Greek festival."

Bales sat quietly for a moment before springing to his feet. "Christ, that place! I was yelling *blasfemo*. Know what that means? It means blasphemer. It's Italian. My momma taught me that. You are talking about the Catholic church, aren't you?"

"Sit down, Mr. Bales," Betts said in a weary voice.

Bales held out his hand but stayed standing. "Hey, I'm cool, I'm cool."

"So you don't remember St. Cosmas? It's a Greek church."

Bales sat down heavily. "Maybe. I just never went back."

"How about Lashad and Rimes. Did they go to the church?"

"Shit, man. They're not my boyfriends. Hey, is that it? You arresting them for slicing up some priest?"

"No, we're just conducting interviews," Worthy explained. He hoped Betts heard the pattern. The guy preferred knives. There was no way he strangled the priest.

"Can you tell us where you were last Wednesday, February first?"

"*Gesù Christo. Un momento, Capitano.* Some other cop asked me that. A nigger. Was the priest a nigger? 'Cause I'd never kill a priest unless he was a nigger. You don't go to hell for that. I read that on the Internet. A preacher in Idaho said that."

"We're asking if you remember being at St. Michael's Catholic Church last Wednesday night," Betts said.

"That the one down by the arena?"

"No, that's St. Paul's," Worthy explained, failing miserably to hide his smile.

"I know that one. It has a soup kitchen."

"St. Michael's is near Suffolk Projects."

Bales sneered. "Suffolk, shit, man. That's for niggers. I live five fucking miles from there."

Betts cleared her throat. "We know where you live, Mr. Bales. But we also know that you hang out at Suffolk." The captain looked over at Worthy. "Anything else, Lieutenant?"

"Just one more question. "Do you remember the policeman who interviewed you last time? His name is Henderson."

Bales seemed confused by the question until Worthy clarified that Henderson was a black officer.

"Hell, I sure do. I scared the shit out of that nigger. He got all fucky in the face." Bales started to rise, but a look from Betts sat him down again.

"How'd you scare him? Did you tell him how much you hated blacks?"

"Hell, no!" Bales snorted. "He'd have beaten the shit out of me if I'd said that. No, I said something that scared that motherfuckin' nigger." He paused to pound on the table again. "I did this girl one time. She really put out until I said something. Then she got all white in the face and ran off. Just ran out the door. No shit. And I was still agoin'." Up again, Bales rotated his hips forward in a snapping motion. "Woo, woo, woo!"

"We know how it works, Mr. Bales," Betts said. "You can sit down."

"So you said something that troubled Sergeant Henderson." Worthy was genuinely curious this time. "Do you remember what it was?"

Bales looked around the room, found the camera on the wall and waved at it. "Hell, I don't know. Wait. Yeah, okay, I remember. He kept looking at me like I was nuts or something, and so I told him he was the one needed shock treatment, not me. Then I got in his face like this," Bales said, standing to lean across the table toward Worthy, "and went 'zit, zit, zit.' "

Worthy saw again the worried look on Henderson's wife's face as she looked in on them the previous Friday. Bales had taunted him not about race, but about shock treatments. His mind stuck on something odd from that visit, but quickly dismissed it. In a day or two, the case should be solved, and the two men would likely never work together again.

DOWN THE HALL FROM HIS OWN office, Worthy stopped and knocked on the door. He heard Henderson's grunt and let himself in. His partner was sitting behind his desk, pencil in hand but nothing else in front of him.

"We just got through with Bales," Worthy said.

Henderson regarded him with dead eyes. "That right?"

Worthy took the unoffered chair on the other side of the desk. "Fortunate for you that he doesn't remember you pounding on his scalp."

Henderson shrugged and tapped the pencil point on his empty desk. "I don't see how that matters. If they want to take me down, they got the tape."

"But then again, you found the diary."

"A diary, huh? You going to tell me we got the name of the killer?"

"Not exactly," Worthy replied. Worthy gave him a quick review of the three people mentioned in the diary, explaining how one confirmed Mrs. Nichols' testimony.

Henderson yawned but didn't say anything as he studied the pencil.

"So, what I'm saying," Worthy continued, "is that we might be closing in. Why don't you and I run by the college and hear what they have to say about this Peggy Hagarty?"

"Sure, sure," Henderson said, but got up slowly. Worthy wondered if he'd even heard what he'd said.

On the way over to Allgemein, Worthy reported on what Captain Betts had said about Bales. "She thinks he's certifiably crazy," he said, immediately regretting his choice of words. "Neither of us sees him as the type to have killed the priest—at least not in that way," he quickly added.

"He's one stupid fuck—that's all I know," Henderson offered, looking out the window. "So you cut him loose?"

"Not completely, but he's on the back burner, especially after I told her about Hagarty."

"You really think the woman did it, don't you?" Henderson asked drowsily. "Sounds like you think we'll be finished in a couple days."

Worthy shrugged. "The pieces fit."

"Fine by me," Henderson responded flatly.

AT THE COLLEGE, THEIR WAIT WAS no more than two minutes before they were shown into the academic dean's office. A tall man in his fifties, dark hair graying at the temples, came around from behind a desk and introduced himself as Dean Wolcott. Worthy glanced around the room as the two of them were seated. Diplomas and archival photos of students lined the wall, along with one prominent photo of the dean in full academic regalia standing with Gerald Ford. The dean was younger in the photo but already had the confident smile he now beamed at them.

"You were on campus some years back, weren't you?" the dean asked Worthy.

"Right. I worked the VanBruskman case."

"How'd that turn out? I don't think I ever heard."

"The girl is still missing," Worthy said.

"Such a shame. What a good family."

I think you mean wealthy and powerful, Worthy thought.

The dean returned to his leather chair and straightened his tie. "I hope your visit today doesn't mean we have some new emergency."

"We're investigating the murder of Father Spiro George," Worthy explained.

"Oh, yes. A terrible tragedy. I knew him, by the way."

"Oh? How was that?"

"We were working together on an icon exhibit. A very gentle man. Yes, I met with him and two of his parishioners who are faculty members here. The church must be devastated."

Worthy nodded. "We're here to talk about one of your faculty members."

"Oh?" the dean responded, his expression blank.

"Dr. William Nichols."

The dean's chair came forward slowly to its fully erect position. "Is Bill in some trouble?"

As if you don't know, Worthy thought. "Not Dr. Nichols himself. We'd like confirmation that he came to see you as recently as mid-December."

Wolcott's eyes twitched slightly. "You'll have to refresh my memory."

"It was a complaint he had with Peggy Hagarty. Are you saying he didn't see you about that?"

The dean looked from one of them to the other. "I'm not sure I'm at liberty to answer that. Not without our lawyer present, anyway."

Worthy looked over to see Henderson. *Time to jump in, partner, put some pressure on this guy.* But Henderson didn't seem to be listening as he studied his knuckles.

"It's part of our ongoing investigation," Worthy explained. "I'm sure Allgemein wants to cooperate."

"Of course we want to cooperate, Lieutenant, but we still have to protect confidences."

"Okay, then let me ask you this. Did Father Spiro ever come to see you about Mrs. Hagarty?"

Wolcott's eyes widened. "And you're suggesting that Mrs. Hagarty has something to do with the murder?"

Worthy studied the dean's face. The guy didn't give too much away. "We both know that you keep careful records, Dr. Wolcott," he said. "So you can either tell us what went on between Dr. Nichols and Peggy Hagarty, or we can subpoena the records."

The dean sat quietly for a moment before looking pleadingly as his visitors. "In your jobs, I'm sure that you have procedures you must follow. You may not like them, but there they are. I believe that's all I'm at liberty to say."

Worthy rose, with Henderson following. "Expect a subpoena by tomorrow morning."

Dean Wolcott rose, but this time didn't come around the desk. "I can assure you, Lieutenant, the file you're requesting will be ready for you."

After dropping Henderson at home, Worthy munched on a burger as he drove toward his old house. The tingling electric feeling from earlier in the day had been short-circuited at the college. But it wasn't the dean's resistance that had caused it. The subpoena would free Wolcott to do what he might have wanted to do anyway, and the damning evidence would be there all the same.

No, it had been Henderson who'd brought him down to earth. The guy had been useless, obviously distracted. He saw Allyson's face and remembered her concern for a man she'd never met. *Let it go*, he told himself.

Again, he saw Allyson's face. He'd tried twice to reach her by phone since their odd weekend, but she hadn't bothered to respond. He turned onto his old street, fully expecting her not to be home. That would mean a few minutes of awkward conversation with Susan before he would take his younger daughter, Amy, out for ice cream or pizza. *Let it go*, he told himself again.

But it was Allyson herself who opened the door, looking surprised, maybe even a bit guilty. "Did Rachel tell you to come?"

Rachel was Susan's psychologist, the one Allyson was also seeing. The idea of Rachel actually being on his side seemed almost funny, but he just shook his head. Allyson stood in the doorway for a moment as if she didn't believe him.

"Okay," she said, turning and walking toward the kitchen. The return of her suspicion and sullenness made him ask the same question he'd asked himself a hundred times since the weekend. What had he said in the restaurant that had turned her away? What had he said about Henderson but the obvious truth?

He sat at the table in his old kitchen and wondered where to begin. Should he inquire about Rachel? No, too invasive. Should he tell her about Henderson coming through by finding the diary? No, that would sound too self-congratulatory, as if he'd been right in not getting caught up in the man's anger problems.

"Where's Mom?" he asked.

"You mean your ex-wife?"

So that's how it's going to be, he thought.

"They're shopping ... again," Allyson added, opening the refrigerator. "I swear, Amy is addicted."

"Is there a Diet Coke in there?" he asked.

Allyson reached in and brought the can over to him.

"Can you sit down?" he asked.

"I'd rather stand," she said as she walked back and leaned against the counter. After a moment's silence, she said, "Rachel said we should talk."

"So I guessed. Something to do with last weekend?"

Allyson twisted a ring on her finger but didn't immediately answer.

He took a sip and waited. He felt butterflies in his stomach and wondered if it was his tension or Allyson's he was feeling.

Allyson sighed. "This is a shitty idea. I don't see what good it's going to do."

"I'd prefer you yelling at me to this silence between us."

Allyson looked up and briefly made eye contact. "Why do people hate silence? Who does it hurt?"

More twisting of the ring. Worthy wondered if maybe Allyson was going to talk about something more important than their weekend spat. Was it possible after all these months that she was going to explain why she ran away? He felt his heart pounding, despite knowing she couldn't tell him anything that he'd hadn't already considered. Pregnancy and an abortion had been near the top of the list, but neither Susan nor he could remember any particular boy. That had raised the darker specter of rape and again an abortion, but during those months drugs and other scenarios had floated in and out of his nearly crazed mind.

"Tell me why you work on murders," she blurted out.

He put the can down. "What?"

She took a deep breath. "I've never understood why anyone would want to be that kind of cop. I mean, dead people and all."

"You don't think solving murders is important?"

"We all know you think so." He was mesmerized by the level of anger emanating from his daughter. He had the sudden feeling that he'd misunderstood absolutely everything about the last several years.

He took another swig of pop. "Allyson, when you see a headline in the newspaper about someone being shot or stabbed or found strangled in a motel room, aren't you hoping somebody like me is out there looking for them?"

"Rachel asked me that. And yes, I'm not stupid. I know somebody has to do your job. But it's different with you."

"What do you mean?"

"It's like some crusade. The minute you got a case, we all knew what would happen. You'd be gone, and even when you were here, you really weren't."

"I don't sell insurance, Ally," he protested. "A city gets scared whenever a killer is on the loose because they suspect something. And they're right. Killing is like a virus. The longer someone gets away with it, the more dangerous he or she is. It's like she's tasted something new, exotic. It's like taking a dangerous drug and finding out that she got away with it. Eventually, she wants that feeling again. I'm paid to find that person, that woman," he added, "before she has that second chance."

Allyson shook her head. "You talk as if someone is forcing you to do this. I think it's you," she said and paused. Her lower lip trembled. "You'd get a case, and you'd run away from all of us."

He felt the heat rising from his chest up to his head. "So now you and Rachel think that I enjoy finding dead bodies? You think it's fun to tell families that they just lost a father or sister? Do you think that I look forward to coming face to face with a killer?"

"Yes," Allyson said without hesitation.

Her look hit him as hard as her response. *She's been waiting to tell me this, practicing it over and over again in her mind*, he realized. "So now I'm to blame for being good at my job?"

"I knew this wasn't going to work. Let's just forget it."

"Allyson, we can't. Say what you have to say."

She stood silently for a moment, tears welling up. "You and Mom made such a big deal out of my running away. Okay, don't say anything. I know it was a big deal, and I know I could have gotten hurt, or worse. But what Rachel says I need to tell you is that what I did was what you did over and over again to us."

Worthy stared at the can of pop. "Rachel told you to say that? Nice to know I'm paying the bill for someone who wants to lay all the guilt on me," he said bitterly.

"Look, that's what I believe, not her. She just wanted me to tell you to your face. I was trying to find a way to say something at the cabin, but I couldn't."

He stirred in his chair. He wanted to say something to wound her in return, something equally unfair. The words came out as if he, too, had been waiting for this moment. "How is my doing my job the same as your scaring the hell out of your mom and me?"

He looked over to see her reddened eyes glaring at him. *My God*, he thought, *she hates me.*

"I'm just saying that you'd get a case and we wouldn't see you for weeks sometimes. It was like you cared more for those damned commendations—"

His fist banged down on the table as if he could force her to listen to reason. "To hell with those. Think of the families. And more than that," he added, "we owe it to the victims."

She began crying openly, then turned away toward the counter. "Dead people. Dead people are more important ... shit, they're more alive to you than the rest of us. Don't you see that?"

"What? That doesn't make any sense."

"Rachel says it makes perfect sense," she blurted out. "Someone would get killed, and the rest of us just disappeared for you. You tell me to think of the families. What about this family, your own family?"

"Allyson, it's my job."

"No, no. It's more than that. Our crime is that we were still living. We aren't dead, so oh, no, we don't count!" she sobbed. "We're just like your partner. You can't be bothered with anybody but your victims. Maybe, maybe you taught us to think it would be better to be ...." She turned and ran from the room.

Worthy sat in his old kitchen and pondered this new reality—his daughter, and apparently his whole family, saw him as a glory hound. He crushed the empty can in his hand. That view was disturbingly close to how Sherrod saw him.

CHAPTER FOURTEEN

———— ✦ ————

Entering the sanctuary of St. Cosmas the next morning, Worthy was surprised to find Mrs. Nichols already waiting. She stood before an icon of the Virgin Mary, her head bowed until she heard his footsteps. She walked toward him amid the sunlight streaming through the stained-glass icons, her arms crossed in front of her as if she were cold.

As he extended his hand, he offered a smile. "Thanks again for coming, Mrs. Nichols. Your husband couldn't make it, I see."

Her grip was weak, and she quickly re-crossed her arms. "No, he's home with Andy. I suppose Bill should have come, but well, he said no."

Worthy pointed to a pew and glanced at his watch. Nine sharp, and where was Nick? All they'd need this morning to wrap up the case was ten minutes.

Mrs. Nichols broke the silence. "As I remember, you have children. Is that right, Lieutenant?"

"Huh? Yes, I do. Two daughters. I'd guess you'd say the older one is pretty much grown."

"All grown up. Wow. People tell me to enjoy these years, but I'm just so tired. It's hard to believe Andy will ever get out of diapers, much less be grown up."

"My older one, Allyson ... well, I'm not sure I remember the diapers, but it doesn't seem that long ago that I taught her to swim and ice skate." He thought of the weekend at the cabin, which might have been months ago, not days. "I guess it's like they say: the years fly by."

He wished Allyson could be sitting next to him for the next fifteen minutes. She'd hear Mrs. Nichols confirm what he already knew, what he figured out by doing his job the only way he could. He wanted Allyson to understand that the pieces in an investigation didn't just fall into place on their own. The discovery of the Jewish book, the interviews with Rabbi Milkin and Mrs. Siametes, Henderson's unearthing of the diary, the coming forth of Mrs. Nichols, the gentle prodding until the name of the Hagarty woman surfaced, and finally the insight into Father Spiro's faltering in the liturgy—none of those pieces came connected. Someone had to drop everything else, *everything*, and put piece with piece until a face emerged. He'd also like Allyson to see that Henderson wasn't there this morning. He'd called Worthy at home to say his wife needed him to help out with something. Typically vague and all too predictable.

Father Fortis entered the sanctuary in a rush, his robe trailing in his wake. "Sorry, sorry," he began, "with Father Spiro's forty-day memorial this Sunday, there couldn't be a worse time for the copy machine to go on the fritz. Thank God for Mrs. Hazelton."

Mrs. Nichols rose quickly to kiss his hand. "Good morning, Father."

Worthy noticed the woman shiver as Father Fortis motioned her to the pew. *We better get this over before she backs out,* he thought.

But Father Fortis interrupted his thoughts. "Are we still waiting for Sergeant Henderson?"

Worthy looked past him toward the narthex, irritated by the question. "Henderson couldn't make it. Working on something else."

Father Fortis gave him a puzzled look. *Don't ask,* Worthy thought. *In a few minutes it won't matter.*

He turned his attention to Mrs. Nichols. "Father Fortis probably told you why we asked you to come back today. We'd like to recreate what happened that last Sunday morning. You and I are going to sit where you did that morning, and Father Fortis is going to take Father Spiro's place. I don't think it will require more than a few minutes. Any questions?"

He liked the sound of that. In ten minutes he'd have an answer for Betts, Sherrod, and even Allyson. *This is the way I do it. This is the only way I know how.*

Mrs. Nichols walked to a pew near the back door.

"Are you sure this is the place?" he asked.

She offered a weak smile. "Yes, we always sit here. People seem to sit where they usually do in church, don't they?"

Father Fortis had moved to the altar, facing it, his arms raised. *Make it a short prayer, Nick,* he thought. As soon as his friend crossed himself and turned back toward them, Worthy called out, "Okay, Nick. Walk us through the service."

"Of course. Ah, let's see. I begin with prayers for the first fifteen or twenty minutes with my back to the people. Those who are here on time, that is," he added.

Worthy turned to Mrs. Nichols. "How long was it before you took your son to the cry room?"

"Hmm, let me think. I think it was pretty soon. I know it was before the first procession. Andy started fussing, throwing the Cheerios, and people turned around to glare at me."

Worthy called up to Father Fortis. "When's this first procession?"

"Right after the prayers. The altar boys and I process the book of the gospels."

We're close now, Worthy thought. His head felt suddenly clear, like the first day of summer vacation at the cabin. He'd taught Allyson to swim on this kind of day. *And this feeling,* he would like to tell her, *is why I do this job.* Maybe, he thought, it was what anyone felt who did something of value. But that feeling had a price, he would have told her. It doesn't come on its own. You have to put everything and sometimes everyone aside to get to it. It didn't mean he cared any less about his family. What his daughter didn't understand was that whenever he solved a case, he came home totally different. He would look at his family—his wife, Susan, Allyson and Amy, in fact, his whole life— as if for the first time. He felt like a man who'd been released from solitary confinement, a necessary solitary confinement. And everything he saw was beautiful.

He rose from the pew. "Give us a minute to get into the cry room, Nick, then start the procession."

They walked through the narthex and down a hallway to the tiny cry room. The room was thickly carpeted, smelling a bit of disinfectant, and sprinkled with a few toys. Through the one-way window, he could see the sanctuary and altar as if on a giant TV screen. He brought Mrs. Nichols toward it as Father Fortis approached them slowly down the side aisle. As he neared the corner, Father Fortis intoned something in Greek.

"What's he saying?" Worthy asked.

"Sorry, my Greek isn't very good. My dad didn't teach us much."

When Father Fortis turned the corner and came to the place directly in front of them, Worthy knocked on the window. "Can you see us?" he called out.

"What?"

"It makes sense that his place is pretty sound-proof," he said to Mrs. Nichols. He repeated his question, nearly shouting.

Father Fortis squinted in from the other side, his nose only inches away from them. "I think I see Mrs. Nichols right about here," he said, knocking in return.

At exactly the right spot, Worthy noted with satisfaction. "Are you sure you can recognize her?"

Father Fortis drew even closer to the window and peered in. "If I stand here, I can make out her face. Yes, I'm sure of it."

And there it was, what he needed to start his investigation of Peggy Hagarty in earnest. He felt the relief of the moment but also the odd feeling that he'd missed something.

He knocked on the window again. "Nick, come in here and we'll finish things up."

Mrs. Nichols sat down in a padded chair, one leg bobbing. As soon as Father Fortis entered the room, she blurted out, "I think I know what this means." There was a slight tremor in her voice. "Father Spiro saw me go into the cry room and thought of my husband's problem—our problem." The words were coming out in a rush. "Then Father decided to do something about it, and that got him … got him killed."

"We don't know that yet," Worthy said, "but we think it's possible." But he did know. He saw the worried look in the young mother's eyes and heard himself uttering all the right phrases about witnesses often feeling guilty, even though their part in a crime was completely innocent. He closed off with the line he loved most, because it was always the last one. "The police department wishes to thank you, Mrs. Nichols, for coming forward and—"

"Excuse me, Christopher," Father Fortis broke in. "May I ask Mrs. Nichols a question?"

Worthy frowned. "Why?"

"It's a small thing, probably nothing. Mrs. Nichols, I can't help thinking that you must have been closer to Father Spiro in that moment than anyone else. What was the expression on his face when he suddenly stopped?"

What a pointless question, Worthy thought.

Mrs. Nichols wore an oddly puzzled expression as she looked from one of them to the other. "But we weren't in here then," she said. "Andy had calmed down, and we'd gone back into the sanctuary, back to our seat."

"What? No!" Worthy's words echoed through the tiny room. Mrs. Nichols stared at him from the chair.

Father Fortis took a seat next to her and glanced up at Worthy. "Be patient, my friend. I'm sure there's a simple explanation. Let's all remember that Father Spiro didn't stop on the first procession, but the second one. That's when we process the communion elements. That comes thirty minutes later."

Father Fortis patted the woman's arm. "My dear, was that what happened? Were you in here for the second procession?"

The woman shook her head. "No, Father. How can I ever forget something like that? Andy was asleep on the pew, and I can still see the look on Father

Spiro's face. He wasn't looking into the cry room at all, but up there on the wall." She motioned toward the wall above the stained-glass icons. "I know I'm right, because I looked down at his feet. I remember wondering who could pick up the communion elements if they fell on the carpet."

With both hands on the window rail, Worthy stared out toward the altar. "You're sure about this?" he asked without turning around.

"Yes. Yes, I am."

Worthy found it odd that he could think of nothing to say. It was as if he was looking at himself as he stood foolishly in the cry room, so close to crying himself. A minute before he'd had the answer for them all—Betts and Sherrod, McCarty and Allyson.

"Then that's that," he said. He hardly recognized his own voice as he repeated, "On behalf of the police department, I want to thank you for coming forward."

Behind him, he heard Father Fortis whisper to Mrs. Nichols, "I'll walk you to your car."

As Father Fortis passed by, Worthy could feel a hand on his shoulder. "Wait here a minute, Christopher."

Worthy nodded. *Why not?* he thought. *Where else do I have to go?*

AS HE WAVED GOODBYE IN THE parking lot, Father Fortis couldn't help but notice how Mrs. Nichols gunned her car. He couldn't blame her. The poor woman's life had been destroyed by the Hagarty woman, but she had nevertheless agreed, because of his invitation in the church newsletter, to put herself through the pain all over again. And what had they discovered? That none of what she said mattered in the end.

He walked slowly back toward the church, his robes blowing in a sudden breeze. It was building up for a snowstorm, he thought, as he looked up at the darker clouds. And there was a storm waiting for him in the sanctuary. Where was the investigation now?

He found Worthy back in the pew where he'd first sat with Mrs. Nichols. To his surprise, his friend was sitting with a Bible open.

"This is the only book that makes sense anymore, Nick. Ecclesiastes. I'm sure you know it."

"Vanity, all is vanity. Yes, I know it."

" 'Nothing new under the sun.' The writer must have been a cop." Worthy closed the Bible and returned it to the pew rack.

He wanted to ask Worthy the question that had occurred to him in the parking lot, but the way his friend's jaw was clenched, he knew he had no answer.

"The old man left us a trail of breadcrumbs, but they lead nowhere," Worthy said, not looking up. "Sherrod chased the altarpiece, and I chased the diary."

"Maybe this is just a slight redirection, my friend," Father Fortis said. He was talking as much to himself as to Worthy, praying that what he was saying wouldn't make matters worse. "Maybe Father Spiro noticed Mrs. Nichols when she came back in from the cry room. Perhaps he had a kind of delayed reaction, deciding what he would do when he reached the cry room on the second procession."

"Let it go, Nick. You're just grasping at straws."

"But what about what she said, about Father Spiro coming around the corner and looking up there?" he asked, turning toward the side wall.

Worthy glanced up at the icons on the wall. "It's more likely that his faltering was simply what most people have been trying to tell us. Some kind of blackout. Why would a blank wall and stained-glass pictures stop him?"

Father Fortis pulled on his beard for a moment.

"Look, Nick, I know what you're trying to do, but let's face it. We're at a dead end."

Father Fortis held up his hand. "Hold on a second, Christopher. Do you remember the first clue you found? It wasn't the diary. It was the way the vestment lay straight on Father Spiro's body."

"So?"

"That led you to think it was someone who knew Father Spiro, or at least respected the priesthood. Right?"

Worthy's eyes lifted to the altar area where the body was found. "Right. I almost forgot about that."

"I remember how you scared me with that detail—it still scares me," Father Fortis said. "The thought that the killer is one of my parishioners, perhaps someone I've given communion to. That was truly a nightmare for me."

"And that doesn't describe Peggy Hagarty. And not Carl Bales, for that matter," Worthy added.

"But I suppose it does bring Lloyd Hartunian back into the picture."

Worthy shook his head. "I don't think so."

Father Fortis sighed. "Then it could be someone else from this parish."

"Maybe," Worthy said, lowering his head again before adding, "maybe. But maybe not. We're here because I pushed too fast, Nick. It's just what I've always hated about Sherrod."

His friend's dejected slump in the pew, his hopeless tone—where had he seen this before? *Of course.* It was like Worthy was making his confession.

"I just thought it was the excitement of everything coming together," Father Fortis said.

"It's like I had to have the case solved today."

"Why? Was it pressure from your captain?"

Worthy shook his head. "At bottom, I guess my motivation is pretty stupid. It doesn't have anything to do with the case—except that *she'd* say it does."

"She? Are you talking about that reporter?"

"No, Allyson. It was something she laid on me."

"Allyson? Do you mean at the cabin?"

"No, last night. She said I used murders to run away from my family."

The two men had been friends for nearly four years. They'd worked together on two cases. Worthy had even saved Father Fortis' life. But this was the first time Worthy had let down his guard about this part of his life. "She was the one who ran away," Father Fortis reminded him.

"In her view, she only did what I'd been doing for years. She said the only people I really care about are my dead victims."

Father Fortis could feel the weight of Allyson's accusation upon his friend. "What did you say?"

"I tried to tell her how I do my job, how knowing the victim is the only way to find the killer." He offered a feeble laugh. "God, it's like she's accusing me of digging up the dead."

" 'Let the dead bury the dead.' "

"Huh?"

"It's something Jesus said, something that's always bothered me, my friend. Even though our Lord wept at Lazarus' grave, he said to let the dead bury the dead."

Worthy turned toward Father Fortis, his jaw clenched again. "That sounds like something Allyson would say. But the dead don't bury the dead, and they don't find their own killers. People like me find them."

Father Fortis noticed his friend's balled-up fist. "I know, I know."

"And before that, Allyson was all hot and bothered about Henderson."

"Your partner?"

"I told her that he's been having problems, but somehow in the way that I said it, she got the idea that because I've kept my focus on the case, I don't really care about Henderson."

"What does she want you to do?"

Worthy shook his head. "I have no idea. Does she really expect me to drop everything and help him?"

"Help him or help her?" Father Fortis asked.

Worthy squinted toward the front. "Maybe that's it. No, probably that's it."

"If that's really what this is about, do you know what she wants help with?"

"I don't know. I don't know."

Father Fortis knew better than to rush his friend. After a moment, he asked, "You said that Henderson was having problems. What are they?"

"I'm sure I told you, Nick. He has this habit of slugging people. First another cop, and then a suspect. The guy's got a career death wish."

"Perhaps he's in the wrong profession."

Worthy shook his head. "That's the odd thing. When he's working at it, he's really very good. Remember, he's the one who found the diary. And he's worried about hurting his family, that's for sure. Hell, Nick, how do I know what makes a person do that kind of thing?"

"But you do, my friend. It's exactly what you do with your victims. You study their lives and get to know them. It seems a bit odd that when you saw Father Spiro's look of anger in that photo, you became instantly focused on figuring out why he was so angry."

Worthy nodded slowly. "But with Henderson it's different. That does frustrate the hell out me—to see somebody screwing up his life."

"And with your victims?"

Worthy shook his head. "With them, I get this weird feeling that they want me to do what I do. I trace their lives, and it's like I can feel them encouraging me to understand them. That's how I find who killed them. I find out who crossed their paths."

"I remember what you said last week. You said victims unknowingly head toward an encounter. I think you also said that murder is like falling in love."

"Imagine how much worse Mrs. Nichols would feel if I told her that her husband let it happen."

"Maybe he did, Christopher. He's an untenured professor hoping to keep his job, right? He has the wife of a senior faculty member in his class. Why wouldn't he try to make a good impression, offer her extra help when she began hanging around? He just misunderstood the cues."

Worthy sighed. "So if I'm so good at understanding dead people, why am I so bad with the living?"

"I wonder how Allyson would answer that question."

"I can tell you. She says I'm a glory hound, that I do it for the commendations."

Father Fortis patted Worthy on the arm. "We both know that's not it, my friend. How about turning the question around? Why *do* you care so much about the dead?"

"I don't think I care about them any more than you do. A half hour ago, weren't you the one saying how much work Father Spiro's memorial service is getting to be? How is that different? Can't people see that caring about the dead is what we're both paid to do?"

"People? Now it's plural?"

"My new captain has been more than a bit disappointed in me. I mean, as a partner. No, as Henderson's mentor."

Father Fortis wondered if Worthy needed him to point out that it was two women who noticed the same thing about him. "You said you don't care for the dead any more than I do as a priest. What was your father like?"

Worthy's brow furrowed. "You mean as a minister?"

"Yes. What happened when someone in your father's church was close to death?"

Worthy was silent for a moment. "I don't remember. I don't think we saw him much then. He would be at the hospital and then planning the funeral."

"You say you didn't see him much?"

Worthy's next words came out slowly, as if he was recalling something from a long time ago. "I remember my mom keeping his plate warm in the oven. And I remember her telling us to be quiet, that Dad needed to rest when he came home. But that's just normal. I mean, the dead …."

Father Fortis gazed up at the altar. "What about the dead, my friend?"

Worthy squinted down at his hands. "I remember that he once said that the dying feel so alone. That they're on the last part of their earthly journey. That they needed our help."

Father Fortis smiled. "Pretty good theology for a Baptist, but maybe not so good for a father. Do you mind telling me what it was like when your father died?"

Worthy grimaced. "He got lung cancer. He was so ashamed. Here he was a Baptist minister who'd never smoked a cigarette in his life, and he got lung cancer."

"Was his passing easy?"

"It was awful. He seemed so … so scared."

"So alone?"

Worthy nodded.

Father Fortis patted Worthy's arm again. "I think this time you should listen to Allyson."

"And do what? Forget that we lost our only lead on this case?"

Father Fortis rose. "Yes, my friend, that's exactly what I'm saying. For the rest of today, forget about the case. I'm serious, Christopher. For the rest of today, let the dead bury the dead."

CHAPTER FIFTEEN

——— ◆ ———

A FTER WORTHY LEFT, FATHER FORTIS THUMBED through the stack of materials Mrs. Hazelton had deposited on his desk. There was a packet of photos from Mr. Bagios of Father Spiro's funeral, with a note: "Thought you might want to see these."

I will look at them, I will, he thought, *but first things first.* He found the phone number of Father Daniel, the seminarian who'd served at St. Cosmas. It was only two days before Father Spiro's memorial service, and contrary to his advice to Worthy, he'd spend every moment of the next two days thinking about the dead.

But even as Father Fortis dialed Father Daniel's number in East Lansing, he found it hard to let the disappointment of the morning go. What would Worthy do now? Peggy Hagarty wasn't out of the picture, but was she any more a suspect now than someone like Lloyd Hartunian?

He had to admit that his concerns went beyond Worthy's feelings. His friend's certainty about Mrs. Hagarty had led him to hope that the case could be resolved in time for Father Spiro's memorial. He had already thought fondly of returning to the monastery and leaving the computer, copy machines, and stresses of St. Cosmas behind. Parish ministry was for a juggler, someone who wouldn't drop the twenty duties when one or two more were tossed his way.

He dialed the number for St. Demetrius in East Lansing and was put through to Father Daniel by a cheery secretary. After introducing himself, Father Fortis explained the main purpose of his call. "I understand the parish council already invited you to attend Father Spiro's memorial. I want you to know that you're invited to serve with the other clergy at the altar."

"Very kind of you to call, Father. I've already asked another priest from the diocese to fill in for me. Let me put you on hold and see if he has it on his calendar." Father Fortis could hear music in the background and was pleased to note that it was jazz. He had seen a number of converts who'd gone into the priesthood and generally found himself uncomfortable in their presence. Many converts were so intent on leaving no doubt about their devotion to Orthodoxy that they went overboard. Some dressed as if they'd taken monastic orders, and from what he'd heard, ran their parishes the same way. He'd heard of one who encouraged his parishioners to adopt the sparse diet of monks and nuns until the metropolitan had put a stop to it. That was the kind who played CDs of Byzantine chant as if it were the twelfth century, not the twenty-first. But jazz was a good sign.

Father Daniel's voice broke in again. "Yes, everything is covered here. And I'd be honored to serve at the altar."

"How's the new parish going?" Father Fortis inquired.

"It's a challenge. We had thirty in Divine Liturgy last Sunday. That's a high number for us, by the way."

"University folk, I suppose?"

"So far it's a mix, really. A few faculty from Greece and Russia. Some Serbian students who are pretty regular. And some converts like me."

"Blessings on you for taking up the challenge."

"I think that I should be saying that to you. When I heard about Father Spiro's death, I felt terrible, of course, but what made it worse was the thought that the metropolitan might ask me to go back to St. Cosmas. Then somebody on the parish council—I think it was Dr. Boras—emailed me about your coming. No, I wouldn't trade with you, Father."

"That rough, huh?"

"You should know by now. St. Cosmas is a typical parish, no worse, I suppose, than most. Are they still pulling in five different directions?"

"You mean about moving?"

"That and the whole issue of language in the liturgy. That's what I like about East Lansing. The liturgy here is ninety-nine percent English, and best of all, no one complains."

"The English has to happen," Father Fortis said. "You're just ahead of the rest of us." He liked the no-nonsense nature of the young man, but he could see how Mrs. Filis and some of the old-timers would have resented him. "Father Daniel, do you have time for a few questions?"

"Fire away."

"How long were you here at St. Cosmas?"

"Let's see. I came right after my course work at the seminary. St. Cosmas started as my field experience; then I stayed on a bit. I was there three long years, but I should also say that I made some great friends there."

"Why did they send you all the way out to Detroit, and especially to St. Cosmas? From what I've been told, Father Spiro wasn't an educated man."

"A few on the parish council, the college types there, said I shouldn't expect to learn much. They thought that I'd been sent to bail Father Spiro out. And at first, it did seem that way. Father Spiro was getting pretty old and set in his ways. But I can see now that I learned a lot from him. Like how a priest has to have broad shoulders and a thick skin."

"The thick skin I understand, but explain the broad shoulders."

"To deal with everything people tell you, and I'm not just talking about confession. In his own way, he really knew those people, and good Lord, did he love them. I'm not sure they realized that."

Father Fortis considered the point. "Did he ever tell you what those burdens were?"

"Some of them, but I could tell he kept a lot to himself."

Father Fortis decided to overrule Worthy's warning. "I'd like to tell you something in strictest confidence, Father."

Father John hesitated for a moment before asking a question of his own. "I'm okay with that, but I'm wondering if Dr. Boras was right when she said you investigate murders."

"I wouldn't put it that way. It's fairer to say that a good friend of mine is heading up the investigation. A very good detective. I help him out when and where I can."

"I don't know that I have anything helpful to add," Father Daniel said, "but please go ahead."

"Thank you, Father. The police have discovered that Father Spiro kept a secret diary of some of the tougher issues. Only Mrs. Hazelton knows that we found it, and we'd like to keep it that way for the present."

"That doesn't sound good. Of course, with Father's memory problems, I suppose what you're saying makes sense. He never told me about it, if that's what you're asking. But to keep it from the parish? Hmm."

"Don't read too much into that," Father Fortis tried to reassure him. He could see now his request for confidentiality would only make Father Daniel more curious. "You talked about Father Spiro's memory problems. Did you see that getting worse while you were here?"

"Parishioners warned me about it, of course, but Bernice—Mrs. Hazelton, I mean—would keep him on track. I'd forgotten about Bernice. I suppose she's taking all this pretty hard."

"She told me the very morning I arrived how guilty she felt."

"Guilty?" Father Daniel repeated.

"Yes, for not being at St. Cosmas that morning,"

"That's so much like Bernice. But then I admit that I felt the same when I first heard. Would he have died if I'd stayed on staff there? Guilt catches you coming and going, doesn't it? But about your other question. Father Spiro's memory did get worse, and quite suddenly over my last months there. It was like someone threw a switch. He missed appointments, couldn't be reached by phone, that sort of thing. He left me in the lurch more than once. That's when the parish council started pushing him to consider retirement."

Father Fortis asked, "All of a sudden? When was that?"

"I'd say sometime in early fall. I asked him if he was okay. He just shrugged."

"Mr. Margolis told me Father Spiro had talked about retirement but then didn't want to consider it for some reason."

"Same with me. I asked him about it when I knew I'd be leaving St. Cosmas. I didn't want him to think that I was trying to push him aside. He told me he had some things he needed to get straightened out. Then he'd retire."

"Were those things at St. Cosmas?" Father Fortis asked.

"That's what I assumed. I suppose it could have been something else. Like I said, he never said what he was so worried about. But then he always saw me as a seminarian, someone sent by the metropolitan. I'm not saying he resented me, but sometimes I got the feeling I was in his way."

Father Fortis would have gladly welcomed some help from a young priest like Father Daniel. He sounded like a juggler, someone who enjoyed the challenges being thrown his way. Funny that an old priest like Father Spiro hadn't appreciated it. "Did anyone ever tell you what happened on Father Spiro's last Sunday, Father?" he asked.

"Someone from the parish council—was it Dr. Boras? No, I don't think so. Anyway, someone told me at the funeral about some fit he had."

"No one really knows what happened," Father Fortis said, "but he did stop right in the middle of one of the processions. You knew the man in a way maybe no one else did. After all, you served in the altar area with him. I'd be interested in your theory as to what happened."

"My theory? Well, I heard he just lost it—blanked out, I guess you could say. What else could it have been?"

"Someone else said she saw him staring at the side wall when he stopped. He could have been looking at the icons in the windows."

"Really?" Father Daniel asked. "I used to do that at St. Cosmas."

Father Fortis sat up. "Oh?"

"Not when I first got there. No, I was too worried about messing up my lines during the procession. But one Sunday, I turned the corner in the back and looked over to the window and read the letters on this one icon. It turned out to be St. Barbara, the martyr, who is my wife's patron saint, and I thought for a moment that she was looking at me. It sounds stupid, but I always noticed her after that. I liked to believe she was smiling, although from the stories we know about her, I'm not sure she was the smiling type."

A fragment of a thought, out of focus and ablur, flitted through Father Fortis' mind, departing as quickly as it had come. He remembered looking up at the stars with his brother when he was a kid. His brother had this unerring ability to see shooting stars, and would call out, "There, Nicky!" But his own luck was always bad. He'd spin around in the yard and stare up, only to hear his brother say that he'd just missed it.

Worthy pulled up in the driveway and left the motor running. He jogged up to the door and knocked. Susan came to the door.

"Chris, what is it?" she asked, giving him a wary look.

"Is Allyson here?"

"She's upstairs, doing homework."

"Can I borrow her … take her somewhere for about an hour?"

Susan hadn't yet opened the door to let him in. "Where? What's going on, Chris?"

"It's hard to explain. Can you just tell her I'd like her to go with me to Henderson's house?"

"Henderson? Who's he?"

"He's my partner. She knows about him. Tell her I need her."

Susan gave Worthy a puzzled look. "You're going to have to ask her that yourself."

"Fine, fine. Just tell her I want her to go to Henderson's with me."

Susan disappeared. He waited, hoping Amy wouldn't try to pull him into the house. Minutes passed, and he expected to see Susan's face again through the screen. What sense would Allyson make of his request? *She probably thinks I'm trying to prove my point, to rub it in*, he thought, acknowledging with a grimace that's exactly what he had wanted that morning.

To his surprise, Allyson came out with her coat on. Without a word, the two walked to the car and drove off.

"Thanks," he said.

"Whatever. Anything to get me away from that chem report," she said, but he noticed she sat erect in the seat, her eyes glued forward.

They drove in near silence across town, as if both were ready for what was about to happen. Worthy, however, knew only how things would start. From there, it was up to Henderson.

He knocked on the door, with Allyson standing next to him. Henderson's wife answered and gave Worthy the same kind of wary look Susan had. *It must be written all over my face*, he thought.

"Carnell isn't here," she said.

"Mrs. Henderson, this is my daughter, Allyson. Will your husband be back soon?"

She looked from one of them to the other for a moment. "Please come in," she said.

Worthy followed Allyson into the house. On the couch, Henderson's boy Jamie sat ramrod straight, watching TV as he had the last time. "Do you mind if we wait in here with your son?" he asked.

Mrs. Henderson started to respond, but stopped and only nodded. "I'll make some coffee. What would you like, Hon?" she asked Allyson.

Allyson pulled a strand of hair behind her ear. "Coffee's fine."

Worthy sat down on the couch next to Jamie, while Allyson took a seat in a chair. Without looking their way, the boy reached for an open bag of potato chips and drew it next to him.

"Hi, Jamie, remember me?"

The boy didn't look away from the TV.

"What's on?" Worthy asked.

This time the boy glanced at Worthy before returning to a cartoon show. "Who're you?"

"My name is Chris. I work with your Dad. And this is my daughter, Allyson." He waited, but the boy's attention was solely on the TV, his hand rummaging in the snack bag.

"Do you know the name of this show, Ally?"

Before she could respond, the boy rose from the couch and walked stiffly toward the kitchen. His pants seemed too high, his belt too tight. At one point, Jamie steadied himself on the corner of Allyson's chair before leaving the room.

Again, Allyson sat quietly, as if she understood her father perfectly.

In a moment, the boy returned and sat down in the same place. "Momma said to tell you it's *Pinky and the Brain*."

"I do remember that," Allyson said. "Pinky's always trying to take over the world, right?"

The boy nodded. Worthy looked over at the boy, whose back was straight despite the soft couch. He remembered what Bales had whispered to Henderson, driving him over the edge: "You look like a guy who needs shock therapy."

"What the hell is this?" Henderson said, coming through the door with a white bag in his hand. Worthy could read the name of the pharmacy on the side of it.

"Carn, don't," his wife pleaded, carrying a tray into the room. "They're guests."

"They?"

"This is my daughter, Allyson," Worthy said, starting to rise.

"Hi," Allyson offered weakly.

"Can we talk somewhere in private?" Worthy asked.

Henderson handed the bag to his wife and walked down the hallway. Worthy followed him into the study, where a computer screen was on. On the walls were more photos like those he'd observed on his earlier visit— Henderson as a young basketball player.

Worthy walked over and stood in front of one. "So you played at Michigan State."

Henderson went over and switched off the screen. He turned around and remained standing. "Two years until my knee blew out," he said tightly. "That was a long time ago."

"You were on scholarship?"

"Like I said, until my knee blew out. They took the money back, so I finished up at Grand Valley State."

"And was that where you met your wife?"

"You out for a drive with your daughter and decide you wanted to find out my life story?"

"No. Something else. May I sit down?"

"No one's stopping you."

"I don't know if you know my daughter's story. She ran away a while back. That just about scared me to death."

Henderson remained standing, eyeing Worthy. "That right? It looks like she's back."

"Yeah, she's back. But she never told us why. It still scares me … and my ex-wife."

Henderson sat down. "That's right, you're divorced."

"Yeah, that happened over a year before she ran away. It doesn't take a genius to figure out the two are connected."

Henderson pulled at his socks. "So, why you telling me this?"

Worthy took a deep breath. "I know why you laid into Bales."

Henderson glared up at Worthy. "So? We already went through that. Over and done."

Worthy's voice was barely louder than a whisper. "I don't think so. I know what Bales whispered, and I'm pretty sure that I know about Jamie."

Henderson rose from his chair and stood over Worthy. *Here's where he uses my head for a basketball*, Worthy thought.

"I know I made it clear that you should mind your own business. You think your daughter is going to keep me from throwing you out? You think you're some goddamned genius. You don't know shit!"

Worthy shook his head slowly, trying to see another way forward. "You take off early because your wife needs you here … with your son."

Henderson didn't move. "That's nothing to do with the case. Let me remind you who found the damned book. So leave my family out of it, and I'll do the same with you. I don't give a rat's ass about your daughter, okay?"

He turned and walked back to the desk. Picking up a coat off the back of the chair, he reached in and pulled out his badge. He gazed at it for a moment, then brought it over and dropped it into Worthy's lap. "Fuck you, fuck the police department, and fuck Detroit. Take that back to the captain. Now, get the hell out."

"No, I'm not going to do that," Worthy said, his own voice tight in his throat. "Is this what you want to do for your wife and son—spend the rest of your life punching people?"

Henderson swayed as he hovered over Worthy. He turned slowly and slumped in his chair, head cradled in his hands.

Worthy rose and walked to the window. "The case threw me for a loop today."

Henderson remained silent.

"I thought I had it all figured out," Worthy continued. "I was sure that the diary made it all clear. I thought your problems and mine with my daughter didn't matter because we'd have the killer. You and I would go our separate ways, and that would be that. But now, I'm not sure I know anything. And I can't go on alone. I'll drown."

"You wouldn't understand if I told you." Henderson's voice was slow as if he were dragging a weight up from a deep hole.

Worthy turned and faced his partner. "You'll have to try me."

Henderson sat in silence for a moment, studying the floor between glances at Worthy. "Last year, the school asked for a conference," he began in a very tired voice. "The counselor looked us straight in the face and asked if Jamie used drugs. An eleven-year-old kid. 'No way,' I said." His voice started to shake. "But we both knew something was up. Jamie's never been social, but then I'm not either."

"I noticed," Worthy said.

Henderson nodded, as if he deserved that. "But with Jamie, it's that he only likes to watch cartoons."

Worthy looked to a side table that held a series of family photos of the three of them. With each passing year, Jamie stood more off by himself, his mother's arm failing to draw him in. "Did you have him tested?"

"Yeah. I thought he might be depressed, but the psychologist started using some other big words. Scary words. I had to look them up on the Internet."

"Like what?"

"Like borderline personality disorder. Then they focused on us and asked that we get tested. Know what schizophrenogenic is?"

"No."

Henderson twisted one hand in the other. "It means you're the kind of parent who makes your kid schizophrenic. Nice, huh?"

Worthy started to say he was sorry, sorry for Henderson's problem, and sorry he'd had to ask. But Henderson cut him off. "This is going to come out better if you don't say a damn thing." He paused before continuing. "I've always made a point of taking what life gives me and making the best of it. You know, letting it motivate me ...." His voice trailed off. "That's not working this time."

The room was deadly quiet until Henderson roused himself and asked, "You remember how high I was right after I found the book?"

"Sure."

"Then I pulled back. Right?"

"Yeah, that you did."

"My wife called me. She said she noticed a mark on Jamie's arm after school. Jamie didn't say anything, but when she rolled up his sleeve there were these marks up and down his arm." His eyes brimmed with tears as he looked down at his own arm. "My boy has been rubbing his skin off with a pencil eraser at school. Can you believe that?"

"Yes, I saw it once."

He watched his partner fold his hands behind his head and stare at the ceiling. Henderson's jaw muscles clamped and released over and over again. "Where was that?"

"I had a job one summer during college. It was in a halfway house."

"For nutcases, right?"

"No. For kids trying to figure things out."

"Fucking nuts."

Henderson's wife poked her head in. "Everything okay in here?" Worthy could tell that she'd been crying and guessed that she'd been listening as well. *What is Allyson thinking?* he thought.

"Fine, baby. Jamie okay?"

"He's okay. Allyson is reading him a story. He's probably already asleep." She offered Worthy a feeble smile and closed the door behind her.

"I told the doctor that I'd seen psychotics before in my job. I told him Jamie was definitely not that. Do you know what he told me? He said that Jamie may not have had an episode yet, but he was probably hallucinating at school. Maybe even while watching TV."

Worthy sat silently, heavy with the vision of what he knew was likely in store for Henderson and his wife. There would be trips to treatment facilities with their smiling staff members. There would be hope held out for new drugs and treatments, as well as tantalizing stories of amazing recoveries. Meanwhile, their eleven-year-old would become a teenager and then an adult, curled up in a bed somewhere.

"So, when Bales whispered about shock therapy—"

Henderson sat forward in his chair. "Why'd he do that? I mean, it was like he was reading my mind." He looked up at Worthy with sad yet hopeful eyes.

Worthy wanted to tell him not to expect any wisdom from him. His wife had divorced him and his daughter had run away, and he understood neither. But then a memory came back from his summer in college.

"There was this guy at the halfway house. Really wired, a lot like Bales. When I'd come into work, he'd be right in my face, pulling his hair, and then he'd say something right out of my life." Worthy could feel Henderson hanging on his every word. All he had was a story that offered little or nothing. "So anyway, we'd just hired this new college kid. He had a girlfriend in town, someone he'd met at a bar. She used to drop him off at work in her convertible, sometimes wearing a bikini top. So one day, the new college boy comes into work ten minutes late and has to thread his way through the clients to get to the nursing station. That's where we gave out meds. Suddenly, this guy grabs the new kid and looks him right in the eye. 'Backseat rodeo, backseat rodeo,' he keeps saying. 'You told her not to stop, told her to ride the bronco until you got done.'"

"So what happened?"

Worthy shrugged and looked down at Henderson. "The trainee just stared at the kid, got white all over, turned, and walked out. Just quit. That's what Bales is like. They just know things."

Henderson sat back in his chair, his brow furrowed. "Maybe that's what happened. The day before the doctor said that Jamie might need to be hospitalized for observation …. I don't remember anyone talking about shock treatments, but who knows? I know I wanted to hit somebody. Man, that Bales. I wanted to pull my gun and kill the son of a bitch."

"But you didn't," Worthy reminded him. "You need to tell your story to the new captain. She's not like Spicer."

"I don't want sympathy," Henderson protested.

"Sure you do. We all do." Worthy walked to the door. "See you tomorrow?"

Henderson offered a feeble nod. "You know I can't promise anything. I got to take care of my family first."

"Yeah, I think I'm beginning to understand that."

CHAPTER SIXTEEN

---◆---

WORTHY SAT ACROSS THE BOOTH FROM Allyson, watching her cut the cinnamon roll into equal pieces. He found it hard to accept it had been only a week since she'd sat across from him at the restaurant up north and quizzed him about Henderson.

"Jamie's in bad shape, isn't he?" she said, offering her father a wedge of the roll.

Though hunger was the furthest thing from his mind, he took it and rested it on the edge of his coffee saucer. "Yeah. It doesn't look good."

"Can't they give him pills or something?"

"They already have, Ally. Some things are hard to fix."

She paused in mid-chew. "He'll never get better?"

He shrugged. "I honestly don't know. It's tearing his folks apart."

"You mean they'll divorce?"

He felt his face redden. "No, no, nothing like that. Well, I guess it's possible, but I think they'll go through whatever happens together." He waited for her to say it, to ask why Henderson and his wife would hold on to each other, when her mother and father couldn't.

He cleared his throat and stared at the untouched piece of roll on his plate. "I want to tell you why I asked you to come with me."

"I think I know."

"Oh?"

"Maybe something I said the other night wasn't completely wrong … about the way you do your job, I mean."

He nodded but didn't look up. "The thing is, I wanted you to be so wrong, and I was sure you were. Henderson was just my partner, and not a very good one most of the time. I thought, to hell with him. I probably thought the same about what you laid on me too. But then ...."

"But then what?"

"Then the proof I had that you were all wrong—my new captain who asked me to help him out, Henderson with his secret, and you—well, that proof turned into smoke. I don't know where we are in this case, and it won't be too long before the media and my boss get wind of that."

"So why are we here?"

He looked up, puzzled. "What?"

"Mom used to tell Amy and me not to bother you sometimes. It always seemed funny to me, because it was when you weren't home much at all. Some case was tough, I guess, and we'd never see you. And then when we did see you, Mom told us not to bother you."

A pain shot through his head as he heard his mother saying the same to his sister and himself. "Your mom never told me that."

"I guess she did the same thing herself. But you didn't answer my question. If things are going bad on this case, why are we here?"

"Where should we be?"

"I'd have thought you'd want to be alone. You know," she tapped her temple, "to concentrate."

"Yeah. Well, someone told me to let the dead bury the dead."

"What's that supposed to mean?"

He picked up the wedge of roll and put it into his mouth. The caramel stuck to his fingers, then to his teeth. "I suppose it means I don't know what you want from me, Ally, especially after you came back, so I can't be sure I can give you anything. Do you remember what you said when I brought back that toy horse for Amy from New Mexico?"

"No."

"You sneered and said that's what I do as a dad. I go on trips and bring back junk." He paused, trying to find the right words. "I've been thinking a lot about what you said the other night, that I prefer being with dead people. I can't tell you how badly I wanted you to be wrong, and I thought my theory on this case would prove that. But then, when my house of cards collapsed, I realized something. I may not know—not yet, anyway—what you want from me, Ally," he said, looking up to see tears in his daughter's eyes, "but I knew what Henderson needed. I wanted you to see that ... that I'm trying. That's why we're here."

✝

"MIND IF I HAVE A WORD with you, Father?" The cheery voice over the phone broke Father Fortis' concentration on the church bulletin. *Yes, I do mind*, he thought, what with this being Saturday, the day before Sunday's memorial and the flowers not yet delivered and the bulletin not yet completed.

"Who is this?" he asked.

"Kenna McCarty. We spoke earlier."

Good Lord, he wondered, *is this woman a psychic or just a vulture?* "You've caught me at a very bad time, Mrs. McCarty."

"It's *Ms.* McCarty, Father. It won't take more than a moment. I'm writing an article on the memorial service for Father Spiro and wanted to know if you'd like to comment."

He relaxed in his chair, feeling a bit guilty for his quick judgment of the reporter. "Yes, certainly. This is a very considerate gesture. I'm sure the parishioners will be most grateful."

"It's a compelling story, Father. Detroit hasn't forgotten about your tragedy."

"No, I'm sure not. How can I be of help?" He wrote a note to himself to call the metropolitan again to make sure about his part in the service.

"I'm trying to imagine what my readers want to know. I suspect not many of them will understand what the service is about."

"Yes, of course. A forty-day memorial service is offered for any Orthodox Christian by family and friends. Forty days remembers that Our Lord ascended into heaven forty days after his resurrection. In the service, we pray that the soul of the departed will be with our ascended Lord."

"Excellent, Father. You're a reporter's dream, the way you explain things so clearly. So this service marks the end of the parish's mourning—officially, I mean."

"Oh no, not at all. St. Cosmas will have another memorial service on the anniversary of his death, and every year after that on the nearest Sunday to the date."

"Really? For how long?"

"What do you mean?"

"Well, will there be one in ten years, for example, or twenty?"

"Very likely, and maybe for twenty years after that. You see, Ms. McCarty, we pray in the service that the *memory* of the departed soul—not just the departed soul itself—will be eternal. These services are our way of doing our part to answer that prayer."

"My readers are going to love this, Father," Kenna McCarty said with real relish. "Yes, that's very touching. Now, who will participate?"

"We expect the metropolitan to officiate as well as other priests besides myself. And the choir, of course, and our chanter will play big roles. The memorial service will be at the close of our Divine Liturgy, and I know for a fact that the parish council president, Mr. George Margolis, will be offering the epistle reading."

"What a marvelous service. Of course, once the article comes out tomorrow, some people will want to know if they can be present. I know you probably have numerous things to attend to, so I don't want them calling the church. What should I say in my article about visitors?"

Father Fortis paused. He hadn't thought of that. The sanctuary would be packed in any case. "Please let people know that St. Cosmas is always open to visitors, but this Sunday is a special moment in the parish's life."

The reporter repeated the words as if she were writing them down. "Perfect, Father. Just one more question. Do you expect anyone else to be there?"

Who else? he thought. "I don't understand your question."

"I mean the police. Do you expect them to be there?"

Yes, he did expect Worthy to be there, but that was none of her business. He felt a tightening in his chest.

"You see, Father, the reason I ask is that I understand there's a break in the case. A new development."

He thought of the diary. Had Mrs. Hazelton broken her word and told someone? He couldn't imagine that, but how else would she have known?

"You'll have to ask the police about that," he said cautiously.

"You mean Lieutenant Worthy? Yes, I tried that, but he hung up on me."

"Just how is this part of your story, Ms. McCarty?"

"Just as I said, Father. Detroit hasn't forgotten about a priest being strangled."

"Meaning, your paper wants to sell copies, no matter if it hinders an investigation or not," he snapped.

"Good Lord, you don't know, do you?" she asked. "No one's told you. I thought Worthy would have the decency to call you, but then, he's a bit of a loner, isn't he?"

A monk's life is a life of discipline. As his abbot had never tired of reminding him, the very structure of monastic life is predicated on self-control, on knowing when to speak and when not to. And so he yearned for the discipline not to ask the question, even as it was out of his mouth before he could stop himself. "What are you talking about?"

"Another cop found the altarpiece, Father. Over at Suffolk, in a Dumpster."

CHAPTER SEVENTEEN

———◆———

CAPTAIN BETTS' OFFICE WAS STANDING-ROOM-ONLY BY the time Worthy arrived. Sitting center stage was Sherrod, on his lap a cardboard box. The guy looked like he'd bought a lamp. Except Worthy knew it wasn't a lamp, but another nail—maybe the final one—in his coffin. Henderson was standing by the window, as he had that first day when the case had been handed over. Captain Betts was also standing against the opposite wall and looking at the box. Behind her desk, in a golf shirt, sat another figure, Michael "Mickey" Livorno, Police Superintendent.

Welcome to my funeral, Worthy told himself.

Sherrod was leaning forward in his chair, patting the top of the box.

Captain Betts cleared her throat. "Okay, it looks like we're all here. Show-and-tell time, Lieutenant."

Sherrod nodded but paused a moment for full effect. "What I have here was found yesterday afternoon, by yours truly, over at Suffolk. I found it in a Dumpster that's about two blocks from Mr. Lashad's current address." He slowly opened the top of the box, as if something could pop out. Reaching in, he pulled out a shiny silver and gold altarpiece. On it, Worthy noted the Greek lettering.

"I believe we all know what this is," Sherrod crowed as he held his trophy aloft, perfect except for a slight dent in the top. "The dent is recent. Notice that there's no tarnish build-up in the crack."

"So you don't think it's been in the Dumpster long, then," Superintendent Livorno asked.

"I can't say for certain, sir. Trash pick-up in on Fridays—that's today—so the longest it could have been in there is a week. Besides that, the item in question was found about halfway down in the garbage, so I estimate it was put there middle of the week."

Worthy stood, detached, watching Sherrod's moment of triumph. Betts had the courtesy not to look his way, though the superintendent seemed as interested in him as the altarpiece.

"Does anyone have any questions?" Sherrod asked, smiling fully in Worthy's direction.

Like when you get to take the case back officially? Worthy thought.

It was Henderson who broke the silence. "I got one, Sherrod. How'd you come to search that Dumpster? In fact, why the hell were you over there in the first place?"

Sherrod didn't look his way, but kept his eyes on Worthy. "Sergeant, you can accuse me of intervention in your case, but the evidence speaks for itself."

Captain Betts cleared her throat again. "The sergeant asked how you found yourself at that particular Dumpster."

Sherrod reddened slightly, gazing at the altarpiece again. "I got a tip. A phone call."

"Who from?" Henderson shot back.

"From an informant, you moron! That's police work. They know me around there and somebody called me and said I'd find something interesting in that Dumpster. And it looks like I sure as hell did."

Livorno rubbed his hands together as he stared at the altarpiece. "I can't see how anyone can argue with Lieutenant Sherrod's results. And I don't have to tell you why it's a relief to the entire department to have this case solved—once that's proven, of course."

Worthy watched the four in the room as if they were characters in a movie scene. His case was over. Livorno's fascination with the altarpiece proved that. *But dammit*, Worthy thought, *Henderson's point is still valid*. Sherrod's victory was too pat. "Why contact you, Sherrod? Henderson's been all over Suffolk. Why didn't they call him?"

Sherrod smirked, looking from Worthy back to Livorno. "Superintendent, do I really have to answer that? I'm a modest man, and Lieutenant Worthy is trying to set me up for self-promotion. That's something I've always detested in others. Not my style."

Henderson's laugh cut through the room. "You're telling us some informant from Suffolk, out of the blue, calls a white cop and tells him where to find this piece?"

Sherrod spun around and glared at Henderson. "Yes, that's what informants do for me, Sergeant. They inform! And I fucking reward them."

"So who called?" Henderson insisted.

Sherrod glanced back at Superintendent Livorno for support. "I'm sure most people in this room will understand if I say I'm not at liberty to say. Hell, I'm not sure myself yet. He'll let me know who he is when the time's right."

Worthy edged over in Henderson's direction. "So, you didn't recognize the voice."

"I thought you were the one teaching at the academy," Sherrod sneered. "Informants call when they know it's safe. He's waiting until somebody has the balls to lock those guys up."

"So this guy, is he Black?" Henderson asked.

"You're a moron, you know that? And this guy is your teacher. Hell, we all know what this meeting means. You blew it," he said, waving the altarpiece again. "Some punks followed the old priest into the church, did the job, and killed the geezer. It wasn't a fucking hard case. It was never a hard case until somebody in this room decided it was."

"That's enough, Lieutenant," Superintendent Livorno said.

"All I'm saying is that I was right. And I deserve—"

Captain Betts cut him off. "The superintendent said that was enough. You can go, Lieutenant."

Sherrod ceremonially placed the altarpiece on the desk, directly in front of Livorno. Glaring at Worthy on his way out, he slammed the door. For a few minutes, no one spoke.

"Anything you'd like to say, gentlemen?" Captain Betts asked.

Neither of them answered.

"What your captain is asking is this: do you or do you not have anything to say which we can use to cover your sorry asses when the papers get on to this?" Livorno asked.

Again, both men remained silent.

Livorno stood, looking like the morning had ruined his golf outing. "Then Captain Betts and I will see you both back here Monday morning, nine o'clock sharp. We'll let you know our decision."

THE NEXT MORNING, SATURDAY, THE DAY before Father Spiro's memorial, Worthy was watching the coffee percolate when the phone rang.

A thin voice on the other end said, "Dad?"

His heart skipped a beat. Why would his daughter call him at eight thirty on a Saturday? "Ally, what's wrong?"

"I just saw the paper."

Steaming water, an anemic brown, trickled into his cup. "You're ahead of me, then. I take it I didn't get another commendation." He hadn't meant it to sound cruel, to throw back in her face what she'd accused him of the week earlier.

There was only silence on the line. "Dad? Does this mean you're going to …?"

"Be fired? No, although like I said I haven't seen the article. I suspect that's what the reporter recommends. What it means is that on Monday I'll lose the case."

"Oh," she said, sounding relieved, then anxious again. "But that's a big deal, right?"

"Yes, a pretty big deal," he replied, seeing no need to explain to his daughter how long public humiliation hung around a cop's neck. *There goes the guy who—*

"They'll give you another one?"

He flipped the switch on the coffee maker. The stream stopped almost immediately. "Probably not this Monday. But yes, they'll give me another one." *Some day.* At least he wouldn't be sent back to the academy. No, he'd spend the next few months sitting at his desk, his ear pressed to a phone as he researched background on other people's cases.

"How about we do something tomorrow?" Allyson asked.

Sunday, the day before judgment came down from on high. And now the day his daughter didn't want him to be alone. "I thought you worked on Sundays," he said.

"Not until six. We could have lunch and see a movie."

"I'd planned on going to church in the morning," he said.

"You've gone back to church? Since when?"

"No, nothing like that. I want to go to St. Cosmas one more time."

"The place where the priest got killed? Why?"

"I'm not sure, exactly," he said. "Why don't you come with me? We can go for lunch from there." He waited for her to refuse, just as she had in the old days when he was still trying to get his family to church. That had been before the wheels came off his marriage and then his life.

"I tell you what. We'll sit in the balcony. After the service, you can meet my friend, Father Nick."

"Sure, I guess so," she agreed, sounding less than sure. "They're not weird, are they?"

"Weird? I don't think so. "There'll be nothing heavy, I promise you that. No pressure stuff." And it wouldn't be heavy, he thought. Of course, the sanctuary would be packed with all those coming for Father Spiro's memorial service. But everyone would be respectful, wanting to do things right. Worthy knew he wasn't going out of respect for the victim. No, he was going for one reason: to look down on the parishioners one last time before having to turn the case back over to Sherrod. The killer wouldn't miss the chance to sit, head bowed and sorrowful, in the midst of the mourners, and feel what—regret, grief, or simply pride? After all, wouldn't tomorrow be the day to secretly celebrate how masterfully he—or she—had kept on top of developments?

First, he or she had had the presence of mind after strangling the priest to take the altarpiece and throw Sherrod off. Secondly, they must have overruled an initial instinct to wipe the piece down and get rid of it, to throw it into the lake or bury it in some field. And hadn't that proved to be a wise decision? How clever the killer must have felt, knowing the value of the altarpiece when he, Worthy, had come on the case and turned attention back on the church. But they had been patient, not playing that card yet. No, they had opted to hit the Catholic church and take something similar. It was as if the killer knew they could still get to Sherrod. And then, the coup de grâce, the killer had disposed of the altarpiece at Suffolk and made one disguised phone call. All that could mean, Worthy concluded, was that the killer thought they were getting too close. *But we aren't*, Worthy admitted. *Or are we?*

FATHER FORTIS' LEFT KNEE CRAMPED AS it did every time he prayed too long on his knees. Always heavy-set, he'd played left guard from junior high through his junior year in college when he'd had surgery on the knee. Technically, he'd been a football player, though he'd never touched the ball except in practice, when everyone would pretend to be quarterback or tight end. The sanctuary of St. Cosmas was dark in the pre-dawn hours, lit only by the candles under the icons that flanked the altar doors. It would be a long day, filled with a myriad of tiny details. The flowers were set in place—*Lord, may they not wilt before morning.* The metropolitan's throne was polished—*Lord, keep the old guy awake. Don't let him nod off like they tell me he did on his last visit.* He'd heard the choir practicing extra long the afternoon before, and once or twice he'd heard the chanter's voice crack. Nerves, he thought, the same as he was battling as he imagined the day ahead. *Lord, give us all a sense of your peace today.*

Nearly forty nights before, Father Spiro, body and soul still intact, might have been on his knees in this same place. Had he been oblivious that Sunday morning to what lay ahead, his accidental death at the hands of some burglar, as the morning article stated was now established? Or, as Worthy believed, had he been praying that night about a confrontation he was to have the next morning?

Letters from the secret diary, in combinations of four, swam in front of his eyes in the candlelight. MRAG, NISP, and finally IOAG. What did they mean? They meant nothing, if the killer or killers had come in from Suffolk.

He'd asked himself the same question a hundred times over the past few days. Last thought at night, first in the morning, he was ashamed to admit, had not been his prayers, but those puzzling letters. As if he could catch Father Spiro's soul before it left this world forever, he whispered, "So what did they mean, Father?" Again, for the second time in the last two days, he felt something vague streak across his mind from one corner to the other like a shooting star. And again, just as it had when he was a boy, he could hear his brother's voice. "Over there, Nicky. Quick!"

CHAPTER EIGHTEEN

———◆———

WORTHY AND ALLYSON ARRIVED EARLY AT St. Cosmas and made their way to the balcony. Worthy watched as parishioner after parishioner brought candles to the icon screen, and after standing quietly and crossing themselves, placed the candles below one of the icons. They seemed like soldiers reporting to duty for a sad mission.

Missing was the laughter and arm-punching he remembered from his youth, the pre-service frivolity that had so disturbed his father. His father's intermittent pleas for a spirit of reverence to prepare for worship would be honored for a week or two, but the chatter of sports and weather would inevitably return. The Baptists he'd grown up with had savored the last few minutes before worship like last drags on a forbidden cigarette.

But again this week, as two weeks before, silence lay heavy in the Greek church. Allyson added to it, sitting quietly beside him without fidgeting. Here at St. Cosmas there was no hint of the breezy familiarity with the Deity. Here, beneath the scowls on the faces in the icons, fear of God made some sense. A part of his first visit came back to mind, when Father Fortis had turned toward the congregation and begged them to forgive his offenses against them: "For I approach God, our immortal King." It sounded like the warning of a landmine ahead.

An African American walking up the side aisle brought Worthy back to the present. Henderson. *Wow, who'd have thought that?* His partner ducked in and sat just behind Mrs. Nichols' usual seat. The man was either loyal or stubborn.

Both he and Allyson stood with the others as the service began. He looked down and picked out those he knew. He recognized Mrs. Filis, the parish council member who'd found the body. Across the aisle and up closer to the front stood Dr. Pappas. Next to him was a thin woman, almost as tall, dressed in respectful black. At the front and to the side stood the chanter and next to him, Mr. Margolis, parish council president.

Worthy looked toward the other side. "Well, I'll be damned," he whispered.

Allyson poked him in the ribs. "Dad! Shh."

"Sorry," he whispered, still trying to make sense of the new couple who had seated themselves along the far aisle. Kenna McCarty was sitting next to Superintendent Livorno. *She must be covering the service for a follow-up story,* he thought, *but why is he here?*

He didn't have much time to puzzle on the matter as Father Fortis appeared in the doorway between the icon screen and the altar and looked down the center aisle. Everyone turned toward the narthex, as if expecting someone.

Soon the scene was explained, as altar boys carrying icons and incense holders escorted an older man in even fancier vestments down the center aisle. Father Fortis came down from the podium, kissed the old man's hand, and led him to the ornate throne set off to the right.

"Who's he?" Allyson whispered.

"I think he's the metropolitan, their bishop."

"Wow. Nice getup."

The service returned to what he remembered from his last visit. By the first procession, the seats below were packed. If the killer was among them, they wouldn't have been the first to come, nor noticeably late. No, the killer would have entered with the crowd—all perfectly normal.

First Corinthians, Chapter One, was read in Greek, then English, by Mr. Margolis. Immediately following, Father Fortis opened the jeweled Bible and read a gospel story about a father with two sons, one who promised to obey, the second who protested but in the end was the only one to obey.

Worthy stood, his legs as heavy as lead, for the second procession. The altar boys inched their way toward the back corner and then turned toward the center. Here, Father Spiro had stopped, frozen for some reason, as unfathomable a mystery to Worthy as the diary's codes.

Worthy looked down and spied Henderson. His voice had held some hope on Thursday when he told Worthy about his son's new psychiatrist. The doctor was a visiting specialist from Peru whose accent was so thick that Henderson admitted he didn't understand every word the guy said. But somehow the doctor had connected with Jamie. "If a shrink from Peru can do that, maybe he can teach me," Henderson had said. Yes, Henderson was stubborn.

A strange rustling had started below him, and Worthy brought himself to attention. He saw Mrs. Filis drop to her knees and cross herself. Slowly, even as he leaned so far over the balcony rail that Allyson pulled at his coat, he realized what was happening. Below him, in the rear of the left aisle, Father Fortis stood motionless, his mouth open but silent. The tinkling of the censer had stopped, and the altar boys and the other priests in the procession stared back at the pale and shaking priest.

Worthy caught a glimpse of Henderson, half-walking, half-running past the altar boys toward the cry room. Worthy turned his attention back to Father Fortis, even as his friend seemed to shake his head and restart the chant. Worthy saw in that moment what Mrs. Siametes had noted about Father Spiro. Father Fortis was squinting up at the far wall. There could be no question of senility this time.

"What's happening?" Allyson whispered.

"I don't know. But I will after I talk with Nick."

Strangely, Father Fortis seemed the calmest person in the sanctuary as he slowly mounted the steps and returned to the altar area. A young priest could be seen whispering something to Father Fortis and Father Fortis shaking his head in response.

Worthy sat back in his chair, slightly nauseated. What had he just witnessed? If it was a charade, some clumsy attempt to spook the killer, then the bluff had worked too well. Many had reacted to the eerie echo of Father Spiro, and who could blame them? Was Mrs. Filis' reaction or Mr. Margolis' beet-red face any more suggestive or incriminating than his own near tumble from the balcony? The only other possibility was that Father Fortis hadn't planned to stop at all. He had seen something, but what?

Worthy squirmed in the pew, waiting impatiently for Father Fortis to finish administering communion. He knew the homily was next, when his friend would have to say something. There was a hushed buzz down below on the main floor as well. He wasn't the only curious one. Finally, Father Fortis approached the pulpit and bowed to the metropolitan before scanning the congregation. "I want to apologize for what happened on the last procession. I can imagine how painful and disturbing it must have been for those of you who knew and loved Father Spiro. It was, perhaps, my own sense of getting to know your beloved spiritual father over these past few weeks that caused my reaction," he said, looking up at Worthy.

Does he expect me to understand something from that? Worthy thought.

"I would invite you on this solemn occasion to think of the majority of Orthodox churches that have an icon of Christ, the Pantocrator, in the dome. When I was a boy growing up in Baltimore, I would sometimes be afraid to look up at our own icon of Christ, which was also in a dome. It was because the face of Christ in this icon is more severe than in any other icon, for here He is depicted as our final judge. As my mother used to say, 'Christ and the saints see everything.' But our faith tells us that only Christ will judge us."

Father Fortis paused to wipe his forehead with a handkerchief before gripping the edges of the pulpit. *He's struggling*, Worthy thought.

"The gospel talks about two brothers and a father. I am reminded again of being a boy myself and yes, a brother. I remember one time when my older brother—may his memory be eternal—told our father that he'd cleaned his room for the holidays. Even I believed him, but actually, my brother had used a garden rake to sweep his toys under the bed."

A number of parishioners laughed appreciatively, no doubt relieved for the service to be back on a more even keel.

"But my father wasn't easily fooled. He knew my brother even better than I did. He could read his face, and he saw it was a lie. Yes, it was what we might call today a 'white lie,' nothing major or damaging in the long run." Father Fortis wiped his brow again. "God is such a father, although it seems from the media that not many people believe that anymore. So many modern Americans are like the fool described in the Psalms, the one who acted as if there is no God Who watches us. Many of us here this morning might have some doubts about such a God. Our hearts might say, 'If there is such a God, would he not prevent the horrible suffering of our world, such as the murder of our own dear priest?' The ancient Psalmist had an answer for that. 'Surely, God beholds our trouble and misery; God sees it and takes it into His own hand.' As surely as the icon of Christ looks down from the dome in traditional Orthodox churches, so God watches us, whether we are inside St. Cosmas or outside her doors. So no one here should miss the chance to be forgiven by this same judge, for as the fourth evangelist tells us, Christ came to save sinners, not to condemn them." Father Fortis crossed himself and moved back toward the altar.

My God, Worthy thought, *do people know he was just appealing to the killer?* By reflex, Worthy looked down on the heads of those below. If he expected some sign of contrition, someone running screaming from the room or falling on his or her knees, he was disappointed. But he didn't expect that. Not from this killer.

Worthy turned to Allyson. "Want to do some detective work?"

Allyson's eyes widened. "What do you mean?" she whispered.

"I need to get down to the priest's office and wait for Father Nick, but I don't want everyone to see me. That means I need to leave before the last part of this service is over, the memorial for the dead priest. Father Nick said it would take about thirty minutes."

"What do I have to do?"

"Right after the service, go to the back door by the parking lot. You know, where we came in. Stand just outside the door and listen to what people are saying as they leave."

"Won't that be a bit obvious?"

"Just act like you're waiting for someone to pick you up. People tend to ignore someone they don't know. Okay?"

Allyson nodded.

Worthy waited until the part of the memorial service when the metropolitan rose to begin his remarks. He moved quietly down the stairs and made his way to the parish office. Slipping through the door, he stood in the darkness. A candle beneath an icon offered the only light. Some saint sat astride an armored horse in the act of spearing a dragon. The warring figures seemed alive in the flickering light, the dragon's tail writhing, like a barbed vine, toward the saint's leg.

After about twenty minutes of waiting that seemed like twenty hours, Worthy heard a single pair of footsteps pause outside the door. Because it was too early for Father Fortis, he waited for Henderson to enter. But just as suddenly the footsteps retreated, even as another set approached from the opposite direction.

Two knocks, but Worthy remained silent. "Worthy, are you in there?"

Worthy opened the door and let Henderson in. His partner's eyes danced. "Too fucking weird. Just too fucking weird."

"Anyone in the cry room?" Worthy asked.

"No, it was empty."

"How about just now? Did you see anyone in the hallway? Anyone walking away from the door, I mean?"

"Nope, just a group setting up coffee down in that big hall. So, what's it all mean?"

"It means something," Worthy said. "Father Nick doesn't go in for theatrics."

"It freaked people out; I'll say that."

The doorknob turned suddenly, and Father Fortis practically fell through the opening. Shutting the door behind him, he moved quickly toward his desk. "I only have a few minutes. I don't have time to explain everything, but I figured out the diary, Christopher. I figured out the code!"

Worthy tried to check his disappointment. They already knew enough about the diary to conclude it didn't help. But he didn't say anything as his friend opened one drawer after another until he placed his translation of the diary on one side and unrolled architectural drawings on the other.

"I have to get back to the metropolitan. Pray to God I can think up a good story to cover things," he said, as he moved from one drawing to another. "I know it has to be here someplace. Yes, here it is." He lifted one out and placed it on top.

The two men stood on opposite sides of the priest. "What the hell is it?" Henderson said. "Sorry, Father."

"It's a scale drawing of the icons in the sanctuary, Sergeant."

"The icons?" Worthy asked. "I don't follow."

Father Fortis pointed a finger at the left door of the icon screen. "Just as I came out this door on the second procession, something caught my eye. Of course, it's been there all these weeks, but I didn't really see it until today. Just like Father Daniel said."

"Father Daniel?"

"Sorry, my friend. My mind is ablur. Look, every icon has a few Greek letters on them to identify the saint being depicted. So, in this first icon of St. Nicholas, for example, the first letters of the Greek phrase, 'the holy Saint Nicholas' are abbreviated NI."

"NI," Worthy repeated. "But the code has four letters."

"Right. I thought the same thing until I came to the end of the aisle and turned the corner."

"Where the dead priest lost it as well," Henderson said.

"Exactly. I was walking down the side aisle, trying to remember what icon was next—up at the front, I mean. My mind blanked, despite all my years in church. But look at this architectural drawing. St. Nicholas is next to St. John the Baptist, who begins with IO. The next icon over is of Christ, but the lettering on His begins with IC." His finger flew across to the other side of the drawing. "The icon of the Theotokos, the Blessed Virgin Mary, begins with MR. Next to that is the icon of the parish, CO for St. Cosmas. Finally, there is the icon of St. George, GE. Do you see now, Christopher?"

See what? he thought. "So you got letters off the icons. But I don't see how they get us to the four letters in the diary."

Father Fortis silenced Worthy with a hand. "It was when I stopped. That's when I saw how the code worked. I turned the corner and saw what Father Daniel said he noticed. That the icons on the far wall look down on us as we profess. And every one of those has Greek or sometimes English letters as well."

"For example?" Henderson said.

Father Fortis sifted through the drawings again until he found the one of the wall icons. "Here's St. Barbara. That's BA. That's when it all hit me. If someone sits anywhere in the sanctuary, their seat could be identified by lining up the letters from the closest icon on the icon screen and the closest icon from the side wall."

"A grid," Worthy said. It was suddenly all so simple, so obvious. "Father Spiro was worried his mind was slipping, but he didn't want to write out the name. So he used a code to remind himself where someone sat."

"But who the hell sits in the same place in church?" Henderson asked.

" 'Creatures of habit.' That's what Mrs. Nichols said. She always sat in the same place and said most people do. And she's right," Worthy added. "It was the same in the churches I grew up in."

"But how does that help us?" Henderson objected. "Hell, they may sit in the same seat, but we won't know who sits where without photos. And tomorrow—"

"Tomorrow isn't here yet," Worthy said, but he saw the same problem.

"Just a minute," Father Fortis said as he searched through a pile of mail on the edge of the desk. "I forgot about the photos Mr. Bagios took at Father Spiro's funeral. Yes, here they are," he said, pulling out a manila folder and tearing it open. "I couldn't see why they'd be important at the time, but thank God for Mr. Bagios!"

Worthy studied each of the photos as Father Fortis laid them out on the desk. He put aside the close-ups of the casket, leaving a series taken of the sanctuary from the balcony. Would they show enough?

"Oops," Father Fortis said as he rose and hastened toward the door. "The metropolitan is probably on the phone trying to find some replacement for me as we speak. Do we have enough to go on?"

Worthy shrugged. "We'll see, Nick. What's your schedule like this afternoon?"

"Very full, my friend. Brunch with the metropolitan, then take him back to the chancery. After that I'm expected to take communion to several shut-ins. Should I cancel some of that?"

Worthy fought off the pressure of tomorrow's deadline. "No, we want everything to look normal. When is the soonest you can be back here?"

"About three thirty. Can I call you if I get delayed? The metropolitan is one of those slow, ponderous types."

Worthy remembered Allyson waiting for him out in the parking lot. "Let's make it four." He reached in his pocket for his address book. "And you can call me on my daughter's cellphone. She doesn't hate those phones like I do." He gave Father Fortis the number before turning to his partner. "How about you?"

Henderson shook his head as he looked down. "Sorry. We're supposed to take a look at a hospital this afternoon. I'm not free until tonight."

"Come when you can. I got a feeling we're going to be here a while," Worthy said. "Nick, before you leave, tell me those letters again."

"MRAG, NISP, and IOAG. Oh, and you might also check out GESP."

"Where did that last one come from?" Worthy asked.

"It's probably nothing, but it was the last thing Father Spiro wrote in the journal. He put a question mark beside it."

"Really? I thought you said the last entry was about NISP or IOAG."

"I did. But there was these four letters on the next page. I couldn't see how they'd mean anything."

Father Fortis opened the door and was halfway through it when Henderson called after him. "Just a second, Father. The old priest must have devised the code months ago, right?"

"So I know why you stopped there, but why'd he stop right there?"

Father Fortis pulled on his beard. "I hadn't thought about that."

Worthy put his own finger on one of the photos. "I think I know. He stopped there because he'd just passed someone in one of the pews, someone he realized he needed to talk to."

"His killer?" Henderson asked.

"Could be," Worthy said cautiously.

"God, I hope so," Henderson said.

"Amen to that, my son. Now, wish me luck."

"Just a second, Father," Henderson called after him.

Father Fortis' head reappeared in the doorway. "I thought the idea was not to raise suspicions."

"Fine, fine, Father, but what are the chances you'd stop exactly where he did?"

Father Fortis blushed. "Maybe we should leave that in the mystery of God."

CHAPTER NINETEEN

———◆———

"**I** STOOD BY THE BACK DOOR, JUST as you said," Allyson told her father, "but all I heard was people asking the same thing I want to know. Why did your friend, Father Nick, stop like that in the service?"

Worthy pulled into the Steak and Shake parking lot and turned off the motor. People wearing what he'd been raised to recognize as church clothes streamed into the restaurant. "To answer that, I'm going to have to tell you some things about the case. I'd rather not do that in there," he said.

"Then let's go through the drive-up and sit out here."

"What about the movie?"

Without looking at her watch, Allyson replied, "We still have time."

Sitting with their burgers and an order of fries between them, Worthy explained about Father Spiro's diary, how he'd been mistaken about Peggy Hagarty, and how Father Fortis had somehow solved the code in the middle of the procession that morning.

Allyson took a long sip from her shake, her brow furrowed. "So the code describes where people sit in the church. Does that mean you know who killed him?"

"It's not that simple. Henderson and I have some photos that might help, but we won't know anything for sure until Nick can join us. I'm to meet with him later this afternoon."

"Can I come?"

"Look, Ally, it's probably going to be boring. Besides, I can't. It's against regulations."

Allyson rolled down her window, pulled a pickle off her burger, and threw it outside. "Now you're going to make up some numbers like thirty-four, dash seven, Section B, about how children of police can't look at evidence."

Worthy smiled. "Something like that, I suppose,"

"At least tell me what you've figured out so far. Who knows, maybe I'll solve it."

"Be my guest," Worthy said. He'd like someone to make sense of what Henderson and he had puzzled over. "We learned enough to find out Father Fortis was right. The code matched some people we knew about."

"Vague. Give me details."

"One series of letters matched a woman we'd already talked to. We also matched up one of the codes with this strange little guy we'd interviewed. Another part of the code showed us a teenaged kid, a boy who has his mother pretty worried."

"Could he—?"

"No, he couldn't have done it, and we're pretty sure the odd duck didn't do it either. But we had one other piece of the code. That proved more interesting. Also more confusing."

Allyson munched on her burger. "So, spill it."

"The old priest wrote one other piece of code on the last page of the diary. No comment, no explanation. But we think we're able to match it with a section of three or four rows of pews. All together, we have about a dozen people in that area. Some of the people we don't know. That's why we need Nick's help."

"But some people you do know," Allyson pressed.

"Some we do. One of the photos shows pretty clearly a woman from the parish council sitting next to a doctor in the parish. He's also on the parish council. Sitting pretty close by is a rabbi."

"A rabbi? Sounds like we're playing *Clue*. The rabbi did it in the sanctuary with the menorah."

"The rabbi is innocent. Trust me. But then we looked at another photo taken from a different angle and realized some other people were sitting close enough to be considered in the area. There was a family of five—three kids looking to be in high school or college—but their backs are to the camera in each photo. Next to them are two people who shouldn't have been there at all. Henderson spotted them."

"Really? Maybe the killers?"

"Not likely. One is the police superintendent and with him is the newspaper reporter." Even now, in repeating aloud what Henderson had discovered, Worthy struggled to make sense of it.

"The bitch who wrote that article about you?"

Worthy nodded, surprised at his daughter's grasp of the details.

"Look, maybe she did kill the priest," Allyson said excitedly. "She needed a good story to boost her career, so she strangled—"

"Stop right there. This isn't the movies. She didn't kill the priest to get a scoop, and she isn't sleeping with my boss. At least, I don't think she is. Still, the photo explains why he wanted me to let her in on the case."

"But what are the chances they'd be sitting in that same area?" Allyson asked, not knowing she was repeating Henderson's earlier question.

"Just a coincidence. We know the killer is from the congregation. At least, that's what the diary suggests."

"Quite a coincidence."

"Nick said it was in the mystery of God."

"Except you don't believe in that," Allyson said, gazing out the windshield. "Do you?"

She didn't look at him. "I don't know. Sometimes I guess I do. Dad? If you don't believe in God, do you still feel bad about things, things you wish you'd done differently?"

He thought he heard a slight tremor in her voice. "Yeah, sure. That doesn't go away."

Allyson sat in silence, ignoring her sandwich, before turning toward him. "I'm not sure I believe there's a God out there, not some angry big being, anyway. But sometimes I get the feeling there's someone out there just wishing better things for me. Do you know what I mean?"

What am I to say, and who am I to say a thing? Worthy asked himself. He felt like the two of them were back at the restaurant up north, just waiting for him to say the wrong thing. "I think I know what you mean. Maybe that's just our consciences."

"Maybe," Allyson replied, not sounding convinced. She returned to her food for a moment before adding, "And your friend Nick believes, right? I mean, he has to, doesn't he?"

"I never think of Nick *having* to believe in God. He just does."

"So does he want you to believe again?"

Worthy fought down an urge to ask Allyson to change the subject. Two and a half years before, he'd had no idea where Allyson was hiding. His only hope, day after anxious day, was that she was all right and would one day come home. One night she had done just that, coming through the door without explanation. His hope had changed. Perhaps one day she would again want to talk to him, to stop blaming him for everything wrong in her life. Since the trip to the cabin, Allyson was talking to him again. How could he complain that everything she wanted to talk about tore at old scars?

"I'm sure Nick would like me to believe in all that again, but he doesn't push. He never does."

"But he prays, right?"

Worthy laughed. "Of course."

"I mean about you both solving this case."

"I guess," Worthy replied, hearing again Father Fortis' last comment about the mystery of God.

"So he thinks God is up there, out there, or in there somewhere, wanting you to catch the killer."

Worthy shrugged. "Maybe."

"You don't sound so sure of that," Allyson pressed.

"It's just that I don't understand exactly what Nick's God is like. He confuses me at times."

"What do you mean? God is just God, isn't he?" Her voice sounded insistent.

"Nick and I don't talk about things like that, but maybe it's what I've picked up by being around him. I think he sees God as this mysterious being who should be respected. How can I put it? It's like I could never imagine anybody in his church wearing one of those stupid religious T-shirts. You know, the ones that mimic beer commercials and say 'this blood's for you' beneath some cross."

"Some kids wear those things to school. I think they're disgusting," Allyson said. "But what's confusing about that?"

"Well, sometimes Nick gives me the feeling that the God he believes in is a trickster who makes odd things happen or leaves little clues around."

"So he'd say God wants this killer to be caught? I suppose, being a priest, he'd say God wants to punish him."

Worthy shook his head. "That's not Nick, somehow. I think he'd say God wants us to find the killer because that's what the killer needs—to stop running, to stop getting away with it, and maybe to be prevented from killing someone else."

Allyson was silent again for a moment. "Wow," she said, "like there's that someone out there wanting something better ... even for a killer."

Worthy didn't know what to say. So he said nothing.

Father Fortis fumed as he drove toward his apartment. The metropolitan had been a carbon copy of his abbot, pontificating widely on matters ranging from the challenges of parish life to the upcoming presidential election. First of all, he had no intention of considering parish ministry. No, the monastery was his true home, even though his own abbot had questioned him openly on more than one occasion about whether he would be better suited to life "outside." And secondly, he had never voted Republican in his life, and he wasn't about to now just because that party's candidate had made it known he began each day with prayer. Pious statements like that always made him nervous, especially from someone who seemed intent on sending troops all over the world.

Father Fortis checked his watch. He had just enough time to drop by his apartment for a shower before getting to the church. Then he and Worthy could finally determine what the events of the day meant. Would the code, now solved, point a finger at anyone? Was that asking too much of Mr. Bagios' photos?

The metropolitan had, as he'd expected, quizzed him about his faltering in the liturgy. *Thank God*, he thought, the metropolitan had apparently forgotten that the shock of the morning had eerily replicated Father Spiro's last Sunday. And thank God, also, that he'd been able to explain his own actions of the morning to the metropolitan with a minimum of lies. Feeling a bit lightheaded from some medication and the stress of the memorial was the excuse that he'd finally come up with.

Just as he was slowing for the freeway exit, his cellphone rang.

"Father Fortis?" The voice sounded scratchy.

"You'll have to speak up," he replied crossly. "The connection is bad."

"Sorry, Father. My name is Alex Portis. You met my mother. She's just been taken to Community North. It looks like she's had a stroke. I was wondering if I could ask you to … to come to the hospital. It doesn't look good."

"Of course, of course," Father Fortis said with a pang of guilt. "I can be there in about a half hour. I just need to stop by the church for a few things."

"For the chrism—the holy oil? Yes, please, Father. I hate to ask, but I think we're at that point. It would mean so much to Mother and to me, of course. Thank you, thank you."

Father Fortis took the exit, drove under the freeway, and reentered it to head back to St. Cosmas. No telling how long this would delay the work on the photos, he thought, as he hunted in his coat for the phone number Worthy had given him. Could the timing be any worse? Worthy had less than a day left on the case, and now his friend would be sitting twiddling his thumbs waiting for him to finish at the hospital. But he had no choice. He said a brief prayer for Athena Portis even as he dialed the number Worthy had given him that morning.

After three rings, he heard a young woman's voice. "This is Ally. I'll get back to you soon. Leave a message."

Great, Father Fortis thought. *Just great.* "Ally, this is a message for your father. Tell him Father Fortis has an emergency at Community North. He can reach me there. I'll be in Mrs. Portis' room. She just had a stroke. Thanks."

He ended the call and tried to relax as he continued on toward St. Cosmas.

The day might still turn out well. Hadn't he heard that situations involving elderly being brought to hospitals often turned out to be less serious than first thought? By the time he parked by the side door of the darkened church, his mood had brightened. It would only take him a few minutes to retrieve his vestments and the holy oil and be on his way. An hour or two at the hospital with the Portis family would still leave them the rest of the evening to work through the new clues. How quickly he'd forgotten his own thoughts of the morning—that the case was unfolding in the mystery of God.

He put his key in the lock. *How funny*, he thought. The janitor had left the door open.

THE COMEDY ALLYSON HAD CHOSEN FOR a movie had no chance of holding Worthy's attention. Allyson's choice of conversation over lunch had only managed to raise the old unanswered questions about her running away. What had happened to her? Something, obviously, that left her feeling guilty, but what? He wished he could repeat her words to him—"Vague. I need details." But he couldn't ask for that. Over a burger and fries in his car, she'd come closer than ever before to shedding light on her disappearance, but he couldn't rush her.

He glanced at the luminous dial on his watch. Three o'clock. Father Fortis should be close to wrapping up his duties with the metropolitan. After the movie was over, he'd drop Allyson off at the house. If traffic was as light as it usually was on Sundays, he could make it back to the church on time. The antics on screen surrendered in Worthy's mind to Mr. Bagios' photos from Father Spiro's funeral. Mrs. Filis had sat with the cardiologist on the parish council. Dr. Pappas, wasn't it? Could Father Spiro have meant one of them by the code? *Maybe*, he thought, as he shifted his weight and tried to find a comfortable place for his long legs. But even as he thought it, he knew he was committing the mistake of premature assumption. There had to be ten people he couldn't identify sitting nearby in the same photo. What if Nick didn't know them either?

Allyson poked his leg.

"Sorry," he said, shifting them again.

"No," she whispered as she handed him her phone. "I just checked my phone. Caller ID. Your friend, the priest, left a message."

"What do I do?" he whispered, staring at the tiny lit window.

Allyson rolled her eyes before explaining what he needed to do to retrieve the message. "But they'll throw us out of here if you don't take care of it in the lobby," she added.

Out in the lobby, he followed Allyson's directions and put the phone to his ear, managing only to catch the end of the message. He hit the button again and this time heard Father Fortis explain the emergency with Mrs. Portis, his need to stop by the church, and his regrets that their meeting might be delayed.

Worthy returned Allyson's phone and returned to his seat, the hope he'd felt earlier in the day fading. More delays and it wouldn't even matter that the code had been solved. He settled down in his seat, trying to pick up the thread of the movie. The lead guy was dropping suitcases and bowling balls out of a car and the girl was driving madly, even as a cop car behind them swerved unsuccessfully to avoid the obstacles. Losing control, the cop car went airborne, only to land among the ducks in a pond. The audience in the theater laughed uproariously, as they always did when his profession was made to look foolish.

The two cops were swimming away from their car, unaware of the angry ducks in pursuit. For the second time that day, a sense of dread gripped him. *I'm missing something*, he thought. He thought back through the day, to the events during the service, to listening to Father Fortis' explanation as to why he'd stopped where he did, to the matching of the code with the funeral photos. All of that was good news. Was it simply the fear that all of that would be wasted if they ran out of time, or had something happened in that litany of good news that was bringing up this sense of dread?

The lead duck on the screen landed full force on the head of the cop, dumping him again into the water. Again the audience erupted in laughter, while Worthy's eyes went wide with realization. He jumped from the seat, Allyson in tow.

"What's going on?" she said, pulling against him.

"I'll tell you in the lobby," he whispered, continuing to pull her harder.

In the lobby, he turned toward his daughter. "We've got to go. No, let me have your phone, Ally."

"Why?" she asked, even as she handed it to him.

"How do I get information on this?"

Allyson explained, even as she looked at her Dad as if he were crazy.

"It's about something I forgot. There were other footsteps."

"What are you talking about?"

He dialed information and asked for the number of Community North hospital. "While I was waiting for Nick in his office, there were these other footsteps. Not Henderson's. Someone else's."

"But it's a big church," Allyson said. "There were lots of people."

He heard a voice on the other end, giving the hospital's name. "This is Lieutenant Worthy of the Detroit Police Department. I need some information right away. Has a Mrs. Athena Portis been admitted there in the last two hours?"

"I'm sorry, we're not allowed to give out that type of information."

"Look, this is an emergency. Give me your supervisor."

"She'll just tell you the same thing. I don't mean to frustrate you, but you have to understand that people sometimes use false names to try to get confidential information from us. I'd suggest you call the family, Lieutenant."

He glared at the phone before handing it to his daughter. "I don't know what I'm doing with this damn thing. Can you get me the number of Athena Portis quick as you can?"

"Portis? Sure."

It seemed to take forever before Allyson talked to an operator and dialed the number.

"So why am I doing this?" she asked.

"You know what it's like to be a detective, Ally? Ninety-nine percent of the time, you hope you're right, and then there's the one percent when you hope to God you're totally wrong. That one percent is now."

She handed the phone to him. "Let's hope you're wrong then," she said as she handed him the phone.

On the other end, he heard a female voice. "Hello, this is the Portis residence."

"Is this Mrs. Siametes?"

"Yes. Who is speaking?"

"It's Lieutenant Worthy. I visited with Father Fortis a couple of weeks ago."

"Oh, yes, Lieutenant. I remember. How are you?"

"I need to know if Mrs. Portis was taken to the hospital today."

"What?"

"Did she have a stroke or something, and was she taken to the hospital?"

"No, Lieutenant. Why?"

"Shit," Worthy said, handing the phone to Allyson even as he pulled her toward the door.

"Where're we going?"

"Back to the church. I forgot that the killer was probably in church this morning and saw the whole thing. I think Father Fortis spooked him."

CHAPTER TWENTY

———— ◆ ————

A s soon as Father Fortis stepped into his office, something made him instinctively step backward.

"Come in, Father," the voice said. "I was hoping you'd hear my confession."

Father Fortis turned on the light but nothing happened.

"I don't think that will be necessary, Father."

From the candle burning below the icon of St. George, Father Fortis saw something glistening in the visitor's lap. The voice sounded familiar, but his brain was lagging behind.

"I don't know how you got in here, but I'm needed at the hospital. An emergency."

"Mrs. Portis with her stroke," the person said, waving the gun at him. "Why don't you sit down, Father?"

Father Fortis came into the office and walked around his desk. He slumped into his chair, where he could see clearly the person who had tricked him on the phone. Of all the possible suspects in Father Spiro's murder, this man had never been on Father Fortis' mental list.

"Relax, Father," the man said. "I don't think I'll need this," he said, lifting a gun, "but I wanted to make sure we'd have our little chat."

"Dr. Stanos, right?"

"Call me John. And you, as I remember, are Nick. Right?"

Father Fortis didn't say anything, his brain racing. Why would Stanos, a history professor, want to kill his priest? He thought of the icon exhibit coming up at Allgemein. No, that couldn't be it. What else was there? Something Father Daniel had told him came back. He'd been assigned by old Father Spiro to work with Stanos in training the altar boys. The altar boys … the altar boys.

Suddenly, Father Fortis made the connection. The boy who came to Father Spiro about his sexual identity fears must have been an altar boy.

"I found your performance this morning spellbinding. At first, I thought you were play-acting, trying to see if I'd bolt for the door. But then, I thought, 'Our new priest isn't that good an actor.' No, I think you figured out something this morning. Something about Father Spiro's untimely, and may I add unnecessary, death."

"You mean his murder, don't you?"

"Patience, Nick, patience. Now, what could you have figured out this morning? That's what I've been wondering all day. What does this monk know, or think he knows? Here I am, thoroughly enjoying your chanting when you stop a few rows past me, exactly where Father Spiro stopped. Did I say how much I was enjoying your voice? Your Greek is flawless, so well-cadenced, so effortless. Really, Nick, don't you think it a sin to hide your gifts in a monastery?"

Father Fortis didn't respond.

"Then I watched you as you took up the chant again. Will you look back at me? No, you're too interested in your policeman friend, who's nearly falling out of the balcony."

"Perhaps I should warn you that Lieutenant Worthy is due here any moment."

"Nick, really. How are we going to have an honest confession if you persist in lying? I believe he thinks you're at the hospital."

"I will hear your confession, Dr. Stanos. If I'm right about Lieutenant Worthy, we don't have much time for you to unburden your soul of this terrible sin."

Stanos laughed uproariously. "Terrible sin? Unburden my soul? Do I sound like someone drowning in guilt?"

Father Fortis studied the man before him. How proficient would a history professor be with a handgun? Yet the man was clearly calm, his tone playful. Too dangerous in his present state to find out. Maybe he could ruffle his confidence at bit.

"You must know the gravity of your sin, of killing someone who brought Christ's forgiveness to you every Sunday. You stand in the shoes of Judas, Dr. Stanos. Your gun can't change that."

Stanos leaned forward, gazing intently at Father Fortis. "I told you already that I don't expect to use this. You see, I'm here to offer you a chance to understand a tragic event beyond the normal issues of fault and guilt. The truth is I killed Father Spiro in self-defense."

"Self-defense? Father Spiro was an old man, while you're obviously still quite fit. Are you telling me he attacked you, and you were forced to strangle him?"

"Nick, Nick. Please try to transcend the surface appearance of things. If someone breaks into a home and holds a gun on that family, would anyone charge the father of murder if he managed to take the gun away and kill the intruder?"

"A ludicrous comparison. Father Spiro—"

Stanos cut him off. "Father Spiro was intent on destroying my entire life— my reputation, my position in the community, and my family's livelihood—as surely as if he was holding that gun."

"You make no sense."

"Sense? What sense does this make? The old man had an appointment with the dean of my college for that Wednesday. Do you know why?"

"We'd been led to believe it concerned the icon exhibit," Father Fortis replied. "I can see now that it was something far more serious."

"Spiro asked to see me that Tuesday morning, and I assumed the same thing. My second guess is that he wanted to discuss his retirement. After all, that faltering in the liturgy made things pretty clear to everyone. I came, intent on assisting in any way I could. I guess you could say I came in a Christian mood."

Father Fortis pondered the comment. Was it possible Stanos still didn't know why Father Spiro had stopped that Sunday? "Don't mock the dead, Dr. Stanos. You came to kill him."

Stanos rose slightly, his hand slamming down on the edge of the desk. "No! And please have the courtesy to let me finish before you decide who was mocking whom." He sat down again, the smile returning. "It was a beautiful January morning, cold but bracing. Perfect weather for gloves. Lucky for me, you might say."

Father Fortis shook his head. "Instead of these rationalizations, I beg you to confess your sins and throw yourself on the mercy of God. Things could be … difficult after the police arrive."

"Oh, my, perhaps I underestimated you, Nick. You're sounding as obstinate as old Spiro." Stanos paused ominously, gazing down at the handgun.

This isn't good, Father Fortis thought. *I have to keep him talking on the odd chance Christopher will come through that door.* "You left a clue, you know," he said abruptly. "That's why we knew it was someone in the parish."

Stanos' eyes rose from the gun. "Don't insult me," he sneered. "The only clues I left pointed to a robbery gone amok."

"Then you left the clue unconsciously, Doctor. Perhaps you wanted to be caught after all."

"Are you stalling, Nick?"

For the first time, Father Fortis detected a break in Stanos' confident tone. "Not at all. After killing Father Spiro, you bent down and straightened his epitrachelion."

"What?" Stanos snorted.

"It's right there in the police photo. Your neatness tripped you up, Doctor."

"Not me, Nick, not me. I took a mental picture before I left and everything looked perfectly natural."

"But murder isn't natural. People do strange things."

"No! It wasn't me!" Stanos lapsed into silence for a moment. "But I believe you. Otherwise, why didn't the police stay in the projects, leaving you and me to plan a fitting memorial for Spiro?"

Stanos gazed down again at the gun. "You see, none of this had to happen. An old man gets a crazy idea in his head, and he decides to destroy my whole life, not to mention my family's. What could I do?"

"You mention Father Spiro's crazy idea. Let me make a guess. A young man, an altar boy, confesses to Father Spiro that he is experiencing sexual confusion. He hints that someone close to him encouraged this, but he won't say who."

Stanos glared up at him.

"You see, I lied to the parish council," Father Fortis continued. "We found that missing book." He waited a moment for the information to sink in. "It turned out to be a confidential confessional diary. The boy's pain is all over it."

"But not *my* name, Nick, or I'd be talking to the police instead of you right now. I want to tell you something, and then I want you to tell me if you think I'm guilty. For twenty years, I've worked with the altar boys here. Never did I violate that trust. Do you want me to count how many have grown up and asked me to be godparent to their children? They came to me when they couldn't even talk to their parents or old Spiro. Sometimes, I was the only one who knew about their girlfriends missing a period, their pot smoking, their brushes with the law. Does that sound like someone who 'confuses' boys?"

Father Fortis remained silent.

"Like I said, I came here that morning and found him by the altar. He was looking all sorrowful, big sad eyes, and I thought someone in the parish had died. He told me he wanted to give me a chance to confess my sin before he went to the dean at the college. So I sat in the front pew, my gloves and coat still on, this coldness seeping into my body. I'm sure I shivered. I thought the old guy had really lost it. I asked him to tell me what he thought I'd done that was horrible enough to cost my family everything."

Father Fortis noticed the lack of remorse as Stanos relived that morning. It crossed his mind that revisiting those moments might be a danger to his own safety. Stanos was too bright not to be considering his options with a second priest barring his path.

"He said I had lured one of the altar boys into homosexuality," Stanos continued. "I laughed at the charge, but he just gave me those sad eyes. That's when I knew he really believed it! I kept asking myself, 'Why does this man want to destroy me?' I asked for evidence. He stood up there by the icons and asked me, like some cheap talk-show host, if I'd hugged boys on occasion or if I'd put my arm around their shoulders. Imagine if you were asked that question, Nick. Given the climate in this country, a rumor like that would drive you right out of this parish."

"So you're claiming the accusation was completely false?"

Stanos stared at him. "The truth is this: a certain percentage of all boys will be oriented that way. This old, senile priest, who should have retired years ago, was isolating a few minutes out of my entire life, minutes of great ambiguity. If I offered back some neutral acceptance to a few who were becoming aware of this orientation, is that damnable or commendable? Look, Nick, I'm not gay or even bisexual."

Father Fortis considered the claim and then realized that Stanos was telling the truth. "No, I can see that you're something quite different, someone obsessed with being adored. You crave being adored by your students, by Dr. Boras, by the altar boys, and by this troubled boy. Yes, I see it now. The boy's physical attraction to you didn't excite you in return; rather, it simply flattered you. You enjoyed his devotion, didn't you?"

"Spare me the pop psychology," Stanos replied in a hoarse whisper. "We're talking about a few minutes … a very few, seen in a very jaundiced light. Think back over your own life, Father. Could you pass such a test?"

Father Fortis tried to imagine some plan of escape. Stanos was obviously nearing the end of his story, and then what? The man sat, gun in hand, between himself and the door. The desk prevented him from throwing his considerable weight at Stanos and praying for the best. His only hope was to keep him talking. "So why didn't you simply threaten Father Spiro with libel?"

"Oh, come on. Every man has his enemies, especially in academia. In the jockeying for recognition, innuendoes and outright lies abound. The hint of a rumor like this would sink me."

There was a note of wistfulness in Stanos' voice. "The college is all about the pursuit of truth, unless it's about a faculty member's personal life. When old Spiro wouldn't see reason, I knew one of us would die that day."

"And so you strangled him."

Stanos studied his face. "It was an unavoidable tragedy, but it was his own fault. That's what I saw clearly that morning and what has remained clear for me ever since. By the way, that's where you and I differ, Nick."

"I don't follow."

"Ever since we began our talk, I've felt your compassion for me. At times like these, Nick, you must remember that compassion clouds reason. I see you don't yet understand. Let me put it this way. My guess is you've lost sleep trying to help this parish along while you help your lame friend, the cop, keep his job. Word has it he's not doing so well there. Imagine while you've been tossing and turning at night that I've been sleeping soundly. Even that very first night. No, I'm not lying. I got up the next day, looked at myself in the mirror as I shaved and went off to work. Same captivating lectures. If anything, maybe I'm a bit wittier. Do you think that's a good cover?"

"I think you're describing life in hell. Is that what all this bragging is about—to convince me you have no remorse?"

"Reason it out, Nick. I was Spiro's angel of mercy."

Father Fortis rose from the chair. "You were his killer! Admit it."

Stanos gave him a knowing smile. "Reason, Nick, reason. I gave him a better death than he had coming to him naturally, slipping away as he was into Alzheimer's. I gave him a martyr's death." Stanos paused a moment, then continued, "I'll tell you something no one else will ever know. He never struggled. I caught him by the vestment and started to pull. The old man just relaxed, absolutely relaxed in my grip, and then he just smiled. We did it together, Nick."

A shiver went through Father Fortis' frame. "Why are you telling me this if you don't want to confess?"

"I want to give you a chance. You see, I trust you can do what I've done. Call it a confession, if you like, but put reason ahead of emotion. Picture what I'm telling you. See Spiro's smile as he saw the truth too. He received a good death—quick, almost painless. See it clearly, and you'll admit that no one will benefit from my life being destroyed. Keep what I've told you in the confidence of the confessional, and let us all move forward."

"And the police? Do you honestly think they'll give up? Do you really believe the city will let them?"

Stanos smiled. "I have always assumed the worst that could happen is the police will yank some good-for-nothings off the streets. So, you see, your silence means it's unlikely they'll ever solve it."

My silence, Father Fortis thought. Yes, that was what Stanos had come for, to make sure one way or another that he remained silent. Perhaps it was time to think of dying as faithfully as Father Spiro had done. But he would not go smiling. If he was to die, he must find some way for Stanos' identity to be known.

"So, either I damn my soul as a priest, or you kill me. Is that it?" he asked.

Stanos shrugged and lifted his gun. From down the hall came the sound of the side door opening, then closing with its characteristic bang. Stanos rose quickly, moving behind the door. Father Fortis' brain raced, searching for a way to alert Worthy to the trap he was walking into.

But it was a woman's voice that echoed down the hallway. "Are you there, Father?"

What is Mrs. Filis doing here? he thought.

The woman stood in the doorway, her eyes seeking his. "Oh Father, I'm so glad you're here. I walked over to tell you something ... about Father Spiro."

From behind the door, Stanos motioned with the gun for Father Fortis to get rid of her.

This is my chance, Father Fortis thought. Stanos had been in control of matters for the last five weeks, throwing a brick through a window and directing the investigation back to the projects whenever they'd gotten too close. But he hadn't planned on this interruption. Should he yell for Mrs. Filis to run for help? No, she'd never understand in time, and then where would they be? Better if he walked calmly toward her and suddenly lurched at the door, slamming it back onto Stanos. Yes, he would throw his weight on him and take his chances. He rose, hesitating for a second to plan his route.

But Mrs. Filis acted first and changed everything. "It was me, Father," she said, stepping through the doorway. "When you stopped this morning in the liturgy, it all came back to me. What I told the police was wrong. I tried to tell you this morning, but you weren't in the office. You see, when I saw him lying before the altar, I ... I straightened the epitrachelion." She reached with her hand to close it behind her.

"Oh, my Lord, John, you scared me. What are you doing?"

Father Fortis heard the splintering sound of bone as the barrel of the gun came down full force on the skull of the woman. Racing around the desk, he banged his leg on its corner, the impact of which sent him cascading to the floor. As he struggled to his feet and pushed himself forward, he saw Mrs. Filis totter for a second, losing consciousness just as the gun barrel hit the side of her head a second time.

Father Fortis dove over the crumpled body of the woman, his full weight driving into Stanos' stomach. He heard the air go out of the man just as the gun barrel glanced off the back of his head. The room began to swim, but he was giddy with the thought that Stanos didn't want to shoot the gun. He grabbed around Stanos' waist and locked his hands, squeezing as he had in his wrestling days. The delicious memory of lifting an opponent off the mat came over him. It was the last thing he remembered before the bullet ripped through his shoulder and headed for his heart.

CHAPTER TWENTY-ONE

———————◆———————

WORTHY PULLED UP BESIDE THE SIDE door of St. Cosmas and parked behind Father Fortis' car. *One car*, he thought, his heart leaping forward in the hope that there'd been a simple mistake. Maybe Nick left the wrong name in the voice message. He would find his friend safely in his office, gathering what he needed for the hospital call.

"Ally, I want you to stay here."

Allyson folded her arms across her chest. "Why can't I go too? Regulations, again?"

"Look, Ally, it's probably nothing. You see, Nick's car is the only one here. I'll be back before you know it."

As he exited the driver's seat, Ally called after him. "Where's your gun?"

He realized he'd misread her. She wasn't being moody. She was scared. "Really, it's just routine," he said, forcing a smile. "Lock the doors if you want."

The normalcy of finding the side door open added to his sense of relief. He closed the door quietly behind him and pondered calling out for Nick. But the silence of the church hushed him, and he jogged toward the office. Still no sound. *Maybe Nick's in the sanctuary*, he thought.

Walking through the secretary's office, he knocked lightly on the inner door. Nothing. He tried the handle and found it locked. He turned to head for the sanctuary, feeling the hair on the back of his neck stand up. Was that a groan? He pushed against the door and felt the frame give slightly. He heard the groan again, but why did it sound like a woman's voice?

His chest tight, his breathing shallow, Worthy stepped back and hit the door full force with his shoulder. It flew open, and he reached in to flip the light switch. Nothing. But he could see two bodies lying on the floor in pools of blood. He raced toward Father Fortis, who was lying oddly on his stomach. Lying next to him, the woman groaned again. *What has she done?* he thought. *What has this crazy woman done?*

He fell to his knees and felt his friend's neck for a pulse. *There it is*, he thought with relief, before noticing how weak it was. Worthy scanned his friend's body, following the blood to its source—a small hole high in Nick's shoulder. An entry wound, but no visible exit. Not good.

Next to him, the woman started mumbling. *Where is her gun?* he thought, realizing his own danger. He watched her rouse herself slightly, wondering how and then why Nick had done so much damage to her head. Blood flowed freely from wounds buried in her white hair down onto her cheek.

He recognized her face from the photos of the morning and from the parish council meeting. She had sat in the GESP section of the photo. She was the one who'd sat next to the cardiologist. "Keep your hands where I can see them," he ordered.

"He shot Father," she mumbled, pulling herself up on her elbows.

"Where's the gun. Just tell me where your gun is."

"*He* did it," she insisted, her voice weakening. "He's gone."

Worthy stared at the woman. "He? Who did? Who's gone?" *Oh, my God*, he thought. *It was someone else.*

The woman's eyes fluttered, then rolled up into her head. He took her hands and felt the life go out of them. *Who is she talking about?* he thought, as he ran to the phone and dialed 911. As he gave the information, the woman's body slumped sideways and fell back to the floor. The pool of blood on the carpet beneath Nick's body was growing larger.

He ran to the side door and called out to Allyson. *She can't hear me*, he thought, as he saw her bouncing in the seat to music on the radio. He ran out to his side of the car and knocked on the window.

Allyson jumped, looking at him with relief for a brief moment before her eyes grew wide. His window eased down.

"Daddy, you're bleeding," she gasped.

He nearly buckled with emotion, first seeing Nick lying in a pool of blood, now hearing his daughter address him in a way she hadn't for so many years. "It's not me, honey. Nick's been shot, and there's a woman not doing too well. Ally, I'm going to need your help."

Tears streamed down Allyson's face as she sat motionless in the car. Slowly, her door opened, and then she was running around the car to her father.

"Oh, my God, Daddy. Is he going to live?"

"Sure, sure he is. It's not that bad," he lied. "But I need you to apply some pressure to the wound while I check out some things." As they ran together toward the church, he pulled out his handkerchief. "You can use this. It's just until the paramedics come."

He led her down the hallway toward the office. "Ally, this looks worse than it is. You believe me, don't you?"

Allyson nodded. "I'm so sorry, Daddy," she said. "I'm so sorry."

He went into the office first, holding her hand. "Yeah, me too, Ally," he said, dropping to his knees. He took the handkerchief and placed it on the wound. "Just hold it right here. Push on it a bit, but not too hard. Okay?"

Allyson knelt beside him, putting her hand gently where his had been. "Is that woman dead?" she whispered.

"I don't know, Ally," he said, even though he did know. "Just keep the pressure on Nick, okay?" He rose and moved toward the door.

"Daddy, where are you going?"

He heard the alarm in her voice, knew he was wrong for making her deal with something like this, but he had a job to do. "I don't think she did this. I have to see if whoever did left any evidence behind. Before the paramedics roll their equipment over everything, I need to look things over. I'll be just down the hall. Do you want me to shut the door?"

With a shaking voice, she said, "No, don't. How long will you be?"

"You're doing just fine there, honey," he said. "I'll be back before the ambulance arrives. Three or four minutes, I promise."

His mind raced as he took another look around the bloody room, then quickly glanced over the secretary's office. Father Fortis had been lured back to the church by the killer and had walked, good priest that he was, into the trap. But what excuse did he have, an experienced cop, for figuring things out so late? The killer had obviously left them to die and was probably miles away by now. The plan had already worked with the woman, he thought, shuddering at the image of Father Fortis lying unconscious, his lifeblood seeping into the carpet.

He backtracked down the hallway to the side door, studying the carpet as he went. *Nothing*. At the door, he bent down and studied the lock. No signs of scratches. He'd have to wait for forensics to check for prints. He stood and looked down the hallway in the other direction. *Where does this go?* he wondered, before remembering that the kitchen and gymnasium led to the parking lot behind.

Of course, he thought. Whoever it was probably came in the back. When Father Fortis had driven up, he wouldn't have seen another car parked back there. And there were exits onto two side streets. The killer could easily have driven away into the neighborhood, hardly noticed.

He moved slowly toward the back door, pushing aside his promise to Allyson. The paramedics would be here any minute, he told himself. Moving into the dark gymnasium, he thought of the photos he'd pored over with Nick only a few hours earlier. The killer's luck was holding. Worthy had to face the fact that if his friend didn't make it, the photos and the code would be useless.

"Hang on, Nick," he whispered, his shoes squeaking on the gym floor. Without his friend, there might be no trail to pick up, no address, no make of car, nothing more than two new bodies. The killer could be anyone, maybe not even someone from the photos, and he could be anywhere by now.

He walked toward the glass door ahead of him, sunlight flooding through the panes. Even before he looked out, he knew what he would find—an empty lot with too many tire prints from the morning service to be of any help.

He stood for a moment in the light, squinting out at the emptiness before dejectedly bending down to check the lock. *No marks again*, he thought. Did that mean the killer had a key? It wasn't much of a trail, but at least it was something.

He rose, surprised how long the ambulances were taking. He turned back toward the office, two emotions oddly warring for dominance. Soon, the paramedics' faces would tell him about his friend's prospects. He could see where the bullet had entered Nick, but without knowing the angle, he couldn't tell if it had ripped through his organs or was sitting benignly in some muscle mass.

But along with his worry, he also felt a sense of pride in his daughter. She may have called him Daddy, as she had when she was a child, but she'd behaved as an adult. She'd walked into a scene from which many would have turned and fled.

As he started his walk back to the office, a third emotion rose within him, a particular anxiety he'd experienced twice before this day. Or was this more a foreboding born of experience? He was missing something regarding the killer, but it was coming to him very slowly. *Yes, that's it*, he thought as his eyes struggled to adjust to the darkness of the gymnasium. *The killer is the careful type.* What would he do if he was unsure of having finished off the two people in the office? What if the killer heard him coming into the church and was forced to leave the scene before he'd finished tying up loose ends?

Worthy paused in the darkness to ponder what the thought meant, so he sensed more than saw the figure coming at him from out of the shadows. He felt a sharp thud, then pain radiating from the top of his skull, as if a piece of the ceiling had fallen onto him. Then the floor rushed up toward him and everything went black.

WORTHY HOVERED ON THE EDGE OF consciousness, his eyes closed, aware only that a hand was going through his pockets as he lay on the gym floor.

Pain radiated from the top of his head down through his neck to his right shoulder and arm.

He heard his car keys jiggle in the hands of the man over him. *I have to play like I'm still out*, he thought, *and wait for my chance.* He didn't dare open his eyes as he waited for his attacker to decide his next move. He tried to wiggle his toes and felt them respond. His right arm, however, felt limp.

He heard the man get to his feet and swear. *Why doesn't he shoot me?* Worthy wondered. The church was quiet. Was that the reason? Had the ambulance already arrived, and did the killer know a shot would be heard?

The man grabbed him by the legs and began to drag him off the gym floor. Did he risk taking a peek at the killer's face? He opened his right eye a slit and saw the man's red face as he dealt with his burden. Though the movement made him woozy, Worthy knew that if he fell back unconscious again he'd never wake up.

Think, he commanded himself. *The man's name is Dr. Stanos.* He tried to work out what the college professor would be planning. He risked another peek and saw that Stanos was pulling him toward a series of doors. *Of course*, Worthy thought, *the kitchen.* Who'd think of looking for me in there?

Worthy assessed his enemy. Stanos' face was red, but he was hardly puffing. That meant he was in good shape and strong. He was the type to think quickly and calmly. In the heat of the moment, Stanos had done a credible job making Father Spiro's murder look like a robbery. Equally impressive had been Stanos' return to professorial life as if nothing had happened. Not only had he avoided arousing any suspicion, he'd listened attentively to Worthy at the parish council meeting, figuring out how a simple brick borrowed from the projects could bring Sherrod back into the mix. The guy didn't panic, which meant, Worthy realized, that Stanos must already know what he was planning to do with Worthy once he got him in the kitchen.

How many minutes did he have to turn the tables on Stanos? As the man glanced over his shoulder, Worthy risked testing the strength in his arms. Okay in the left one, and the right was getting better. But any hope was immediately quashed by a tightening in his stomach. Allyson was still in the office and no doubt wondering where he was. *Please God, don't let her come looking for me.*

He welcomed the increased throbbing in his head as proof his brain was coming back online. He had to think clearly, to figure out Stanos' plan for him so that he could make a plan of his own.

Stanos' object was clear—to finish him off and get away without being noticed. That meant Stanos believed that the two in the office were already dead and couldn't implicate him. Now he had just the one loose end. But why the kitchen? Why not one of the education classrooms off the gymnasium? They were just as close.

Worthy tried to remember the details of the church kitchen from his initial tour of the church. Pots and pans hung from hooks over the large ovens and the two sinks. Various utensils, knives, and cutting boards were usually put away in drawers beneath the metal work station. *Maybe Stanos intends to stab me with one of them,* he thought. As the door swung back and Stanos pulled harder on his legs, Worthy remembered a pantry in the back for dried foodstuffs. *Is he going to kill me and leave my body in there?* The smell wouldn't attract attention until morning. Was that enough time for his plan to work?

Then it dawned on him, just as his careful peek proved him right: Stanos was pulling him in the direction of the walk-in freezers. *I'm going to be left to freeze to death, my body not discovered for days. And before he leaves, if he's smart—which he is,* Worthy conceded—*he'll wipe down the gym and kitchen floor and in the commotion in the office he may even take my car. Please God,* he thought, *make Allyson go with the medics.*

Worthy had to admire the plan, improvised as it was. No weapon meant little blood to clean up. And dumping his body within an existing crime scene, while sending everyone in search of his car, meant he had time once again to slip back into his routine. The guy didn't make obvious mistakes.

Worthy was now close enough to the freezers to hear their distinctive hum. *That's his plan. So what's mine?* How crazy that he could die in the belly of a church. *No, I have to find a way out, and not just for myself.* Allyson would hold herself responsible, thus carrying on the Worthy family trait.

His fingers twitched until he made a fist in the semi-darkness with his right hand. He could feel his nails dig into his palm. Yes, there was some strength, but was it enough? The door of the walk-in freezer was only ten feet away. Its metal handle, once closed, would seal his fate.

The metal handle. Yes, that was his chance, maybe his only one. Stanos would have to drop his legs for a few minutes to reach back and pull on the handle. What if he jumped up at that moment and turned the tables on Stanos, pushing him backwards into the freezer and closing the door?

His heart beat faster as his body was dragged closer to the door. *Give me all the strength you got,* he commanded his body. Through the slits of his eyelids he confirmed what he could feel. Stanos had slowed down and was readying himself for the final step.

Stanos lowered Worthy's legs and stood where he was for a moment. *What is he doing?* Worthy thought. Was it possible that he'd guessed wrong, that Stanos had brought him into the kitchen only to shoot him? The shot would echo off all the metal and surely be heard in the office. *No, that can't be it.*

Stanos remained where he was, looking down on him. Then he began flexing his arms, shaking out his muscles, and Worthy understood, even as his heart sank. *Damn, the bastard thinks of everything,* he realized. If Stanos hadn't done that, Worthy realized, he'd be jumping a guy with cramped muscles.

"Time to sleep, buddy-boy," Stanos muttered.

Buddy-boy? The way Stanos said those words, so casual and light, uncapped a new rage within Worthy, so that when Stanos turned, unlocked the door, and started to open it out, Worthy nearly flew to his feet.

"Fuck you, buddy-boy," Worthy snarled, hitting Stanos full force on his left shoulder and sending him reeling toward the open freezer. But in his fear that he wouldn't have enough strength for the task, he'd executed his plan too quickly, so that Stanos' other shoulder hit the edge of the freezer door and slammed it shut.

Stanos fell back against the door and then down to one knee, even as Worthy felt a wave of lightheadedness roll up from his stomach toward his brain. He tottered back toward the metal work table just as Stanos regained his balance and rushed toward him.

With his left hand, Worthy opened the nearest drawer on the table and grabbed a handful of utensils. With his right, he reached out, and just as he'd been trained, straight-armed Stanos directly at the base of his nose. Stanos' head flew back, but only momentarily, and Worthy had no time to confirm what weapons he held in his hand. He gripped the largest handle and let the other utensils fall to the floor.

He swayed a bit as he raised his arm toward Stanos and saw what he'd chosen. A soup ladle.

"How terrifying," Stanos muttered hoarsely as he ran at Worthy again. He hit Worthy full force in the chest and drove him to the floor. Worthy went down grasping Stanos as they fell, aware that his opponent had made his first mistake. On the floor, Worthy wouldn't have to waste energy trying to keep his feet and his balance, dubious propositions at best.

With one arm, Worthy tried unsuccessfully to break free before searching for what he'd dropped. In the gloom of the kitchen, he spotted what he wanted—a big meat knife, only three feet away and best of all, out of Stanos' sight.

Stanos struggled quietly, not wasting energy with words, as he tried to force Worthy's torso and head down to the floor. With all his might, Worthy pulled himself and Stanos toward the knife. He managed a few inches, only to lose purchase when Stanos found Worthy's free arm and grabbed at it. Worthy dove down and bit into Stanos' hand, freeing his own hand in the process.

"You fuck," Stanos muttered, his breathing heavy.

"Not so fun when it's not an old man or woman, is it, Professor?" Worthy whispered, hitting Stanos in the ear with his fist before the man's head rammed into his side again.

"You don't understand a damned thing," Stanos spat back. "None of this had to happen."

Stanos went back for the free hand, and in the process, the two bodies edged a few inches closer to the knife.

"Let me guess, a high school wrestler, right?" Worthy muttered, his own breathing heavy now.

"You bet. And you fight like a basketball player."

Worthy felt a fist hit him in the ribs, and he fell willingly in the direction of the knife. With his one free hand, he reached to grab it. The cold metal burned his hand as he raised it and swung it down on Stanos' arm. The blade glanced off, sliding down the hand until it caught on three curled fingers. Worthy leaned all his weight on the blade, felt the blade hit bone then slice through. He watched two fingers explode with blood even as they hung by flaps of skin from the retracted hand.

If he'd expected Stanos to panic, he was mistaken. Stanos pulled away from Worthy and rose to his feet. Without a word, he grabbed a towel off the table and wrapped his hand.

Worthy also managed to rise to his feet, the knife in his hand.

"It's no use," Worthy said, as the two began to circle each other. "Whatever happens, they'll find your blood in here."

"You think I've got a record? They'll never be able to match my blood. Once I kill you, that is."

"You figure to kill me with this knife?"

"Oh, yeah," Stanos said, circling to Worthy's left. "That very knife in your hand. The way I figure it, that head wound must be making you feel pretty dizzy."

Worthy rotated to face him. "My head's fine. But let's say you do kill me. Then what? You expect to lecture tomorrow with two missing fingers?"

"A garden accident. The hedge clippers jammed. I may even be able to have them reattached, so don't worry about me. You see, Lieutenant, that's what I do for a living. I exercise my brain. If you didn't have so little time left, I'd advise you to try it some time."

Worthy knew Stanos wouldn't wait much longer. He'd caught his breath and felt a wave of nausea, despite what he'd said to Stanos. He also knew from the look in Stanos' eye that he feared nothing.

Stanos took a deep breath, feigned low as if to grab at Worthy's legs, then drove high toward his face, his one good hand reaching for the knife.

Worthy twisted away from the force coming at him, swung the knife in a high arc away from Stanos' arm, and sank it deeply into his upper thigh. Gasping and off-balance, Stanos stumbled forward, even as Worthy held the blade in place, letting it rip through the muscle as Stanos fell to the floor.

With a scream of agony, Stanos rolled onto his back. "Oh, God! Oh, fuck!" He looked momentarily at the gash and the blood pooling from it before his eyes began to roll back in his head. His head hit the floor with a dull thud.

"I guess I should have told you, Stanos," Worthy stammered, breathing heavily as he rested his hands on his knees. "My little high school didn't have enough guys for both basketball and wrestling. So they let us play both sports. One-fifty-four weight class, three years running."

CHAPTER TWENTY-TWO

FATHER FORTIS OPENED HIS EYES AND squinted at the two faces before him. The one was a younger, quite beautiful version of the other: fair-haired, tall, with a similar open countenance. "You must be Allyson," he whispered hoarsely. "I heard one of the doctors tell a nurse I owe my life to a beautiful young woman. The doctor was right."

Worthy stood next to his daughter at the bedside. "I see your eyesight is okay. How're you feeling?"

Father Fortis looked over at the tubes running from both his arms. "Better than the alternative. Thanks to you, my dear."

Allyson coughed and crossed her arms across her chest. "I'm just glad you're okay, um … Father, I should say."

"Call me Nick, my dear."

"Okay. And you can call me Ally." She put a small bag on the stand next to Father Fortis' bed. "These are for you."

"What are they, my dear?"

"Mints, the kind you like," she replied.

"That's so thoughtful," he said, trying to smile. Every breath felt as if his chest was pushing against a wall. He glanced up at Worthy. "Is that a turban you're wearing? Christopher, I hope you're not going to tell me you converted to Hinduism or Sikhism while I was out of commission. I thought it was clear that I had dibs on your soul."

Worthy touched the bandage over his left ear. "Just another bit of Stanos' handiwork. Like that bullet they took out of your side. What did the surgeon say? It passed half an inch from your pericardial sack and ended up even closer to your liver."

"The benefits of being fat, my friend," Father Fortis replied. So Stanos was in custody or maybe dead. "When did you catch him?" he asked, looking toward the window.

"Sunday. Not long after he shot you."

"Sunday. What day is it today?"

"Thursday," Allyson offered.

"Really?" He'd been aware of being conscious several times, but never long enough to know anything except that he was in a hospital. Four days ago. He looked up again and caught Worthy's eye. "So Mrs. Filis has been buried."

Worthy nodded. "I wasn't sure you knew about her."

"I remember coming to when the paramedics were working on me in the office. I heard one of them say she was gone. That's going to haunt me, my friend."

Worthy reached over and touched his friend's hand. "Why am I not surprised you'd feel that way? Listen, Nick, if it's anyone's fault, it's mine."

Father Fortis watched Allyson as she looked over to search her father's face. Did they know how much the two of them looked alike? He took another breath and felt the wall again. "I don't see how it could be your fault."

"I'm the cop, so I know. It's simple. If I'd figured out your voicemail ten minutes earlier, I'd have gotten there about the same time she did. I could have prevented it."

"Or you could have been shot, too," Allyson said.

"She's right, my friend. Anyway, my message was all wrong," Father Fortis protested. "There was no clue."

"That's not exactly right, Nick," Allyson said. "He pulled me out of this great movie. Okay, it was a stupid movie. But Dad had a bad feeling the killer might have set you up." She looked up again at her father. "Once again, you were right."

"Oh, your father is amazing, my dear."

Worthy cleared his throat. "It's easy to forget that Stanos chose to kill the old woman, though I can't for the life of me figure out why he wanted her there. I mean, you I understand. But why'd he lure her back?"

"But he didn't want her there. And I'm not sure he meant to kill anyone that day. My stunt in the Sunday morning liturgy scared him, but he came to tell me why he had to kill Father Spiro."

"*Had* to kill him?" Worthy asked.

"Not exactly a confession, I admit. He seemed to believe that if I understood the truth—at least as he saw it—I'd keep his secret."

"But he shot you," Allyson protested.

"But did he want to? No, the gun was there to make sure he'd keep the upper hand. Mrs. Filis, may her memory be eternal, shouldn't have even been there."

"Then why'd she come?" Allyson asked.

Father Fortis shook his head slowly, still wondering if there was something he could have done to save her. "Christopher, do you remember what the first clue was that pointed to the killer being someone from the parish?"

"Sure. It was the way Stanos straightened the vestment on Father Spiro after he killed him."

"And what if Stanos hadn't done that, my friend?"

Worthy was silent for a moment. "I'd probably have gone with Sherrod's robbery angle."

"Exactly." Father Fortis took another deep breath. "You see, Stanos didn't straighten the epitrachelion after all."

"Mrs. Filis did," Allyson said, almost in a whisper.

"Wait a minute," Worthy protested. "She told Sherrod she hadn't touched the body."

"I know, my friend, but maybe at the time she didn't remember what she'd done."

"Shock?" Allyson offered.

"Or maybe Sherrod scared the hell out of her," Worthy added.

"We'll never know, but that's what she wanted to tell me Sunday afternoon. Apparently, she tried to tell me that morning, but she missed me in my office."

Worthy looked puzzled. "She tried to see you after the service?"

Father Fortis nodded. "That's what she said. Why?"

"Because that's when I was in your office waiting for you. I heard someone at the door. I think they tried to turn the knob. Anyway, that's what I remembered when I was in the movie with Ally. I thought it must have been the killer. I thought he or she'd try another way to get to you."

"Like inventing the story of the other woman's stroke," Allyson mused. "So it was Mrs. Filis who really put you on the right trail."

Father Fortis considered Allyson's perspective. In a way, wasn't she right? And that brought another thought to mind.

"The code in the diary, Christopher. I was wrong about that, too."

"I can't see how, Nick."

"If Father Spiro had really meant the code to be unbreakable, wouldn't he have used only Greek letters to make it even harder to decipher? But he used both English and Greek, as if he expected, one day—"

"That someone like a cop with no Greek might need to understand it," Worthy finished the sentence.

"Mysterious are the ways of God, my friend."

"God, the trickster, right?" Allyson asked.

Father Fortis was puzzled by the odd term. "Trickster? I guess God may seem that way sometimes. And Stanos would agree. I don't think I'll ever forget the look on his face when he was behind the door and heard Mrs. Filis explain about the epitrachelion. That was the first moment I saw murder in his eyes. Christopher, I notice you haven't said if he's alive or dead."

"Sorry, Nick. He's alive, but not saying much. He's probably thinking about this same thing. How Mrs. Filis ruined all his careful plans."

Father Fortis nodded. " 'Ruined his plans.' Yes, that's how he would see it. He called Father Spiro an old senile priest who was out to ruin his life."

"Stanos is listening to his lawyer and not saying anything, though he didn't expect you to survive. Why did he kill Father Spiro?"

"Ah, I'll give you a couple of the puzzle pieces. The pain of NISP was caused by GESP."

"You've lost me," Allyson said. "Is that part of the code?"

"Yes, it is. 'The pain of NISP was caused by GESP,' " Worthy repeated. "That was the boy worried about his sexuality, right? If Stanos was GESP, that means there was something to that."

Father Fortis frowned. "He's trained the altar boys for years. Apparently, he got closer to this boy than to the others. I'm not sure what really happened, but Father Spiro thought he knew and confronted him on it. And then Father Spiro said he felt morally responsible to tell the college authorities in case—"

"In case Stanos was a predator over at Allgemein as well," Worthy again finished the thought.

Allyson patted the priest's leg. "Nick? Do you want me to tell you the real reason you didn't die?"

Father Fortis' eyebrows arched. "Please do, my dear."

"Because my Dad would go nuts if he couldn't solve the puzzle. He was pretty miserable to be around this week, even though his picture was on the front pages for two straight days."

"Not just mine. Henderson's and Nick's, too," Worthy interrupted.

Father Fortis rolled his eyes.

"You want to know what's ironic, Nick? The story accompanying the photo was written by Kenna McCarty. Unlike Sherrod, who is licking his wounds, Kenna McCarty came out looking good. Thanks to Henderson's willingness to share some of the lesser-known details of the case with her, the reporter got her scoop after all."

"What does your captain say?" Father Fortis asked.

"Captain Betts is harder to read," Worthy replied. "I know she's grateful she didn't make the mistake of giving the case back to Sherrod. And I can tell she's genuinely pleased that Henderson can stay on the job, at least for the time being. But my guess is that Captain Betts also knows that she's made an enemy of Sherrod. Rather than admit his approach would have let Stanos off the hook to maybe kill again, Sherrod will accuse her of robbing him of the credit for solving the case."

"My dad may be a big shot again," Allyson said, "but he wouldn't be satisfied until he knew why Mrs. Filis was there, and Stanos sure wasn't talking."

"The man is clever, and he's got a good lawyer, I'm sure," Father Fortis said. "So I'm happy to know my survival is helpful. Be sure you tell the metropolitan. Speaking of the metropolitan, the dear folks at St. Cosmas are going to need a priest now more than ever. The grief over their murdered priest is now compounded by the death of Mrs. Filis and the arrest of one of the parish's most prominent members. I wonder if the metropolitan would see the wisdom of bringing Father Daniel back to St. Cosmas, at least temporarily?"

"Not your problem to fix, Nick," Worthy reminded his friend.

"Of course, you're right," Father Fortis agreed. "Now, I believe I feel a nap coming on. But before you two go, I want to apologize, my dear, for … how should I put it? I guess the best way to express my feelings is to say that I'm grateful you saved my life, but I'm sorry you had to see all the blood in that room."

Worthy sighed heavily, shaking his head at Father Fortis.

"Did I say something wrong?" the priest asked.

"No, Nick. It's just that I've been trying to tell her the same thing all week. I was worried she'd be traumatized, but all she's been doing is smiling a lot."

Allyson blushed. "You should know by now that I have my secrets."

"Just no more big surprises. I don't think your mother or I could take it."

"Well, I guess it will seem like a surprise. Maybe to you more than Mom."

"Another mystery to solve, my friend," Father Fortis said. He could see that Allyson was making no moves to change the conversation. Did she want her Dad to know?

"So what clues has Ally left you?" Father Fortis asked.

"Maybe you're one of the clues," Allyson said with a smile, looking down at Father Fortis.

"Me? Well, now. I don't think it has to do with an interest in the priesthood. We Orthodox aren't that progressive."

"I suppose it's too much to hope that you've decided to go to college after all to become a doctor," Worthy added.

"Please. With my grades in chemistry? But you're warm."

"So it has to do with going to college," Father Fortis posed.

Allyson nodded. "Dad's not going to get it, Nick."

"Oh, Lord. Is this what I think it is?"

"Okay. I'm lost," Worthy confessed. "Though I'm happy you're going to college."

"Think, my friend. What's been new between the two of you over the last few weeks."

"You mean besides all your questions?" Worthy asked, looking at his daughter.

"God, you're so dense sometimes," Allyson said.

Worthy's mouth dropped. "No, it can't be. I thought you were just interested in your old man."

"I don't know whether to offer my sympathies or congratulations, Christopher. Your daughter wants to study criminology."

Worthy groaned. "Nick's wrong, isn't he?"

"Oh, come on. Why not?" Allyson asked, looking from her father down to his closest friend. "The way it looks to me, life is just a bunch of puzzles. Why not get paid to solve a few of them?"

Photo by Leif Carlson

DAVID **CARLSON** WAS BORN IN THE western suburbs of Chicago and grew up in parsonages in various cities of Illinois. His grade school years were spent in Springfield, Illinois, where the numerous Abraham Lincoln sites initiated his lifelong love of history. His childhood hope was to play professional baseball, a dream that died ignominiously one day in high school.

He attended Wheaton College (Illinois) where he majored in political science and planned on going to law school. Not sure how to respond to the Vietnam War, he decided to attend seminary for a year to weigh his options. To his surprise, he fell in love with theological thinking—especially theological questioning—and his career plan shifted to college teaching in religious studies. He earned a doctorate at University of Aberdeen, Scotland, where he learned that research is a process of digging and then digging deeper. He believes the same process of digging and digging deeper has helped him in his nonfiction and mystery writing.

Franklin College, a traditional liberal arts college in central Indiana, has been his home for the past thirty-eight years. David has been particularly attracted to the topics of faith development, Catholic-Orthodox relations, and Muslim-Christian dialogue. In the last thirteen years, however, religious terrorism has become his area of specialty. In 2007, he conducted interviews across the country in monasteries and convents about monastic responses to

9/11 and religious terrorism. The book based on that experience, *Peace Be with You: Monastic Wisdom for a Terror-Filled World*, was published in 2011 by Thomas Nelson and was selected as one of the Best Books of 2011 in the area of Spiritual Living by *Library Journal*.

Much of his time in the last three years has been spent giving talks as well as being interviewed on radio and TV about ISIS. Nevertheless, he is still able to spend summers in Wisconsin where he enjoys sailing, fishing, kayaking, and restoring an old log cabin.

His wife, Kathy, is a retired English professor, an award-winning artist, and an excellent editor. Their two sons took parental advice to follow their passions. The older, Leif, is a photographer, and the younger, Marten, is a filmmaker.

Let the Dead Bury the Dead is the second in the Christopher Worthy/ Father Fortis mystery series, which began with *Enter by the Narrow Gate*. Carlson's second book on religious extremism, *Countering Religious Violence: The Healing Power of Spiritual Friendships,* will be released by New City Press in 2017.

For more information, please visit:
www.DavidCCarlson.org.

Enter by the Narrow Gate

A Christopher Worthy and Father Fortis Mystery

David Carlson

A Detroit detective and an Orthodox priest
team up to solve two mysteries unfolding
in the Santa Fe area: a missing person's case
involving a teenage girl and the ritualistic
murder of a young nun. Their dangerous quest
will require them to delve into the secret lives
of Trappist monks and alienated teenagers and
gain insight into obscure religious practices
and the cultures of the Southwest.

FROM COFFEETOWN PRESS AND DAVID CARLSON

T HANK YOU FOR READING *LET THE Dead Bury the Dead*. We are so grateful for you, our readers. If you enjoyed this book, here are some steps you can take that could help contribute to its success and the success of this series.

- Post a review on Amazon, BN.com, and/or GoodReads.
- Check out David's website or blog and send a comment or ask to be put on his mailing list.
- Spread the word on Social Media, especially Facebook, Twitter, and Pinterest.
- Like David's Facebook page and the Coffeetown Press Facebook page.
- Ask for this book at your local library or request it on their online portal.

Good books and authors from small presses are often overlooked. Your comments and reviews can make an enormous difference.

DEC 2 1 2017

Made in the USA
San Bernardino, CA
08 August 2017